KRAKEN'S KEEP

JEAN KILCZER

copyright©2013 Jean Kilczer
all rights reserved

ISBN:1481074857
ISBN-13:978-1481074858

DEDICATION

Anthony Martino

To a Great Bro.
Love, Sis

ACKNOWLEDGMENT

My sincerest thanks to Millie Ehrlich, my friend and reviewer, who made this a better book with her intelligent, perceptive, and supportive comments. Thanks, Millie!

Other Books by Jean Kilczer

Adult Science Fiction:
Sojourner to the Stars: Book One - The Loranth
(The Jules Rammis series)
Sojourner to the Stars: Book Two - Halcyon Nights
(The Jules Rammis series)
The Empty Hands

Children's Books:
Snowflake's World: Book One - The Deadly Sulphur Mine Snowflake's World: Book Two - The Enchanted Portal
at Haunted Lake
Snowflake's World: Book Three - The Quest for New Eden

jeankilczer@centurylink.net

CHAPTER ONE

On a cold December afternoon, Culley and I were eighty feet down, scraping barnacles and plants off concrete columns of the North California Steinbeck Bridge to check for cracks and corrosion.

"Tess," he called through the communication system in his full-face mask, "C'mere, I want to show you something."

The visibility was poor and the outgoing tide had begun its inexorable pull to the open sea.

"*Now*, Culley?" He knew what I meant. Our bottom time was limited with the swift tide and a decompression stop on our way up. The frigid water had me shivering in my wet suit and I looked forward to finishing our work and heading topside.

"*Now*, Tessie."

Culley's a commercial diver. One of the best in the field. But if you tell him that, he lowers his head, kicks dirt, and says *Ah, shucks. Ya think?* But I knew he took his underwater work and safety very seriously. I swam to where he was shining his light on a bridge column.

"This one needs a marine biologist," he said and backed away so I could get a clear view. When I did, I held my breath. It's a thing we're trained never to do underwater.

"I want to see bubbles, Tess."

I breathed again.

The column had been burned open to make a four-foot high narrow den. Within that den I saw things that had no place in the known world of marine life.

"What do you make of it?" Culley asked in his deceptively casual tone.

My God, I thought. What do I make of clusters of five-inch-long octopus eggs? The average egg of the Giant Pacific octopus, the largest known species, is the size of a grain of rice.

The babies hung in their egg sacs like bunches of elongated brown speckled grapes, swaying in the current that kept them aerated, which is usually the mother octopus' job. Within each sac a pair of developed eyes stared out. The larvae pulsed and were turning.

"My God, Culley, they're ready to hatch!"

"That's what I was afraid of."

"They'll be monsters."

"Oh, yeah. There could be other dens in the columns, too."

Enough dens, I thought, *could compromise the bridge and cause it to collapse.*

The outgoing tide was stronger. The eggs leaned in that direction, as though the hatchlings knew their seaward destiny.

"You see what the mother *did?*" I asked.

"Now, Tess, no need for swearing."

"The real mother, you klutz. She left her eggs for the tides to aerate, instead of starving to death in an effort to keep them oxygenated."

"Kudos for the mother." He checked his dive computer and looked up.

"I'm going to take some specimens." I unsheathed my dive knife.

"Wait a minute. If the mother -- "

I grabbed one cluster in my gloved hand and cried out as something burned my palm. Acid was eating through the neoprene glove! Culley ripped it off my hand. By the time it swirled into the depths, the fingers of the glove were gone. I held my burned hand.

"Let me see it." Culley took my hand in his and shined his light on it. A red slash ran across my palm.

"Tess, if the mother burned through concrete to make this cradle, you think her offspring might use acid, no?"

"Let's go home!" I shook off his hand and followed the anchor line to our decompression stop. A fresh tank hung on the line for emergencies.

I was chilled to the bone and the outgoing tide was trying to take me with it. My hand burned in salt water, but these were the least of my concerns. "Culley, what if these creatures have laid their eggs on the hulls of ships? They could be all over the world." My voice was shaky, not only from the cold.

"Ships, bridges, oil platforms, and docks." He rubbed my arm to add some warmth. "So where do you think they came from?"

"I don't know. Maybe a genetic twist from the radiation leaking out of the Japanese power plants thirty years ago. Maybe a quantum leap in their evolution. Maybe..."

"Yeah?"

"Maybe they've been down in the depths for millions of years and we never knew it. Maybe for some reason the warming seas brought them up. I wish I could have taken some specimens."

Boats rumbled by overhead as we started toward the surface. Jellyfish drifted in the current.

"Would be nice," I added, "if the mother's just a mutation, you know, one of a kind that doesn't breed true. The babies might not live or breed."

"You think? Those critters looked pretty healthy to me. I think they were sizing us up for future meals. But what do I know."

We were quiet as we climbed into *Shearwater,* Culley's sixteen-foot Boston Whaler. Ice, my white, blue-eyed Siberian husky, ran across the deck to greet us, but when I reached out with my ungloved hand to touch his head, he sniffed it and ducked away.

Culley stripped off his gear but stayed suited up. His brown hair was plastered to his angular face and his neck. He has the look of a poet, with his pensive dark eyes, his hooked nose and sensitive lips, his loose-jointed ambling walk, but he has the soul of a field marshal. He sat down and contacted Alex "Ace" Foley, the harbormaster, on the boat's radio, and told him what we'd encountered.

"Get a pontoon shaver out here, Ace," Culley said, "and block off the harbor mouth before it's too late. Tess said the eggs are ready to hatch. And hang a fishing net from the pontoons so the little bastards can't go under the pontoon."

"Culley," I said, "*Culley,* tell him the mother could be a hundred feet long."

Culley swiveled in his captain's chair to look at me. "That's *feet?*" The fear in his eyes was a rare thing. I'm sure he had his quota of anxiety, but in the two years we'd known each other, he'd usually masked his feelings with glib remarks.

"Tess says," he told Ace in a strained voice, "the mother could be a hundred feet long." His lips were pressed as he peered out at the harbor.

Colored lights from land and boats shimmered in black water.

I couldn't believe it when Ace chuckled over the radio. "Hundred-foot-long octopussey? You guys get nitrogen narcosis down there?"

Culley has a way of convincing people when he knows he's right. He yells louder than they do and finds just the right swear words to fit the occasion. People usually give in just to shut him up.

I stripped off my gear and wet suit. My hair is thick and long, and hard to dry with just a towel. I did my best and got into a woolen shirt and pants.

"OK. Awright!" Ace finally agreed to get in touch with the offshore patrol boats, the Coast Guard, the town government, a local dive company, and the Pacifica National Laboratory, where I work. "I'll see what I can do."

"See what you can do *now*, Ace," Culley said. "This is going to make international news. You want to be a hero or a do-nothing-dumb-shit-sat-on-your-hands?"

"I said I'll see what I can do!"

Culley slammed the mic onto its holder. "Only thing he'll do is figure out the best way to cover his ass."

I got on my Apple Q-Tree, a quantum device that does everything except read your mind, and contacted Brad Bellows, my boss at the Pacifica Lab. As I waited for Brad to answer, I scanned the surface for hatchlings or their mother. Night is the time when baby octopuses hatch and make their way to the surface for protection from predators. In the distance, seagulls cawed.

What would happen to seabirds, I thought, *if they tried to eat the acid-coated hatchlings?* This was becoming more of a nightmare with every turn.

"Hi, Tess," Brad said. "Where are you?"

"On the Whaler. Listen, Brad -- "

"Are you still helping Mr. Self-contained-underwater-breathing android instead of doing your real work here?"

"Will you *listen,* Brad? We have -- "

"Tell Mr. Nice Guy," Culley threw over his shoulder, "to go fuck himself."

"What did he say?" Brad asked.

"Brad! We have a problem." I told him about our encounter with the octopus nursery.

He was quiet for a moment, then he said "Do you think they're ready to hatch?"

"They were already turning in their sacs. I'm looking for hatchlings on the surface now, but it's dark."

"Good God, what have we done to the oceans this time?" Brad said.

I drew in a cold breath "Oh, no."

Around the boat five-inch baby octopuses surfaced and lit their wakes with streams of stirred phosphorescence as they pulsed toward the open sea and avoided the jellies who were on the same voyage. The babies had a shiny brown coating. I'd never seen that on any octopus. I suspected that it was the source of the acid.

My knees weakened and I sat down. "They're hatching." I chewed a fingernail.

Culley turned in his chair.

"Tess?" Brad called.

I held the Q-Tree limply. Culley looked over the side of the boat and I saw his body stiffen.

"What's happening?" Brad asked

"They're hatching," I said.

"Oh, shit! I've got to get the staff together for a meeting. We've got to put our heads together on this one."

A seagull swooped out of the sky and scooped up a hatchling. He squawked and dropped it. He continued to squawk as he flew away in an erratic path that dipped into the water.

Culley watched him disappear into the sky.

"Yes, Brad," I said, "put your heads together. Good luck." I broke the contact.

I opened my mesh bug bag, dipped it over the side, and scooped up two hatchlings. They burned through the bag before I got them into the boat and flopped back into the water. "Dammit!" I muttered. "The fishing net won't hold them."

Culley nodded.

It seemed that as with some vipers that are born with a full complement of poison, these giant octopus babies were born with full sacs of acid.

Culley strapped his buoyancy compensator onto a fresh tank.

"What are you doing?" I asked. "The mother might have returned to stimulate her eggs to hatch."

"I'm counting on it." He sat on the gunnel and strapped on his fins.

"Culley, let the Coast Guard stop the hatchlings with pontoons and that surface scraper. You told me yourself the mother could use acid for defense."

Culley patted the underwater torch he'd clipped to his weight belt. "I've got some acid right here. How many of these little horrors does an octopus lay?"

"I'm not sure. Mollusks aren't my specialty. Maybe fifty thousand." I knew I was underestimating. "But usually only a few survive."

I swear Culley turned pale in the dark boat. "Yeah," he said, "I guess we better hang out while the Coast Guard tells the government this isn't their area of expertise. After all, the pontoons and sea scrapers are for oil spills." He fitted the full-face mask over his head. "Then the politicians can blame the other guy's party for not taking action while the world's ocean structures go to hell."

He stared at me through the mask. I couldn't read his expression but I felt that he was imprinting my features on his mind in a last goodbye. It scared me.

"Culley..."

"Take care of yourself, Tess. And take care of my boat." He unclipped his light and went over the side.

I shivered even with the woolen pants and shirt as I watched his light fade into murky water. I rubbed the white, shriveled tips of my fingers and scanned the water. More hatchlings pulsed to the surface and were swept past the boat with the outgoing tide.

Ice licked my foot and sat next to me. I scratched him behind his ear. "I can't just sit on my hands, either," I said.

I stripped down in the cold night air, put on my clammy wet suit, and got into my gear, with fresh gloves. "Take care of the boat, baby." I kissed Ice's snout, put on my mask, took a torch, a light, and went over the side.

I swam down quickly to avoid the baby octopuses who might brush by me. My burned hand hurt again in the salt water but I gripped the anchor line to hold myself against the full-running tide. Visibility was down to three feet. Water seeped like fingers of ice into my suit.

There is no night like night in the ocean. Here, real dangers might lurk just beyond your narrow beam of light. I love the sea, that wise and brutal unconscious of the planet where life probably first stirred, but we are creatures of light and we embellish the dark with monsters of our own creation.

Below, my light lit a circle of brown, swirling particles and jellies. I reached the den and watched baby octopuses pour out and join their siblings from other dens. They avoided me in their quest for the open sea. Out there, they could sink into rocky crevices for cover, and grow.

Into what?

Here, there were creatures that needed no added horrors of the id.

"Culley!"

Only my bubbles and the silence of the sea. My heart was a fist that beat against my chest as I clung to the anchor line and scanned with the light. Culley's always a bit negatively weighted. If he were...I mean, if something happened to him, he would slowly sink to the bottom. I didn't want to go down there to look. I was breathing much too heavily, with the danger of hyperventilating. I knew I was on the verge of panic. I wanted only to get back into the solid boat, the world of air, sharp colors, my warm clothes, and sounds besides my own breathing.

"Culley!" I shouted hoarsely into the mask

Only the black water and the octopuses. Panic is one of the biggest killers of scuba divers. I felt well up in my throat as lashes of heat flashed through my suit from hundreds of baby octopuses that jostled each other and slid across my body. "Culley!" If I stayed much longer, I'd have to decompress.

I took long, slow breaths to calm my thoughts and my shaking body. I owed Culley more than just scrambling to the surface for my own safety. I started down the anchor line. With low visibility I came to the muddy bottom at ninety-six feet very suddenly. A crab snapped open his claws and scuttled away.

"Culley," I called. I squeezed away tears that I couldn't wipe from my eyes.

Something huge, white, and blurry moved just beyond my light. I swung it in that direction. And then I panicked. I clung to the anchor line. "Please, God," I whimpered, "don't let me die alone down here."

A white tentacle, thick around as a column itself, uncurled in my direction.

"Breathe. Breathe!" I told myself as I started up the anchor line. I screamed and hid behind the column as the tentacle tried to catch me. With my heart slamming in my chest and my teeth chattering, I unclipped my torch, made it hot, and held the line as I went toward the tentacle. It jerked back before I could burn it and disappeared in a cloud of black ink and stirred mud. I backed off quickly and rose. That ink could well be caustic.

"I tried, Culley," I called dismally as I rose to the surface.

I had one last hope. He might be in the boat.

But only Ice greeted me with whines and wags of his tail.

I didn't realize how exhausted I was until I climbed onto the deck. The tank, the weight belt, seemed to weigh a thousand pounds. The wet suit was clammy against my skin. I sank to the deck and Ice licked my face, thinking I wanted to play.

I got out of my gear, stripped off my wet suit, my bathing suit, and got into the woolen shirt and pants, then wrapped myself in a blanket.

I sat in the captain's chair, Culley's chair, and poured a cup of hot coffee from the thermos. The coffee spilled in my shaking hands. I kept the unlit torch tucked in my lap. I would wait. Culley was not an easy man to kill. A couple of sharks had tried it over the years. Their whitened jaws hang in the Pine Coast Museum.

I patted the torch. "I've got some acid right here."

Ice sat next to me, then yawned and curled up, as though he knew we were in for a long night. I chewed a fingernail.

He was right.

CHAPTER TWO

I awoke to shouts, the rumble of inboards, and swaying boat lights from the inlet between the two jetties. I jumped up and shined my light in the water around the boat. "Culley?"

No answer.

Media and Coast Guard helicopters beat the water into circles of white foam as they hovered above the inlet. Their lights shined down like pointing fingers on an eerie scene of swaying Coast Guard cutters and frothing waves.

Suddenly a great white tentacle lifted out of the water and crashed down on a cutter. The boat's lights swung wildly. The crew shouted as they threw themselves into the waves. The cutter's bow lifted like a breaching whale, then sank with the tentacle wrapped around its stern.

Oh my God! I mumbled as boats pulled survivors out of the water. Rifle shots followed the huge octopus.

The tide was incoming now, and on the off chance that a survivor might be dragged toward the bridge, I started the motor and slowly cruised along the columns, staying far enough away so the Whaler wouldn't be rammed into the bridge. In this frigid water, a survivor without a dive suit wouldn't have long before hypothermia set in. Death would follow quickly.

I saw the orange life vest first in my light, then I realized that a hefty man with white hair was jammed, face down, against a column.

I got to him quickly, caught his life vest with the boat hook, pulled him to the side of the boat and turned him over, in case he were still alive. When I saw his face, I screamed and clutched my throat with both hands to prevent myself from throwing up. One side of his face was burned away. White bone showed in a death grin. Hanging flesh floated around his head. His burned-out eye socket seemed to stare at me.

Suddenly his head lifted out of the water. I fell back onto the deck, dizzy with terror. I dropped my light. It went out. I groped for it, surrounded by night, found it and turned it back on. I crouched on the deck and gathered my thoughts. I was a scientist, after all, and I shouldn't be subject to the appearance of supernatural occurrences. The Milky Way hung like a dome overhead.

"If you're really up there, God," I said, "please let Culley be alive." I realized then that our friendship went deeper than I'd realized.

With a deep breath, I looked over the side again. A rockfish was under the man's head, lifting it as he chewed on shreds of flesh. I slammed the water with the boat hook. The fish darted away.

I forced myself to look at the man. This had been a living, breathing human being just minutes ago.

"There's nothing to fear, Tess," I told myself. In the sea we find our true place in the natural order - just another step on the food pyramid.

I tied a line to the body's life vest and towed him to three pilings that stood in shallow water. I tied the line securely to one piling and headed toward the inlet to see if I could help. But what I really hoped for was to find Culley alive, involved in helping survivors of the sunken boat.

The sound of an inboard grew louder. A Coast Guard cutter approached and shined its light on the Whaler.

"Tess? Is that you?"

I recognized Tom Crowley's voice. "Yes. Tom! Did you see Culley?"

"No. I'm searching for Trace. Bruce Tracy. That *thing* out there sank his boat. We got the rest of the crew on board, but Trace is missing."

"Oh." I went to the side of the Whaler. "Is he an older man, heavy-set, with white hair?"

"You saw him!" Tom gripped the rail of his boat with both hands. "He's a big man, white hair."

"Yes. He's...uh -- " I looked back at the three pilings. "He's..."

"Oh Christ! He's *dead,* isn't he?" Tom slammed a fist on the gunnel. "I knew it. And he was ready to retire."

"I'm so sorry, Tom. I tied his body to one of the pilings. I have to warn you, it's pretty grim."

Tom stared at the three pilings. "Don't mention this to the press. They'll want to take pictures of Trace. Goddamn it!" I saw him wipe his eyes. "His wife an' kids are gonna be devastated! You know where that nightmare came from?"

"No. Not yet. Did you see Culley?"

"He's missing too?"

I nodded. "He tried to kill it."

"All by himself? He would. He didn't come up?"

I shook my head and wiped away my own tears. "I went back down and searched for him, but...I don't know, Tom. I think he's gone."

"Don't think that way, kid. We'll look for him."

Tom drove toward the pilings to pick up his dead friend, and I drove toward the boats in the inlet to look for a friend I might never see again. The wind brought an acrid odor that mixed with the salty smell of the sea and got into my throat. Wind wiped the tears from my face.

Before I reached the inlet, I heard more rifle shots. The boats headed full speed toward the open sea. Coast Guard and media helicopters followed. The noise of their blades was deafening. I avoided the shredded pontoon and ripped fishing net that floated in with the tide, and drove to the side of a remaining cutter.

Captain Jen O'Malley, a friend, came out of the wheelhouse. "Tess! Are you OK?"

"I guess. Did you see Culley?"

"Yeah. He's down on the bottom."

"Oh. He's on the bottom. He's dead," I said numbly, admitting my worst fears.

"*Dead?* For Christ's sake, Tess! He's tying a line to the sunken boat so we can put a buoy on it. It's a navigational hazard out here in the inlet. We'll have to tow it to the dock."

My relief was like a wash of summer air. "I'll *kill him* when I get my hands on him! I swear I'll -- "

"Don't kill him yet. He's too cute. He floated here on the tide. Said he couldn't get back to the Whaler. So we asked him to put out a marker buoy and then we'd give him a ride back to his boat. We tried to contact you on the Whaler, but you didn't answer."

"I was in the water, looking for him."

"That's what he figured. He's been worried about you."

"Did he say that? He said he was worried?"

"No, Tess, I made it up." She leaned over the side. Her short red hair lifted over her square face in the wind. "Do you know where that monster came from?"

"I have a few theories, but nothing solid."

Tom's cutter was returning from the pilings.

"Jen, I'm sorry, but Trace is gone."

"Gone?"

"I think Tom's bringing back his body."

"Ah, Trace! We were afraid of that. Son of a bitch." Jen watched Tom's boat approach. "He was one of the nicest guys you ever want to know. What the hell is that thing, anyway? This is your field."

"Not really. My field is jellyfish. She's a giant octopus, bigger than any that's been known up till now. I estimate she's about a hundred feet long."

"A hundred feet! How do you know it's a *she?*"

"She came in to help her babies hatch."

"Is that what we saw floating by?"

I nodded.

Jen shook her head. "Then they all got away."

More rifle shots from beyond the inlet.

"They're wasting their time," I said. "They'll be lucky if she doesn't sink another boat and kill more people."

I didn't tell Jen what I was thinking. Why worry her even more while things were so bad? But I knew we were up against a real fight, possibly worldwide, to save our ocean structures and ships.

"Hey," Culley called from near the bridge.

Jen shined the boat's light on him and he waved. "Hey! How about a ride in?"

"Go get your boyfriend," Jen said.

"He's not my -- "

"Yeah, yeah. Go get him. And don't let another woman claim him. I might make a play for him myself." She grinned a toothy grin.

"You're married, Jen."

"So?"

"I'll go get him."

I passed Tom's cutter as I went to pick up Culley. I waved and he waved back. I didn't see Trace's body being towed. Tom must have brought him on board.

I pulled up alongside Culley and cut the motor. The boat drifted near him. I threw over the anchor and lowered the ladder. "Need a lift, mister?" I said in a sad attempt at humor.

"Considering I own the taxi. Yeah."

CHAPTER THREE

It was morning, two days after the night of the octopus.

I watched the Giant Pacific octopus emerge from his rocky lair in the Monterey Bay Aquarium, and slither to the side of his tank where a woman keeper held up a small dead fish.

The large crowd, gathered around the tank, was hushed as the keeper stroked the octopus' tentacle with the fish and pushed it toward the beak between his tentacles. He took the fish gently from her hand and retreated to his lair.

People kept glancing at me. The press had hounded Culley and me, and our photos were all over the news media.

The keeper turned to the silent crowd. "The octopus," she said, "is the smartest fish in the ocean. That's *fish,* ladies and gentlemen, not sea mammal." She smiled at me, nodded, and walked away without further explanation about the hundred-foot octopus.

I fielded a few questions.

"Miss Hoffman," a teenaged girl with long, brown hair approached me, "do you think it's a mutation? I'm, well," she said shyly, "I'm majoring in marine biology."

"That's great," I said and smiled. "It's a fascinating field. It's possible that the octopus is a mutation, but at this early stage, I couldn't venture a guess on an unknown species of cephalopod."

I looked at my watch. "I have to leave now. Good luck with your studies."

I turned and left. There was nothing more I could tell anybody about our short encounter with the Kraken. Some glib journalist had christened the octopus with the Norwegian mythological sea monster's name, and of course it stuck.

It was raining again, not unusual for December in Monterey. I picked up a copy of *The Pebble Beach Comber,* a daily newspaper, and a cruller and coffee from old Jason who sat behind his cart of snacks, outside the aquarium, with an umbrella tied over his head.

"Is it today's paper?" I asked him.

"December ninth, 2041. One more rainy day on the sunny West Coast."

I laughed. "Take care, Jason."

I skirted puddles as I held the folded paper over my head and ran to my car with my collar up.

The car was warm but had a musty smell from all the rain. I took off my wet jacket and wiped my hair and neck with a towel. Funny, I don't mind being wet on a dive, but I hate being out in the rain. I drank some hot coffee and felt it warm my stomach, then I ripped off a piece of sweet cruller and chewed as I opened the paper. Above the fold of the first page, a photo of an older man, perhaps between sixty and seventy, broad-faced, with white hair and an impish grin, stared out. I stopped chewing. The headline read:

KRAKEN BURNS COAST GUARD RETIREE TO DEATH WITH ACID

At least they didn't get a photo of his body, I thought sadly and read on.

WORLD COMMUNITY ON ALERT As Scientists Predict the KRAKEN Can Come Ashore And DESTROY CITIES! MILITARY VOWS TO DESTROY KRAKEN FIRST!

It sounded like an old B grade Japanese sci-fi flick, but in reality the octopus *could* come ashore. Smaller species were known to climb into fishing boats, steal bait, and plop back into the ocean to eat it.

The paper was full of stories about the "Kraken and her spawn." News had spread like wildfire. Pleasure boats remained at docks or in dry dock. Vacation cruise liners canceled all voyages until further notice.

The call went out across the seagoing nations for commercial and sport divers to check out bridges, freighters, docks, oil rigs, platforms, and underwater scientific habitats. The Navy employed SEAL teams to check military ships and installations. Rewards for dead giant octopuses were posted at international ports. Chemists worked on developing a substance that would prevent the eggs from gluing to any metal or wood.

I sighed and looked up from the paper. A patter of rain drummed on the car's roof. Through the silver rivulets that streamed down the windshield the bay and sky met at the horizon in a misty tangle of clouds and water. Seagulls were perched on pilings and rocks. From somewhere offshore a sea lion barked. It all seemed so normal, yet the lead-colored waters hid a threat to humans who still dared to venture out there, and to our seagoing way of life.

I opened the paper and read on. A California representative who was up for re-election referred to the killer bees that had escaped from a lab in South America way back in 1957 and came north into the U.S.

"If I'm elected," *The Pebble Beach Comber* quoted the candidate, "I'll make certain this dangerous monstrosity is blown out of the water!"

"You've got my vote," I muttered. Nothing like simple solutions to complex problems.

"Oh my God!" At a university in Arkansas, two geneticists who were growing heart tissue from human embryos were shot and killed. A radical religious group who called themselves The Church of the Hands Of God's Vengeance are persons of interest in the murder case. A note was found near the bodies: "The Kraken is God's revenge for a civilization gone awry, and for the scientist spawn of Satan who refused to heed the laws of the Good Lord."

I nibbled a fingernail.

The paper reported that U.S. President Cuomo gave a TV address pleading with the nation to maintain order and peace in this crisis.

"Scientists and the military," he explained in a direct quote, "are our only hope to eradicate this menace, which is most probably the result of a quantum leap in evolution and not God's revenge or the result of genetic engineering."

I turned the page and drew in a quiet breath. A tribal community in South America had tied a young virgin girl to a rock below the high-tide mark as an offering to the sea god to keep the tribe safe from the devil fish. The authorities heard about it and raced out there. They rescued her before the incoming tide was above her head. I let out a breath.

I put down the paper and drove to my apartment, north of Monterey.

Culley was parked near my front door in the RV he calls home. "Tess," he said, when I trotted up to him with the newspaper over my head, "I want you to stay away from the Pacifica Lab. Who knows where these religious nut cases will strike next?"

"How can I keep you in beer if I don't work?" I smiled lamely. "The Lab just hired retired police persons as guards. They'll escort us to and from our workplaces."

He stared at me and his pressed lips softened into a grin. "Got any?"

"Beer?"

He nodded.

"Don't I always?"

*****

Ice came through the doggie door from the backyard to greet me.

"Hi, baby." We played for a while, then I fed him and put on fresh coffee. I went to the bedroom and changed into casual pj's. When I came back, I opened the refrig. Culley sat on the living room sofa across from me, petting Ice.

"You can't be all bad," I told Culley, "if Ice likes you."

Damn! I realized as I reached for a beer that my silk pajamas were see-thru in the refrigerator light. I grabbed the beer and shut the door quickly.

Culley approached me with Ice walking beside him.

"Uh, here's your beer," I said. There was a look in his eyes that excited and frightened me. I shoved the cold beer at his chest to hold him off. "Your favorite brand."

He took the beer, set it aside and stared into my eyes.

"What?" I said. "It's not your favorite brand?"

He stroked my cheek and smirked. Culley's good at smirking.

I pressed back against the refrig. He was so close I could smell the scent of his body. "Go drink your beer and look at a football game or something."

"I'd rather look at you."

"OK, but back off. I can't breathe. Did I tell you that Ice is an attack dog?"

Ice heard his name and wagged his tail.

"I've been backing off for months, Tessica. I've been staring at my favorite brand and trying hard not to wrap my hands around it." He sniffed my hair. "Trying hard not to drink in its perfume."

"I don't wear perfume."

"That's what you think."

He kissed me lightly. His lips on mine were sweet and exciting. I felt my breath come quicker.

"You think it's easy for me to watch the curve of your breasts when you bend down to put on your fins, or your tight little tush when you wiggle into your wet suit, and not touch?"

"I don't wiggle."

"Whatever you call it."

"Well, I have to watch you too, you know."

"Oh, yeah? What part of me are you watching?"

"Never mind. Call me old-fashioned, but I don't believe in casual sex." I tried to push him away.

He put an arm on the refrig and blocked my path. "Who said it would be casual?"

"Culley, if I allowed my heart to go where it wants to take me, someday I'd wake up and you'd be gone and there'd be a note on your pillow: *Got a great dive job in Timbuktu. Take care of the kids. I might return some day.*"

"Timbuktu? I thought it was landlocked. I'll have to check that out. There's no guarantees in this life, Tess." He grinned. "I've always been a sucker for willowy blondes with dark eyes."

My hair is long and thick and close to black. My eyes are hazel, and my body type is more athletic than willowy. "Do I have to dye my hair blonde, stop exercising and wear dark contacts?"

"For you, Tess, I could change my preferences."

"But could you overcome your aversion to commitments?"

"I could commit to you." He stroked my cheek, my lips. I felt fire rising in my loins. He pressed against me and I knew there was a fire in him too. I pushed him away.

"That's what you say, Culley. But your heart is wind and I don't think even *you* know where it will take you." I went to the coffee maker. The aroma of fresh brewed filled the apartment.

Culley followed and embraced me from behind. "You want it in writing?" He kissed my neck. "I'll make up a contract. I, Ryan Culley, promise to commit to Tessica Hoffman."

I shivered with excitement. He felt it and his hands slid beneath my pj's and up to my bare breasts.

"Culley."

"What?" His hands on my breasts were more than I could resist. I turned and put my arms around his hard back, stroked his muscled arms. He tightened his muscles to impress me.

It did.

I felt myself weaken in his arms. The fire rose up and my breath came quick and deep. He kissed me and I arched my back against him.

"Oh, what the hell," I whispered.

He picked me up in his arms.

"Where are we going?" I asked.

"Someplace softer than your kitchen floor."

He put me down on my bed and kissed me again.

Ice jumped up on the bed and wagged his tail and whined. He wanted to play.

"Is this going to be a *ménage à trois?*" Culley asked.

"Well, if you're willing to leave, it doesn't have to be."

Culley got out of bed and picked up Ice. "I'll make the choice for you." He carried Ice out of the room and closed the door.

He came back and I helped him pull my pj top over my head. He embraced me and pressed me down to the bed. His weight on me was sweet. He was hard and ready against me.

Ice whined and scratched at the door.

"Tessie," Culley murmured. "Tessie. You're so beautiful."

"But will you love me in the morning? Oh!" I breathed as he pushed into me. Ice's whine faded in my ears and then there was only Culley and me and the world went somewhere else.

He was gentle and caring, as I knew he would be. I dug my nails into his back. "Oh, Culley," I whispered as the fire intensified and my breath came in gasps.

We climaxed together and I moaned as that feeling of ecstasy swept through me in waves. It's nature's ultimate gift. *Reproduce your kind and for a while, I'll raise you to heaven.*

When it was over, we lay there, still together, breathing hard. Culley kissed my lips, my cheeks, and down to my breasts. "You got anything in the frig? Damn, you made me hungry."

We both laughed. "You bastard," I said softly and nibbled his ear.

"Why don't we just stay like this?" he said. "I can reach the phone and call out for pizza."

I chuckled and baited him. "Do you like hot sausage on top?"

"Tessie."

"What now?"

"Did I ever tell you I love you?"

I shook my head. "Not in so many words."

"Well, in three words. I love you."

We parted and I sat up. "You're serious, aren't you?"

He nodded.

"That's quite a commitment." I brushed his long hair off his forehead.

"That's me, Tess, all about commitment." He raised his head and cupped it in his hand. "I've been on enough dive jobs in foreign countries, ever since dear ole dad took off for greener pastures when I was sixteen. I've been working dive jobs even before I got my commercial license. I don't need to see Timbuktu or the Fiji Islands." He stroked my face. "I need you."

I felt a welling of love for him. It had been there for a long time, I realized, but I had held it down. It frightened me. "I...I don't know, Culley. I'm not sure. Your father took off?"

"I'm not my father."

"I'm just not sure I'm ready for a commitment."

"Oh, Christ! Give me a break."

"You like kids?"

"They're all right, as long as you keep them in a closet."

I slapped his chest.

"I'm the oldest of five, Tess. I know all about kids. All you need is a good whip."

"What did your mom do after your father left?"

Culley took my hand. I felt his tremble and I realized I had asked a very sensitive question. I cuddled against him.

"She got in her car." He cleared his throat. "Turned it on and just sat there."

"She didn't drive anywhere?"

"She was in the garage."

"Oh." I kissed his cheek. "I'm so sorry."

"It was a long time ago."

"Did your father ever contact you?"

"He came back for a visit two years later."

"Did you tell him what happened?"

"Yeah. I wanted him to know why I put him in the hospital. I hope you had better luck with your parents."

"Oh, they're good people. Rachel and David. When I was a kid, my dad took me everywhere with him. He loves sports. He even taught me how to use a rifle."

"He took you hunting?"

"Oh, no. Dad would never shoot an animal. Target practice and skeet shooting. We even competed in local contests."

"Guess I'd better stay on your good side."

"Well, if you ever need a back-up woman," I said with a sneer and a Western accent, "I'm your gal!"

"You're scaring me." He peered at my tank of hydrozoan jellyfish that hung in the water like glowing white lanterns with horns. "Why do you keep those things? Don't you see enough jellies on dives?"

"I'm studying their behavior. Jellies are the oldest multi-organ animal. Somewhere between 500 and 700 million years old."

"Gosh, hon, they don't *look* that old."

"Close, wise guy. You're looking at animals with no internal organs, no bones, no brains, that can regenerate their entire bodies over and over. There are a lot of scientists studying how they manage to bypass death."

"I guess only a critter with no brain could live forever and not go nuts." He kissed my cheek. "I suppose I could manage it with you by my side."

"But could you give up your organs?"

He stared at the tank. "Question is, how do you know you're immortal without a brain?"

"Maybe that's what prevents them from going nuts."

"Speaking of nuts. Did you catch the news? They had a terrorist jerk yelling his head off that 'this monstrosity' was caused by the U.S. meddling with God's Order."

I sighed. "We're all meddlers, hon. Overfishing, lawn fertilizers that wash into the oceans as nutrients. We have met the polluters and they are us."

Ice whined behind the door. I got up and let him in. He jumped all over Culley. "Was it good for you, Ice?" Culley rubbed his ears.

"You're a pervert," I told Culley, and joined him in bed with Ice between us. I thought about the flip in ocean ecosystems. Years ago, fish had dominated. Now, in 2041, the jellyfish are dominant. "Maybe the jerks are right, after all," I said, "if there's such a thing as God's Order."

"Yeah. Retired divers still talk about the good old days when there were plenty of fish in the ocean and you could dive without a wet suit and not get eaten alive by stinging jellies, especially box jellyfish."

"Oh, they're killers. I've been thinking about the octopus," I said.

"So has the whole world. What are your thoughts?"

"If she were just a mutation, who would she have mated with to produce those giant babies? There must be giant males too."

"Well, that's encouraging," he said.

"The question is, Culley, if they're deep-sea dwellers, what brought her into shallow water? My intuition tells me she's just the avant-garde."

"Tess, any chance that you could just go back to studying jellies in tanks?"

"You want me to stay out of the water, don't you?"

He nodded.

"Are you going to stay topside?" I asked.

"Probably not. I'll go where I'm needed to do what I can. Would you want me to just cover my ass, like Ace? That's a trick I never learned."

"No, I suppose not." I stroked his cheek. "But that's what you want me to do."

He stared at the tank of jellies. "Promise me you'll only dive when I'm there to be your buddy."

"It might not work out that way."

"I just found you, Tess, now you've got me worrying I could lose you."

I laid my head on his arm. "And I could lose you. We've got tonight, Culley. That's all we know for certain. You said it yourself, there are no guarantees in life."

CHAPTER FOUR

The choir sang the Ave Maria as Culley and I filed into the Catholic church with the long line of mourners at Bruce Tracy's funeral. The smell of flowers was thick and cloying. Dust swirled in the light that filtered through stained-glass windows. Culley and I stood quietly in the back. The priest, a sixtyish bald-headed man, began his eulogy from the pulpit, above Tracy's coffin, which was draped with an American flag. A photo of Bruce, the same photo I saw in the newspaper, stood framed on the coffin. Behind the priest, a cross hung on the wall with a figure of the crucified Christ.

A solemn hush fell over the mourners, broken only by the crying of an infant, as the priest began to speak.

"He was my friend, faithful and true," he said and wiped a tear. "I loved Bruce Tracy like a brother."

I heard soft sobs from the front pews. "The Lord is my shepherd," the priest said. "I shall not want." Neither Culley nor I are Christians. Both of us lean toward a pagan belief in the sanctity of nature. But many of the mourners responded: "Though I walk in the valley of darkness, I fear no evil, for you are with me."

I hadn't known Bruce, but by the end of the mass I was shaken. How many more deaths, how many more church masses and tears, before this creature would be killed or driven back to the deeps? I chewed a nail. Culley took my hand and lowered it as we listened to the choir.

> So I leave my boats behind
> Leave them on familiar shores
> Set my heart upon the deep.
> Follow You again my Lord."

Culley and I were quiet as we held hands and filed out of the church with the mourners.

"Hey, Tess. Culley!" It was Jen O'Malley. Tom Crowley was with her.

They walked up to us.

Tom's eyes were red, from crying, I assumed.

"So, Tess," Jen said, "does Pacifica Lab have plans on how to destroy this monstrosity?"

"Right now, they're just holding conferences. They're trying to formulate a plan of action."

"Well," Tom said, "I hope they formulate soon! We just got word that a barge was sunk. The hull was burned through with acid."

"They lost two crewmen," Jen said.

"this is terrible," I said. "The Lab's working with the government, and the

Navy. That's all we can do right now."

I looked at Tom and shrugged.

"It's a pretty desperate situation," he said.

"The Lab knows that. They might get a scientific expedition together to go out and see what we can find."

Jen shook her head. "Let us know, OK?"

I nodded and watched them walk away.

"That's a lot to put on Pacifica's shoulders," Culley said.

"Well, they've got broad shoulders."

We kissed goodbye and went to our vehicles.

I wiped tears that blurred my vision as I drove to the Pacifica Lab, more determined than ever to help destroy this creature that killed humans, or drive it back into the depths, where it belonged.

CHAPTER FIVE

"Tess!" I heard Culley call.

I turned with the heavy box of frozen food in my arms. Culley ran down the dock to where I stood, helping to load provisions on Pacifica Lab's sixty-foot research vessel, R/V *Reverence For Life*. By the look in Culley's eyes I felt an argument coming on.

"What are you doing?" he said.

"My job, Culley."

"I don't want you going out there!" He waved toward the harbor. An early sun spread diamonds across the quiet water of Monterey Bay. The box felt heavier and I shifted it. "We've already had this discussion in my apartment." I saw the pain in his eyes. "It's my job, hon."

Brad Bellows came out of the cabin. "Oh, hi, there, Mr. Nice Guy," he said to Culley. Brad jumped easily to the dock, threw back his shock of blonde hair, and took the box from my arms. "Here, let me help you with that heavy box, lady." He glanced at Culley, whose expression had turned stony, and smiled. "There are still gentlemen left in the world."

"Gentleman," Culley responded, "who let a woman to go out on a dangerous job?"

Uh, oh, I thought.

"I suppose you're not familiar with the equality of the sexes," Brad said. "It's an old concept that postdates keeping females barefoot in the winter and pregnant in the summer."

They had never met. I saw Culley's lip curl as he took stock of Brad's tight white pants, his blousy blue shirt, his captain's hat pushed back to show his hair, and his necklace of plastic shark teeth. His features are too heavy to call handsome, but he's a charmer and some women are drawn to him. Myself, I always wonder what's in a charmer's quick smile. Are they afraid to show their real nature? But he's my boss, and so I'm tolerant. It's a survival trait. Anyway, sometimes I like him.

But I didn't like the look in Culley's eyes. "C'mon." I took his hand and led him away from Brad.

We sat on a bench on the dock.

"Look, Culley, just because we declared our love for each other and consummated it, that doesn't give you the right to run my life. I'm sorry. I'm scared too, you know, but we have to study these creatures and find a way to destroy them or drive them back into the depths."

"Yeah, we're good at destroying anything that moves. You know for sure there's more than one?"

The breeze blew my hair around my neck. He brushed it behind my ear.

"Reports have been coming into the Lab. There's a lot more than one."

"How bad is it?"

I stared out at the bay. Sea lions barked and seagulls cawed. "As bad as it gets," I said. From somewhere there came the clicking of a sea otter breaking a shell with a rock. It's a symphony that I love. "Reports are coming in from states and countries in the Pacific ring of fire," I told him. "You know, where tectonic plates grind against each other and cause earthquakes."

He nodded.

"It's the most active volcanic area in the world." I chewed a nail and wondered if that could have something to do with the Krakens coming into shallow waters.

Culley took my hand and lowered it. He's on a mission to stop me from biting my nails.

"From the reports coming in," I said, "the Krakens are all females."

"What does that mean?"

"For some reason, the females don't lay their eggs in deep water anymore." I shrugged. "It could mean many different things. We just don't know. We're dealing with a spectacular new species, in our experience, anyway." I nibbled a nail on my other hand. "We need answers. They're wreaking havoc on sea-going trade. Chinese goods have stopped coming into the Los Angeles ports. And that's just the beginning." I leaned against him and he put an arm around me. "That's why I have to do my part."

"OK."

I smiled up at him. "I knew you'd understand."

"I'm coming, too."

"What?"

He nodded toward the boat. "They can always use an extra diver."

I thought of Brad and Culley in the relatively close quarters of a sixty-foot boat and rubbed my forehead. *This is not going to work,* I thought.

He read my thought. "I'll behave myself."

I nodded. "OK. Thanks."

"As long as dandy pants does too."

It's not going to work!

"Tess!" Brad called. He stood in the stern, his wrist raised, and jabbed a finger at his watch.

"Where's Ice?" Culley asked as we walked toward the boat.

"I left him with a neighbor."

"Wish I could leave you with a neighbor."

Culley jumped into the boat and extended a hand to me. I took it and jumped in.

"Whatever happened to 'Permission to come aboard'?" Brad asked Culley.

"Brad," I said, "we could always use another good diver."

Two men came out of the cabin. They both wore crew cuts and had the self-assured look of athletes who know their physical limits are beyond the norm. They moved with the grace of big cats.

The taller, light-haired man called Culley by his first name. "Ryan." He nodded a greeting. "Are you in on this job?" I detected a slight British accent. A cigarette dangled from his mouth. There was a look in his blue eyes that was cold and devoid of emotion. I took an instant dislike to him but I told myself, *Give the guy a chance,* The fact that he and Culley didn't shake hands only added to my gut feeling.

"You'll have to ask the boss," Culley told him. He turned to the shorter, dark-skinned man who extended a muscled arm. "Rámon," Culley said. They shook hands. "Good to see you." He glanced at Brad. "Am I in on this job?"

"Well." Brad fluttered his hands. "If our Navy SEAL team wants you on board, I suppose I can't say no. Anyway, it'll keep Tessica happy."

Culley introduced me to the two men. The light-haired guy was Phil.

"I'll get my gear," Culley said. "It's aboard my boat." He smiled at me. I turned my back to Brad and smiled back at him.

Phil and Rámon accompanied Culley to his boat, which was berthed not far down the dock, to help with his gear.

Brad watched Culley go. "Nice tuckus," he said. "Too bad he's such a shit."

"It doesn't matter, boss. He's taken."

Brad shrugged. "There are plenty of fish in the ocean."

If you like fish, I thought but didn't say.

"Are Mini and George on board?" I walked toward the cabin.

Brad nodded. "Mini thinks we should tag a sea-cam on one of those creatures to study its movements. That is, if we *find* one of them. I'd prefer to have our SEALS kill the bitch and tow her back to the lab's private beach for Mini to dissect. Well?"

"What do I think? We may not have a choice in the matter, but I vote for the camera. I'd like to know if they return to their deep homes after the eggs hatch. If that's their pattern of behavior, we might be able to drive them back for good by destroying as many of their eggs as possible. Although, the sea-cam data might suggest a different course of action."

"We'll just have to wait and see."

Mini opened the cabin door and ducked under it. The smell of frying bacon and eggs wafted out. "Hi, Tess. I thought I heard you."

"Hi, Mini."

She gave me that broad smile that lights up her face. Mini's real name is Minerva Johnson, but with her playful sense of humor, my six-foot tall, slender and graceful African-American friend towers over most of us.

"C'mon," she said and waved me into the cabin. "It's my turn to slave over a hot stove." Her ebony skin shone with blue highlights in the sun. Her bushy hair was tied back with her usual brightly colored scarf, making a halo around her angular face. Mini could have been a runway model with her striking good looks, but she'd opted for marine biology, with a specialty in cephalopods, which included octopuses.

I hugged her. "How are things?"

"Which things?" She gestured toward the open sea. "The ones out there?"

"I'd like to compare notes on that."

"Me too, Tess. But first let's eat."

George Backer was at the table, scarfing down eggs and bacon. His plate was heaped with food.

"George!" Mini scolded, "you're going to eat up our provisions before we leave the dock."

George grinned as he chewed and brushed crumbs off the stained shirt stretched across his bulging belly. At forty-two, his hair was already going fast. He sweeps what's left over his scalp. His complexion is ruddy. His smile is quick and a bit shy. He knocked over the salt shaker as he reached for another pancake from the platter. He's clumsy, awkward, and is a brilliant marine ecologist. But he loves to eat and we worry that it could be his undoing.

"Hi, George." I sat next to him and rubbed his arm. George loves shows of affection.

He nodded and chewed. "Tess," he said around a mouthful, leaned over and gave me a wet kiss on the cheek. "Are you hungry? I saved some pancakes for you." He stabbed one from the platter with his fork and plopped it into my dish.

"I'll wait for Culley."

"Oh?" Mini turned from the stove and raised her eyebrows. "Is Culley coming too?"

I smiled. "Culley, too."

"Speak of the devil," George said as Culley, Phil, and Rámon entered the cabin, followed by Brad. Phil turned and coughed into his hand.

Culley sat next to me and I smiled at him. The others took seats. I introduced Culley to George and Mini.

"Do de black maid get to eat too?" Mini sat down and speared a pancake with her fork.

George stopped chewing. "Mini, I wish you wouldn't talk that way." A piece of pancake flew out of his mouth. "It makes me think you have some unresolved issues with slavery."

"Oh, ice down," Mini said. "If I had unresolved issues I wouldn't talk that way."

I glanced around the table. We could have been representatives of different countries at the U.N. Brad Bellows, with his Scandinavian hair and skin coloring. Phil, whose grandparents immigrated here from England. Hispanic Rámon, Culley's black Irish coloring, George Backer, of German descent. Mini Johnson, my Nubian friend, and me, Tessica Hoffman, with my Jewish heritage. I thought of a Hollywood film from the last century: *The Magnificent Seven*. We'd have to be magnificent to challenge the deep-sea creatures we were about to seek.

CHAPTER SIX

The day turned cold and drizzly as we headed southwest, toward the coordinates, northeast of the Hawaiian Islands. Swells hissed around the boat as we sliced through three-foot waves and left white lashes on the heaving back of the sea. I lifted the hood of my rain jacket, wiped my wet cheeks, and squinted into the foggy distance.

Sightings of two giant octopuses had been reported by fishing boats and we were underway to the location. Navy boats from the Pearl Harbor Naval Station were also on the hunt for giant octopuses.

The depth at the location was over 6,000 feet. Could *that* be where the species originated? I thought of the Japanese radiation spills from their nuclear power plants back in 2011, after a tsunami, and the U.S. atomic-bomb tests on Bikini atoll in the last century. Nurse sharks had been spotted near Bikini with just one dorsal fin, when they normally have two. Radiation can cause tumors and tumors in the pituitary glands can cause gigantism. I'd have to ask Mini if octopuses had pituitary glands. But what about those acid sacs? That seemed more like a natural defense and an improved mechanism for killing prey, instead of the ink sacs other octopuses have for defense. Was that also a mutation or did it evolve in the deep sea, where prey is scarce, over millions of years? As usual in science, we had more questions than answers.

We needed to collect data and compare notes with scientists around the Pacific ring. I sighed. In the end, just killing the octopuses or destroying their eggs wasn't going to give us the information we needed to address this threat.

A ray of sunlight off the starboard side pierced the gloom of gray clouds. What lay beneath these waters? We had a mini remotely-operated vehicle on board, an ROV for short, so we could view the bottom when we reached our destination.

Culley was at the helm. Brad was taking his usual three p.m. nap. Phil and Rámon were working in the stern on some problem they discovered with the air compressor we used to fill our scuba tanks. Phil used his cigarette butt to light the next cigarette, then threw the butt overboard. If it were anyone else I would have explained that fish eat the filters, then die, and are eaten by other fish, who also die. Somehow I knew that Phil wouldn't be open to the suggestion. I heard him cough. He did that a lot lately.

Mini and George came on deck. Mini sported a beautiful red silk scarf tied around the back of her hair. The scarf was striking against her ebony skin, her slanted eyes, and prominent cheekbones, and one of the few luxuries she allowed herself in her dress.

We both preferred casual pants and shirts for working. She towered over George, whose bald pate showed as his strands of hair were lifted by wind. George was eating a candy bar and hurrying to keep up with Mini's long stride. As usual, they were arguing about some moot point in the interrelationships of sea life.

I was glad they were such good friends. George had been bullied as a child, and abused by his own father, who couldn't cope with anger. George had been a lonely child, he once told me. But he was good at math, and was curious and bright. He turned to science, he said, not only because he loved it, but because it gave him some prestige. He also turned to food, as a way to comfort the emptiness he felt inside.

"The cosmic emptiness," Brad called it. I wondered if Brad felt it too?

"Oh, look!" I said as a school of bottlenose dolphins suddenly appeared and leaped through bow waves like sprites that rode the worlds of air and water with equal joy. "Oh, look at them." Something within me swelled and I felt a surge of love for these wild, exuberant creatures. I wanted to jump into the water. I wanted to see the world through frothy veils of sea foam. I wanted to join them in their search for schools of sardines. I spread my arms. "Wait for me!" I called to the dolphins and laughed.

"Hold her down, George," Mini said as they approached, "before she jumps in and starts living on sushi."

"Sushi?" George asked. "Do we have sushi in the freezer?"

"Oh, for God's sake, George," Mini said, "If I told you we have a package of rats' asses in the freezer, you'd be defrosting it!"

"That's not very nice," George said. I saw the hurt look on his furrowed brow. He fished a candy bar out of his pants pocket and opened it.

"Mini," I whispered and shook my head.

Suddenly the dolphins veered to starboard and plunged away.

"Wonder what scared them?" Mini said.

"Hey, you guys!" Culley called from the helm. "Take a look off the port bow, and tell me what you see."

We made our way to port side, holding onto the rails.

A huge mat of brown kelp glistened and undulated in the waves. It was longer than our sixty-foot vessel and wider. In the distance a smaller mat floated.

"Fucales," George said.

"What did you say?" Mini asked.

"Kelp," George answered, "of the order fucales."

"Oh," Mini replied. "I thought you were saying fuck in Italian."

"What's it doing in such deep water?" I said. "Kelp only grows in shallow littoral zones."

"That's true." George nodded. "That's true, but it could have been torn from its holdfasts in a storm." His eyes widened as he studied the closer, great mat. He stopped chewing.

"There haven't *been* any storms. It's getting closer! Culley, does it look like it's getting closer from where you are?"

He leaned forward to peer through a window on the bridge "It's creeping up on us," he called.

George had a death grip on the rail. Mini studied the mat with a hand pressed to her throat. "Octopuses can mimic just about anything they want to."

"Oh my God!" I said as the closer mat morphed into a huge oblong shape that jetted toward the boat. Its brown color deepened to bright red, denoting anger in an octopus. The air bladders that hold kelp upright suddenly elongated into knobby octopus skin.

"There's your sushi!" Mini said. "C'mon!" She headed for the cabin. George and I followed. I slammed the door behind me. Brad mumbled something and fanned his face as though he were chasing flies. He turned over and resumed snoring as the boat lurched to starboard and the engines roared.

Mini took out the sea-cam she wanted to attach to a giant octopus. She fastened it to the end of a dart gun that had a barb designed to penetrate thick skin and hold it securely in place. The cam would extend and right itself with its air bubble, and rotate for a 380 degree view.

Phil and Rámon barged into the cabin, silently unzipped their duffel bags and pulled out rifles. I'd never seen such scary-looking weapons. Phil had an assault rifle with a grenade launcher. Rámon had a submachine gun. I had the shakes. I could see the octopus from the porthole. She was gaining on us. I stared at the weapons. She was going to be sorry.

Mini took her dart gun and paused at the door. "You realize," she looked from Phil to Rámon, "that while you two are hot to make bite-size chunks out of her, this is *still* a scientific expedition. Priority one is to tag the octopus with this sea-cam and collect data on the species' behavior and movements."

Rámon grabbed her arm. She towered over him like a sapling over a stump. "Our mission," he said, "is to also protect the crew of this boat."

Mini tried to break free but couldn't. "Let go of my arm!"

Rámon did.

"Stay in the cabin," Phil ordered Mini.

I saw the fear in Mini's eyes. She backed a step.

George faded into the background and for a moment there was only the sound of Brad snoring.

Culley kept us ahead of the octopus. I think he was waiting to hear our plan. Rámon and Phil loaded their weapons.

"Suppose you give Mini a chance to attach the sea-cam," I said to Phil. "If the octopus puts us in danger, then you can kill her."

"There's one problem with that plan, lady." Phil covered a cough. "Our orders are to kill every damned one of them that pops its head out of water." He went out the door, followed by Rámon.

"How are we ever going to learn what these creatures are about," I asked, "with those guys on board?"

"The thing is," George said, stepping out of shadows, "with the octopuses' high degree of intelligence, the other one will learn from its companion's death and use different tactics in the future. We'll just be breeding for a smarter species of octopus. You know, like house flies."

"House flies?" Mini asked.

"Yes," George answered. "When you swat a housefly -- "

"Save it for some other time," Mini told him. "In the last three decades octopuses have been observed teaching the young ones. They're evolving."

I went out on deck. "Listen, guys," I said to Phil and Rámon, "Mini is an expert on octopuses. She says that if you kill this one, the other one is going to learn some new tricks. We'll just have a more powerful enemy."

"More powerful than this?" Phil tapped the rifle. "Culley!"

"What's up?" Culley called from an open bridge window.

"Throttle down," Phil told him.

Culley looked at me.

I spread my hands. "They've been ordered to kill it."

Mini and George came out of the cabin. Mini had the dart gun in hand. George had a candy bar.

Culley nodded toward the dart gun. "What about that?"

"We've got our orders," Rámon called.

"They tell me this is a scientific expedition," Culley said, "not a sea hunt."

"It's a military operation first, Ryan," Phil called. "Now goddammit, throttle down!" The strain on his voice made him cough again.

My throat tightened. "Culley? Culley, do what he says, hon. Please."

Culley smiled at me. "OK, Tess. Don't worry. Come on up here with me."

I went to the bridge. He opened the door and pulled me in. "Whatever the military wants."

He slammed the door, locked it and went back to the wheel. I heard the deep-throated roar of engines grow louder and faster. I held on as the boat plowed forward. The octopus was left behind. It sank beneath the waves, probably exhausted. The other one also disappeared.

Phil's face, framed in the window of the door, was distorted with rage. He slammed a fist on the window. "Goddamn you, Ryan!" He raised the butt of his rifle to smash the window. "Open the fucking door!"

"Open it, Tess," Culley said.

I did, and stood between Phil and Culley, my heart pounding.

Culley set the helm on automatic and moved in front of me. "You're in the line of fire, Tess."

Phil threw Culley aside and went to the wheel. "Where the hell do you come off interfering with a military operation?"

"Leave him alone!" I shouted at Phil.

"The same place you get off interfering with a scientific expedition." Culley pushed Phil away from the wheel. "A dead Kraken isn't going to tell these people *anything* about the animals. This isn't a war, Phil, but you kill enough of them, you just might start one."

"Damn you, Ryan, I've got my orders!" His pale complexion flushed with anger. "Now get the hell out of my way!" He lunged at Culley. They both went down.

"Stop it. Phil!" I pulled at the back of his shirt. "Stop it!"

Rámon came in, pushed me aside, and got them separated. "That's enough, *amigos*," he said gently.

Mini stood outside the door. George was gone, probably hiding in the cabin.

"Take it easy, Phil," Rámon said and put a hand on Phil's shoulder. "Take it easy, OK, buddy? We'll launch the ROV. With some luck, we'll find those creatures of the devil again."

"Look, you two," Mini said to Phil and Rámon, "it's pretty clear that we're at odds. The ROV belongs to Pacifica National Lab and we don't intend to loan it out to the military so you can kill octopuses." She shook her head. "I can't believe" you guys. We'll drop you off at the Pearl Harbor Naval Station. Then we can all get on with our missions." She went out on deck.

"You heard her, boys," Culley told Phil and Rámon. He led me onto the deck. "C'mon, Tess, let's go chain the ROV to something strong."

"Take the wheel, Rámon," Phil said and coughed again..

Rámon did.

Phil came out of the bridge and stood in front of Culley, staring into his eyes. I've seen dead fish that looked friendlier. "I'd like to feed you to the crabs," Phil said, "but I'm afraid they'd choke on your big mouth."

Culley extended a protective arm in front of me. "Why don't you try it anyway, Phil?" he said too softly. "You were always hot to kill something."

Anger flared in Phil's eyes. "I'll ask you one more time, big mouth. Are you going to interfere with our mission again or can I trust you to obey the military laws of our country?"

"The only laws I obey," Culley said, "are the ones that make sense. When you start making sense, let me know." He took my arm. "C'mon, Tess."

I was surprised when Phil moved out of our way. I heard him cough from behind us.

Culley and I were walking back to the cabin when I heard a thud. Culley cried out. He dropped my hand and crumpled to the deck.

Phil stood behind him with his rifle raised, butt forward.

"Culley!" I kneeled beside him and cradled his head. "Culley." I stroked his face. "Oh my God! Wake up."

His eyes were half closed. His jaw was slack. A trickle of blood from the back of his head wet my arm. "He's bleeding!" I cried.

"He'll live." Phil grabbed Culley's wrist and in one motion he lifted him over his shoulder. "Now I'll chain the big-mouth to something strong."

"You bastard!" I jumped up and pummeled his back with my fists. "Why did you hit him?"

He shoved me away. "Go dissect a frog or something, lady. I'm through pampering you nerds."

Mini came out of the cabin. "Tess? Tess, what the hell's going on?" She saw Culley and gasped. "Oh, no! He's not *dead?*"

Phil pushed her aside and went into the cabin. He dumped Culley on his bunk.

I grabbed a towel and pressed it to the back of Culley's head to stop the bleeding.

"Are you crazy?" Mini said to Phil.

Brad was still sleeping in his bunk.

Phil remained silent as he took a pair of handcuffs from his duffel bag.

"No, don't," I pleaded.

"Get out of his way," Mini told me. "He's nuts."

Phil handcuffed Culley's limp wrist to the bunk. He lit a cigarette and left the cabin. The door to the head slowly opened. George peeked out. "Is he gone?" He peered around the cabin from a crack in the door.

"He's gone all right," Mini said. "He's out there with Pluto!"

I sat beside Culley. I was shaking badly. Mini patted my shoulder. "He'll be OK, Tess."

Brad stirred, sat up and yawned. "I had a good nap." He rubbed his eyes and nodded at Culley. "Oh, Mr. Nice Guy's taking a nap too."

He got up, scratched his butt and went to the head. "You finished in there?" he asked George.

"I guess so." George tiptoed out.

Culley moaned and rolled his head.

"Culley?" I said softly. "Hon?"

He moaned again and blinked. Then he grimaced as the pain hit. I gently dabbed beads of perspiration from his face with an edge of the towel. He stared up at me and mumbled something.

"What, baby?"

"I should've seen it coming." He pressed a hand gingerly to his head. "He always had a rotten temper." He tried to move his handcuffed right hand. "Oh, Christ."

"It's all right." I wiped his clammy forehead and hoped he wasn't going into shock. "Mini?" I said shakily, "could you please bring him a blanket?"

She nodded, took one out of the closet and covered him.

I tucked it around his shoulders.

"Your lady takes good care of you." Mini smiled.

Culley rubbed his forehead and moaned.

"Does it still hurt bad?" I asked.

"Yeah, but I've got to pee."

Brad came out of the bathroom zippering up his fly. He saw the handcuffs and made a face. "Can't you two save your kinky sex for when you're alone?" He glanced at Mini and raised his eyebrows. "Or is this a *ménage à trois?*"

CHAPTER SEVEN

I left Culley alone with a bucket to give him privacy and went to the bridge. The sea had calmed. Rain dappled the surface and small fish leaped.

Rámon was at the helm. Phil maneuvered the ROV from the controls on the console. George and Brad watched the screen. Mini turned in her chair and smiled at me. "How's Culley?"

I shrugged. My knees felt shaky. My throat choked up and tears burned my eyes. "I...."

Mini got up and led me to a chair. I sat down. "I think he'll be all right," I said.

"I told you he'll live," Phil threw back.

"Why don't you go fuck yourself!" I said.

He nodded without turning. "Sometimes I do."

"Your chances of finding the octopuses now," I told him, "are about one digit away from zero on the negative side."

The ROV was at a thousand feet. A passing bioluminescent fish inspected it and moved on. A red jellie pumped past and disappeared into the black gloom of this eternal night.

"Wait," Mini said as a small deep-sea lobster, caught in the vehicle's lights, scuttled by with four claws raised.

George leaned forward to stare at the screen. "It's...it's a -- "

"Another mutation," Mini said.

"You know what?" George said, "We need a sample of the bottom sediment and the water to test for toxicity."

"Did you *hear* that?" I asked Phil.

"He's commandeered the boat for a military emergency," Brad told me. "There's nothing more we can do on this trip. In fact, we're ordered by law to help them. I should have never given them permission to come aboard." He fluttered a hand. "What can I say?"

"Is that legal?" I asked Brad.

"It's legal," Phil said. "The military is authorized to use lethal force if necessary in situations of a perceived threat to the nation." He sounded as though he were reading it from a book. He turned to us. "Keep that in mind if you suddenly decide that science is more important than the safety of the populace, or the life of a fish!"

There was no use arguing with him. He was just following orders. It's a concept that goes way back to World War II. I sighed. The fact that those orders might increase the threat just didn't fit in with his mindset.

The ROV showed nothing more than a few jellies, a sea cucumber with modified arms for clinging to the mud, and two normal deep-sea crabs mating.

"Now that's a turn-on," Brad said.

I was always amazed at the evolutionary twists and turns in deep-sea creatures as they adapted to the conditions of cold, and pressure, and endless night, thousands of feet down. Life had a grip wherever it could eke out a living.

The ROV passed above what seemed to be a large mound of mud. I slid Mini a look. She nodded discreetly. *A giant octopus!* I thought. I glanced at George.

He raised his brows. "Mini, I'm getting hungry. Is there any sushi in the frig?"

"Oh, yes, George. It's on the bottom shelf."

Brad glanced at Mini. "Cephalopod sushi?" he said, meaning, in this case, octopus.

"Absolutely," Mini answered.

Phil began to spool in the ROV by its spider-optic cable. "Is food all you people ever think about?"

I went back to see Culley and emptied the bucket. He was sitting on the bunk. I sat next to him. "How do you feel?" I gently brushed his hair back off his forehead.

"Better, now that you're here." He gave me a crooked smile and put an arm around my shoulders. "I know how important this mission is. I tried, Tess."

"I know you did, hon. They've commandeered the boat. Phil calls the giant octopus invasion a national emergency. He's right, of course. Too bad we're at odds on how to handle it. Culley, he says it gives him the authority to use lethal force, if necessary. In fact, we're legally obligated to help him kill as many giant octopuses as we can find."

Culley put a hand to the back of his head and gingerly felt around. His hand came away dry. "Yeah. It overrides the captain's authority. I want you to stay as far away from Phil as you can. He's dangerous, Tess. Don't cross him. I was on a dive job with Phil before he became a SEAL. He got a local diver killed when he told the guy to use a torch inside a cave. The oxygen built up under the ceiling and exploded. He should've known better."

"There were no ramifications?"

"He told the authorities the diver did the cave work on his own. Phil never mentioned it again. I don't think he had a minute of guilt."

"Was Rámon with him?"

"He met Rámon when they became SEALS. I don't know how Phil squeezed past the SEAL's screening. Their qualifications are pretty tough."

"Maybe he's a charmer. What about Rámon? Doesn't he see through Phil's facade?"

"Rámon's an OK guy, but I don't think he has a clue about the real Phil. My friendship with Phil ended when the diver was killed."

A thud suddenly rocked the boat. I jumped up. "What was that?"

Culley forgot he was handcuffed and tried to get up. He fell back. We looked at each other. Another thud made the boat shudder. I tripped over Culley's feet and fell. He helped me up.

"I'm going to get the key!" I said.

"Tess! Don't cross him."

The boat's collision alarm went off.

"Dammit!" I muttered and ran onto the deck. Brad was there. I froze as a great red tentacle rose above me from the water.

Brad grabbed my arm and yanked me away as the tentacle crashed down onto the deck. The boat rocked and we were thrown against the side. I screamed as the octopus put her weight into tipping it. I would have slid over the side but Brad grabbed my leg and dragged me back. We crawled to the bridge. Mini came out, with George braced against the door, holding her wrist in a fireman's grip. His eyes bulged. Brad grabbed Mini's other wrist and held mine too. We scrambled onto the bridge. Brad slammed the door as the octopus lifted herself and tipped the boat again. I heard it take on water. "Oh my God! Culley!"

The bilge pumps automatically turned on. Brad got to the helm and swerved the boat hard to port in a wild circle calculated to shake the creature loose. Mini grabbed the dart gun. She opened the door.

"Mini!" George cried, "for God's sake, don't go out there!"

Phil and Rámon were in the stern with their weapons, holding on as they sloshed through water in an attempt to get close to the octopus.

"Phil," I screamed. "The key." I went onto the deck and held on.

He ignored me. Mini fired the dart. It hit its target and the tagged octopus jerked back and sank beneath the surface.

The boat righted itself. I made my way to Phil. "Give me the key!"

He turned his weapon on me. There was a look in his eyes that made me think of barracudas. "Please, Phil," I said softly, "just...just give me the key."

He pushed me aside and peered over the gunnel. The swirling water calmed. There was no sign of the octopus.

Phil's jaw tightened. He ripped the dart gun from Mini's hand and flung it overboard. "You black bitch!"

Mini's lip curled into a smile. "I've been called worse."

Brad and George emerged from the bridge. George was as white as a sheet. He staggered to the side of the boat, leaned over, and threw up.

"Well, this has been an interesting day," Brad said and laughed. "I hope we don't have any more like it."

"Brad," I said, "you just saved my life."

He pursed his lips. "Well I hate to lose a good employee." He took my chin in one hand and shook it. "Think nothing of it. Culley would have absolutely murdered me if I let *you* go over the side."

"As captain of the ship," I said to Brad, "can you order Phil to give me the key to Culley's handcuffs?"

"When I'm good and ready," Phil said and went to the cabin.

I followed.

Culley was standing. "Tess! You all right?"

"I'm fine, Culley. I'm fine." I went to him.

He hugged me with one arm. "God, Tess...."

"How's your head?" I asked.

"Not bad." He glared at Phil. "If anything happens to her, you're lunch for the fish."

"Heartwarming, Ryan, heartwarming to see there's something you finally care about." He sat down heavily, laid the rifle on the table, and covered a cough. "Besides yourself." He looked exhausted and drawn.

Culley raised his handcuffed arm as far as it would go. "Do I have to chew off my wrist or are you going to unlock this?"

"You're an honorable man," Phil said. "Give me your word that you won't interfere again with my mission. Let's say for old times sake. It's your call."

Culley looked at me.

"Mini tagged the octopus," I said. "It was a good shot."

Phil leaned back and rubbed his eyes. He lit a cigarette, inhaled, and coughed again.

"For old times sake." Culley smirked. "You bastard."

Phil reached into his shirt pocket, fished out the key and threw it at Culley's feet.

I picked it up, smiled at Culley, and unlocked the handcuffs.

Culley rubbed his wrist. "Now I know how a dog feels, chained to a tree."

CHAPTER EIGHT

We sat in the cabin the morning after the octopus attack. It was George's turn to cook breakfast. He was dressed in a white apron and chef's hat. He loved to play the part. He also loved to pick at the food while he cooked. "Today's special is blintzes with chopped nuts." He grinned at me. "I'm making this just for you, Tessica."

"Thanks, George." *Blintzes with nuts?* "It's been a while since I've had real home cooking."

Culley sat quietly at the table next to me. Phil and Rámon had cooked their own breakfast and were eating on the bridge.

I knew Culley was saddled with an invisible bond, his word. It was sacred to him, and one of the reasons I loved him, but it put restrictions on what the rest of us could confide to him while on this voyage. Phil was mean and dangerous, but he wasn't stupid. He had forced Culley into an agreement not to interfere with him and Rámon. Not only could Culley no longer interfere, it covertly suggested that he was now on their side. While the rest of us could plot and conceal our scientific research when it was at odds with Phil and Rámon's plans, for Culley, that would mean breaking his word.

Brad appeared to be off in another world. He fingered his necklace of plastic shark teeth and stared at the wall. "I've been thinking about our encounter with the octopus," he finally said.

"What are your thoughts?" Mini asked.

"If it wanted to board the boat and kill us, or sink the boat, don't you find it hard to believe that a small dart in the ass of a hundred-foot-long creature would deter it?"

"They have no asses," Mini told him. "Head, foot, visceral mass, mantle, equals octopus."

"The dart seemed to deter her," I said.

"That's the point, Tessica," Brad replied. "It *seemed* to. You told me yourself, Minerva, that they're the smartest fish in the ocean."

George turned from the stove, spatula in hand, to listen.

"And so they are," Mini said, "but get to the point, Bradford."

Culley looked from Mini to Brad. "Is this a private conversation? I'll go eat on deck."

"No, no, stay," Brad told him. "The point is, suppose the creature had another plan."

"Another plan?" George asked. "Like what kind of other plan?"

"Oh my God!" I sat back and looked at Culley. "Suppose she planted eggs in a burned-out den in the hull?"

There was silence, while oil spattered in the pan and smoke rose. George stood, open-mouthed, the spatula held up, like a statue of a chef.

Brad leaned on the table with his chin cupped in his hand. "George, your nuts are burning."

*****

While I had no use on God's green earth for Phil, I had to admire his diving style. He, Rámon, and Culley were three of the most efficient divers I had ever dived with. Not one wasted motion to use up air. They moved as though they'd been born in the sea.

We scanned the hull, and there, amidships, where the octopus had surfaced, was a burned-out area of the outer hull, about three feet wide and four feet long, with strands of eggs glued to the inner hull. If *Reverence* hadn't been a double-hull vessel, the octopus would have sunk her.

The plan was that I could take some egg samples and then Phil and Rámon would torch the rest. Culley held a glass jar that we hoped was impervious to this species' form of acid, while I carefully scraped off a few strands of eggs. He guided the strands into the container and screwed on the lid.

Culley and I returned to the deck with the specimens. Neither of us wanted to watch the remaining eggs being torched. It's not that we disagreed with the action. We just didn't want to see it happen.

Mini accompanied us to the lab. It was small, but on the cutting edge of technology. We put the strands in an aquarium and set the water conditions for octopus eggs. Mini kept some eggs to study under the microscope and compare with photos of eggs from other octopus species in her research files.

"I want to dissect a few," she said. "Mother octopus doesn't know what a boon she gave us." She scraped a sample off a dead egg and spread it onto a glass slide with a glass pipette. Glass seemed to be the only element that was impervious to the acid.

"I'll do an in-depth analysis later," she said and peered through the microscope. "Right now I don't see any difference between these embryos and normal octopus eggs, except that these guys are much larger for their early stage of development. Oh, wait a minute." She picked up a slide and carefully scraped the sample with the edge of it.

We waited.

"It seems...they have a mucus coating. I suspect that's what protects the eggs from their own secretions of acid. "She looked up. "I need to do further tests."

Culley went to a window and stared at the ocean. We were both dripping water from our wet suits. "I hope Mom octopus doesn't come back," he said, "and see what we did to the kids."

*****

Culley and I stripped off our neoprene dive suits in the wet room. I was anxious for a hot shower.

"If I take off my bathing suit are you going to give me a hard time?" I said. "I really want a shower."

"Probably pretty hard." He hugged me. We kissed. *Yes, pretty hard,* I realized.

"I'm not going to lie down on this cold, wet cement floor," I told him. "So forget it, Ryan. In fact, take a cold shower."

"Would I ask my lady to lie down on this cold, wet, cement floor?"

I wanted to have sex with him, too, but right now, I wanted a hot shower even more. Salt from the wet suit was drying in streaks on my body.

"Whatever," I said, took off my bathing suit and turned on the shower.

Culley stripped off his bathing suit and got under the water with me. It felt so good to wash off the salt, the sweat from the wet suit, to scrub my hair with shampoo. I gently soaped up the back of Culley's head. The wound had scabbed over. "You heal faster than a crocodile," I told him.

"Tess, is there any chance you'd leave this expedition? The Pacifica Lab could send out a helicopter to pick you up."

I put my arms around his chest from behind and leaned my head against his back. "I wish we could both leave."

"I will if you will."

"Culley, your word is sacred to you, and I love you for it. Would you really want me to do the dishonorable thing and leave my colleagues, especially with Phil and Rámon on board?"

He rubbed his forehead. "Then just promise me you'll let me protect you."

I took his shoulder and turned him around. "I promise, if you'll let me protect you too."

"Whatever."

I saw the anxious look in his eyes. It was then that I realized Culley still had some major issues over the death of his mother. He was the oldest child. He had found her. I intuited that he blamed himself for not seeing the signs of her coming suicide. Christ, he'd only been sixteen! I remained quiet. If Culley ever wanted to talk about it, he'd have to initiate the conversation.

We kissed. The fire rose in both of us. It was just more apparent in him.

The damn cement floor was rough and cold and wet!

After a while, I no longer noticed it.

We emerged from the wet room in our fresh clothes. My hair was damp. Brad was in the cabin doing paperwork. His expertise is in administration, but you'd never know it from his personality and mannerisms. Actually, he's a very good administrator, and business people consult him on various projects and investments.

He looked up as we came in and waggled his head. "L'amour, l'amour," he sang from the opera *Carmen*. *How did he know?* I wondered. He yawned and closed the lid of his computer. "Time for my nap." He went to his bunk and stretched out.

I yawned, then Culley did too. We chuckled. Culley looked at me with such love in his dark eyes, I felt warm and safe. We laid down together, squeezed onto one bunk, and I fell asleep with Culley's arm around me, and for a while, I let the world go away

CHAPTER NINE

Six thousand feet of water separated *Reverence* from the sea floor as Mini, at the helm, cut the engines and we sea-anchored the boat in the warm waters northeast of the Hawaiian Islands. We had reached the coordinates.

"Hello, Mom?" I said into my Q-Tree.

"Tessie," Mom replied. "How are you, baby?"

"I'm good, Mom. Is everybody OK?"

"We're all fine. Where are you?"

"We're northeast of Hawaii. I miss you, and Dad, and Chris. Is Chris doing well in school?"

"Oh, you know Chris. He hates school. He wants to join a circus and travel around the country."

"That's Chris," I said with a sigh.

Our conversation was mundane, but my connection to my family was important. It gave me a sense of my roots out here in the grasp of endless sky and sea.

"Give Dad and Chris my love, Mom. And tell the brat that when I come home we're going to have a long talk about school and circuses."

"OK, Tessie." Mom laughed. "Take care of yourself. I love you, baby."

"I love you too, Mom. Bye." I broke the connection.

Mini was in the lab, doing an in-depth analysis of the biological acid and consulting other scientists around the world with her high-tech quantum computer. It could send millions of messages, if she chose, at the touch of a key, or a word.

Rámon was at the helm, humming a romantic Spanish tune. Phil watched the screens. The sea cam, still attached to the giant octopus and rotating, showed the flank of a small uncharted volcanic island at a thousand feet down. Culley, at the controls of the ROV, guided it toward the octopus so we could get a full view of her activities. George watched silently. I think he was afraid to say anything while Phil was around.

Mini came onto the bridge, followed by Brad, who left the door open. A salty breeze swept through the bridge and ruffled papers. George closed the door. I felt a twinge of fear at Brad's grim expression. It takes a lot to shake him.

"What's up, boss?" I asked.

He sat down heavily and stared at the sea-cam screen. "It doesn't look good."

"What doesn't look good?" George asked.

"Reports. They're coming in from all over the Pacific," Brad said. "Divers go down to inspect the hulls of ships and bridge columns, but they don't come up. The ships' radios pick up muffled screams and then nothing."

We were all silent.

Brad drummed his fingers on the table. "Two fishing boats were sunk off the coast of Japan with no mayday, no debris."

"Like the coast guard cutter," I said to Culley and bit a nail.

He nodded. "Is it worldwide?"

"It seems to be confined to the Pacific," Brad said. "In fact, the Marshall Islands appear to be the nexus of the creatures' population explosion."

The Bikini atoll, I thought. It was part of the Marshall Islands and the site of past atomic bomb testing.

"This morning the Nanue Bridge in Hawaii collapsed," Brad told us. Culley and I looked at each other. Bridge collapses were what we both feared after our encounter with the giant octopus at the North Steinbeck Bridge.

"It was all very sudden," Brad continued. "People died inside their cars. When the authorities inspected the remains of the bridge, they found large holes with giant octopus eggs."

Phil swiveled in his chair. "But you still don't want us to kill them, right?"

The rest of us remained silent.

"Did you finish your tests on the eggs?" I asked Mini.

She nodded. "I saw signs of a point mutation in their cells."

"Well, would that lead to the adaptation of the acid sacs and the mucus?" George asked, "in response to something dangerous in their environment?"

"It could," Mini told him and nodded.

"Then these giants," I said, "are a species that have been around, possibly for millions of years, no?"

"It's very possible," Mini said. "I suspect that the giant Squid ancient sailors reported, the ones that sank ships, were really this species of octopus."

"You know the old cliché," Brad said, "'we know more about the surface of the moon than the bottom of the ocean'."

"So the real question," George said, "is what brought them into shallow water? We need samples of the water, the rocks, and the bottom sediment."

"Look at that!" Rámon said from the wheel. "Are those birds?"

I stood up to look out a window. A flock of dead seagulls floated in the waves.

"Oh my God," I whispered. "Brad, they could have been eating hatchlings! We've got to pick up those birds before fish eat them and die too."

In the ocean a foreign substance can kill many fish as they prey on each other. It used to happen with shiny tabs from soda and beer cans before the improved cans no longer had snap-off tabs. The filters on cigarettes have the same dire effect.

"Ryan," Brad said to Culley, "would you consider collecting those birds? I would really appreciate it. As Tessica says, we need to find out what killed them."

"We'll launch *Nomad,*" Culley said, meaning our fifteen-foot inflatable boat. "George, take the wheel, will you? Hey, Rámon, you want to help me bring in the dead birds?"

"*Si.*" Rámon followed Culley to the deck.

Phil elbowed George aside and took over the helm. George stared at the birds through a window. mini, Brad and I went on deck and helped Culley and Rámon launch *Nomad.* Brad threw in a boat hook and plastic sacks. "From now on," he said, "one of us will be on watch twenty-four-seven, and we all work together."

"Phil *too*?" I asked.

"Tessica, it's obvious that we're at war with the Krakens. So, yes, Phil too. Let bygones be bygones."

"I can't forgive him for what he did to Culley," I said.

"No one's asking you to *forgive*, sweetheart." Brad cupped my chin in his hand. "You just have to work with him. OK?"

I bit my lip. "OK!"

"We'll refuel in Hawaii," Brad said, "and take on provisions. Then we're off to the Bikini atoll."

"Oh." *The nexus,* I thought.

"If anyone decides to leave the expedition," Brad said, "they can disembark when we reach Hawaii and take a plane back to California."

The line drawn in the sand that separates the dedicated from the timid. I wondered which choice George would make. I'd hate to lose him as a team member.

Culley and Rámon gathered fourteen dead birds and put them into the sacks. It was a sad sight.

We winched *Nomad* up to the deck.

"This is a bad day," Rámon said as he and Culley came onto the deck with two sacks of dead birds. Rámon looked up at the sky and crossed himself. We all remained silent as he fished out his gold cross from beneath his shirt, kissed it and said a prayer for the people who perished in the Nanue Bridge disaster, the lost boats, the lost divers, and even the dead seagulls as being the least of God's creations.

I lifted one of the seagulls out of a sack. The bird smelled of acid and wet feathers.

Brad and Culley brought the sacks to a freezer for future studies.

George accompanied me as I took the bird to the lab.

"What happened?" Mini asked as she turned from the computer.

I shook my head. "We're not sure, but something killed a whole flock of seagulls."

"Oh, what a shame," Mini said and got up as I laid the dead bird on the autopsy table.

I told her about the other catastrophes Brad had reported.

"The Nanue Bridge?" she said. "I've been on that bridge. How many people died there?"

"I don't know," I answered. "I wonder where this is going to end?"

George put on his autopsy gloves and took out his instruments.

"He's just a juvenile," George said, studying the bird. He opened the package of instruments and shuddered. "I hate autopsies!"

Mini came to the table and put a hand on George's shoulder. "Think of it as preparing a chicken for dinner."

George nodded, picked up the rib cutter and cut through the bird's breast bone.

"You smell that?" I said as the ribs separated.

"It's hard to ignore!" George replied.

The smell of acid was bitter and overwhelming. Mini and I backed away. George fished out a surgical mask from the package and tied it over his nose and mouth, but he still coughed.

The seagull's stomach and esophagus were blackened and in shreds. George picked out a dead octopus hatchling.

Mini examined the dead bird. "Poor bastard."

"It wasn't an easy death," I said and shuddered as I thought of the divers who had been killed.

"Are you all right, Tess?" Mini asked.

"I'm OK. I was just thinking that there's no end to nature's brutality."

"True," Mini said, "she's a two-faced entity. She gives. She takes. We humans are definitely her children."

"Ah me." George placed tissue specimens in jars. "But pain is pain, and death is death, no matter the species." He labeled the jars and put them in the freezer.

"I've been studying the mucus coating on the eggs," Mini said. "There's an outer layer that contains the acid, much like gastric acid in our own stomachs, but gastric acid doesn't eat through metal. I suspect this cephalopod acid is much more concentrated. I've never seen anything like this."

"Nature doesn't give a fig about our human categories or the limitations we put on her," George said. "Someday, we'll realize that there are more things in heaven and earth than are dreamt of in our science."

"And in the sea," I said.

"Especially in the sea," George added.

"Amen," Mini said.

I smiled as Culley walked in. "Hi, hon."

He smiled back. "Hi, Tessie." He looked at us and furrowed his brow. "Am I interrupting?"

I went to him and kissed him on the cheek. At times I think Culley doesn't feel he measures up to scientists. I had an intuitive sense that he was afraid I'd find another scientist who was more my peer. I studied his face and smiled. A mop of dark brown hair; deep-set hawk eyes; a hooked nose; a sensitive mouth. His face is a contradiction that I love. I'm pretty tall at five feet nine inches, but I love it that he's five inches taller.

I told him about our findings on the dead bird as George put it into a plastic bag and took it to the freezer. Mini washed the table, then disinfected it.

"Suppose we all go into the cabin and have a cup of coffee," I said, to draw Culley into our group. "Oh, and a beer."

Culley nodded.

"Brad's decided to have a person on watch at all times," I told the group over coffee and beer.

"Yeah. Phil's on watch right now." Culley said. "I told Brad I'd take over after this watch." He stared at his beer. "You know, Brad's not such a bad guy. He's tougher than he looks."

I let out a silent sigh of relief. "I'm glad you feel that way, hon."

Mini chuckled. "A newborn bunny looks tougher than Brad."

"He's very smart, too," George said. "That's probably why he's the boss."

We all laughed, and somehow it drew Culley into the club.

A dangerous club, I thought, with our course set for the Bikini atoll, after Hawaii. Would we blunder into a swarm of Krakens? It might get us the data we needed, but at what cost? I thought of the dead divers and glanced at Culley. Now that we'd found each other, the thought of losing him was unbearable.

He looked at me. "What?"

"I just like to look at you," I said.

He grinned. "The feeling's mutual."

"Oh, Romeo, Romeo," Mini said.

"As long as I'm his Juliet," I said. "Brad wants to refuel and take on provisions in Hawaii," I told them. "Then he intends to set a course for the Bikini atoll."

George choked on his coffee. He wiped his mouth.

"He says," I continued, "that anyone who wants to disembark in Hawaii can do so and take a plane home."

Culley pressed his lips together and looked down.

"Into the lion's den," Mini said. "But I suppose that's where you have to go if you want to study lions."

"Maybe...." George started.

"That's an incomplete sentence," Mini said in a show of bravery, but her hand shook as she raised her cup. "To the advance of science." She gulped the coffee.

"Maybe," George continued, "it's not such a bad thing that we have two SEALS on board." He threw Culley an anxious glance.

Culley looked from George to Mini. "I'm going to tell you guys what I told Tess. Phil is dangerous. He's a killer."

"Oh, great!" George squeaked. He gestured with his pudgy hands. "Like we don't already have enough on our plates!"

I chewed a nail. Culley gently lowered my hand and held it. I remembered his words the first time we made love, in my apartment: *There are no guarantees in this life, Tess.*

Brad opened the door. "All hands on the bridge," he said and lifted his brows.

"What's up, boss?" I asked as we filed out the door.

"We found her."

Rámon was at the wheel. Phil maneuvered the ROV closer to a dying giant octopus on the ocean floor. The sea cam was still attached. Fish already tore pieces out of her.

"I wonder why she's dying?" George said and turned to Mini. "Do you think there's some element in the metal sea cam hook that's killing her?"

"It could be," Mini answered and threw George a glance. She discreetly shook her head, but Phil caught the motion.

"Answer the question!" Phil said. "Or would you prefer that I report you as a traitor during wartime?"

"Get off it," Culley told Phil. "She's not exactly collaborating with the enemy."

Phil turned to him. "Withholding vital information is the same as collaborating."

"Maybe in *your* book," Culley threw back. "The one that's written in blood!"

"I see you've already forgotten our agreement," Phil said. "I thought at least you had some semblance of honor."

"Culley," I said softly and put a hand on his arm as tension between them silently grew.

"All right!" Mini pointed to the dying octopus on the ROV screen. "It's the optic nerve in females. It produces a secretion that causes them to stop eating, to brood their eggs, and to die after the eggs are hatched. They die even if they don't brood their eggs."

"The poster child," Brad said. "Live fast and die young."

"How young?" Phil asked.

"It depends on the species." Mini watched the ROV screen. The octopus' tentacles drifted down to settle around her body as death claimed her. "Usually no more than a few years."

"But what if they continue to eat after they lay their eggs?"

"She might have just been old," Mini said. "Three years is old for some octopus species, but obviously, we don't know what's old for this species."

Phil turned to Rámon. "If the military destroys enough of their eggs, in a few years we'll be rid of this threat for good."

Rámon shrugged. "It's too bad we have to destroy so many of God's creations, you know?"

"If enough eggs are destroyed," I said, the females might return to the ocean floor and resume laying their eggs there. In that case, the hatchlings could *still* return to shallow waters."

Mini nodded.

"But first we have to find out," George said, "why they came into shallow water in the first place. Brad, we really need samples of the water and bottom sediment."

The sea cam screen showed wild swings in the camera as more fish and crabs moved in to rip chunks out of the dead octopus.

Phil stood up and lit a cigarette.

George went to the ROV controls and maneuvered the vehicle to the octopus. He used the ROV's cutting arm to remove the sea cam from her head.

"I hate to see anything die," Rámon said and crossed himself.

"Then you're in the wrong business," Phil told him, and went on deck to smoke.

"What's his problem?" Brad asked Rámon. "He's not happy unless he's miserable."

Rámon shrugged. "It's just his nature. Some people are never comfortable with themselves."

"He's managing," I said, "to make the rest of us uncomfortable, too."

CHAPTER TEN

The sun shone bright as we drove toward Hawaii. The water was green velvet, with rippling folds of darker hues. The sky was a sheer blue curtain drawn between the ocean and infinity, with patterns of cream-colored clouds. A warm breeze seasoned with salt riffled my hair. I was rocked by wavelets that slapped the vessel's sides.

I stood in the bow, gripping the rail, and listened to the siren song of the sea. These are the days that make me love the ocean.

It was hard to remember that I was on watch. I lifted the binoculars and scanned the surface. How could anything monstrous and menacing emerge from these gentle waters? I expected Poseidon Himself to rise up out of the depths. But only flying fish swooped into the air, sailed for a short while, like guests in the world of air, and fell back to their real home.

*****

We arrived at the Aloha Photon Station on the island of O'ahu in Hawaii to refuel, stock provisions, and catch some R&R. One of the many meanings of *Aloha* is respite. I think we all needed it.

Phil came on deck. His skin was pale and he looked haggard. He rubbed his forehead and I saw him squeeze his eyes shut. It was obvious that he was in pain. I couldn't help feeling sorry for the slime ball.

"Don't leave port without us!" he ordered Brad as he and Rámon left *Reverence* to check in at the Naval Station and report their findings. I wondered if he'd return to the boat. I hoped not, for everyone's sake.

Brad, Mini, and George left to sightsee and check out a favorite restaurant George remembered from when his parents took him to Hawaii as a child.

Culley and I rented a hotel room for the night. It was our first chance since the day in my apartment to be alone for our own form of R&R.

While Culley went to a dive shop to buy a powerful underwater Mark 3 gun, I showered and went clothes shopping.

As I strolled through a shopping center, a teal green evening dress in a store window caught my eye. I went in and was greeted by a plump, pleasant Hawaiian saleswoman with heavy jowls and a broad smile. She had my size in the dress. I tried it on and looked in a long mirror. *Not bad,* I thought. My suntan contrasted nicely with the color of the dress. It was tight at the waist and flared out into blue and green folds, Culley's favorite colors.

"I'll take it," I told the saleswoman.

She smiled. "It's lovely on you. Do you need shoes to go with it?"

I looked down at my bare legs and my sneakers sticking out from under the dress. We both laughed. "Yes, white," I said, "and pantyhose. Oh, and a blue scarf."

She smiled. "A necklace and earrings?"

"Why not? Shells?"

"Shells." She nodded.

I bought makeup too, and applied it at the shop's table and mirror. I swept my hair up and tied it with the scarf. The saleswoman clipped on the necklace and I fastened the earrings and put on my new shoes. They had a short heel and I was wobbly. It had been a long time since I'd worn heels.

"Perfume?" she asked.

"OK, perfume."

She brought out a tray of elegant little bottles and I chose one that was a delicate blend of Hawaiian flowers.

The saleswoman gave me a broad smile. "You were beautiful when you came in, lady. But you will leave even more beautiful. You have a man to show your new clothes to?"

"Yes." I smiled.

"He will be pleased."

"Thank you."

I paid her and walked back toward the hotel. I noticed men turning to look at me and I almost fell over my heels. A car screeched to a sudden stop, just short of plowing into the car in front of it. The driver put his hands to his head. He looked frightened at the near miss.

I took the hotel elevator rather than walk the one flight to our room in my new heels.

"Culley," I called and knocked.

"Who is it?"

"Wise guy. Open the door."

He did, and his laugh remained frozen. "Oh, wow," he said softly. "Do I know you?" He looked down the hall. "Did you see a lanky broad in shaggy pants and a shirt go out the door?"

"Yeah!" I said. "She told me she was running away from some wise ass boyfriend of hers."

"Tessie." He took my arms. "You're as beautiful as a Hawaiian goddess of the sea. Come in and let me pray at your altar." He bowed.

I swished past him, and shoved the bag with my pants and shirt and sneakers into his hands. "That's more like it." I looked around. "Where's my pedestal?"

"I don't have a pedestal, my goddess, but there's a throne in the bathroom."

"Wise ass."

*****

It was a night I'll always remember. An interlude between dangerous waters. We danced at an outdoor restaurant by the harbor, where strings of colored lights reflected off the water and yachts were anchored offshore. Hawaiian singers enhanced the romantic mood. We ate, and we drank too much and were both giddy.

I took off my shoes and carried them as we walked on white sand. From somewhere the strings of a guitar echoed across the beach. The sun set in a blaze of fire that torched the clouds and left behind a blackened sky with silver embers of stars. Waves sizzled up to the high-water mark. I took off my pantyhose, stuffed them into a shoe, and let wet sand squish between my toes.

Culley sniffed my neck. "You're my Hawaiian flower," he whispered. We kissed.

I laughed and ran through splashing water. The hem of my dress was wet. Culley followed me. We kissed again.

"Let's go back to the hotel," he said.

We held hands and walked back to our room.

That night we sipped love like red, red wine.

CHAPTER ELEVEN

Morning lifted the veils of sleep as I lay curled beside Culley in our hotel bedroom. His arm was draped around my waist. He still slept.

Why did I feel anxious? Oh, yeah. Today we had to return to *Reverence* and set a course for the Bikini atoll. I looked at my new dress, draped on a hangar to keep it from wrinkling. Shreds of last night's sweet memories clung to my mind like falling petals as reality intruded.

From somewhere a rooster crowed. I turned around to face Culley. He looked so innocent in sleep.

"Hon," I said softly and kissed his cheek. "Wake up. It's morning."

The rooster crowed again.

He blinked his eyes open and smiled at me.

"Naw. It's just a nightingale." He hugged me close to him and sighed.

"A nightingale with a severe sore throat," I said. The wall clock showed six fifty-seven.

"We have to leave in an hour," I told him. "Do you want our crewmates to think we decided to jump ship?"

"What would you think, Tess, if someday we came back here, to this very room." He stared at me and I felt our love like a candle that warmed us. "Say for our honeymoon," he said. "Yes?"

"Oh, Culley." I kissed him. *If we both make it back from this expedition,* I thought, and smiled to cover my anxiety. "You've got a date."

*****

We set a course for the Bikini atoll. I sat in the stern with Rámon. Culley was at the helm. Brad, George, and Mini had arrived late and were just now having breakfast. I was surprised that George had returned, but I said nothing. It must have been a difficult decision for him to make, and I admired him for it. It's hard to be courageous when you're really scared. I think his close friendship with Mini had something to do with it. Phil was in the cabin, taking a nap. He'd been more sullen and aloof than usual since he'd returned to *Reverence*. The few times he spoke, I noticed that his voice was raspy.

"Why the hell is Phil always so angry?" I asked Rámon. "OK, he's uncomfortable in his skin, but why is he always pissed?"

Rámon's smile was sad. "I think that is the only way he knows how to handle life. My mother used to say when she saw an angry person, 'His mother didn't hold him enough when he was a baby'."

"Very insightful," I said. "Do you ever try to get him to stop smoking?"

"*Sí.* He just says that smoking is all he has."

"That's pretty grim."

Rámon stared at the sea. "I am one of nine children. My mother and father

50

loved each one of us as though we were their only child. You know what I mean?"

"I think so. My parents are loving people too. I have a younger brother. He's only fourteen. He's a good kid, but he wants to run away and join a circus."

Rámon laughed and scratched his short-cropped hair. "When I was a young boy, I wanted to join a rodeo and see the world."

A school of sardines leaped out of the water, probably chased from below by larger fish.

"Even the fishes have each other," Rámon said.

I nodded, but I wondered if he knew they were leaping to save their lives?

"Tessica," he said, " I would ask you for a favor. Say no if you don't want to do it."

"Ask, Rámon. If I can, I will. If I can't, I'll just say no."

"I went with Phil to the Naval Medical Clinic yesterday, after we were debriefed." He pressed a hand to his mouth, but I saw his lips quiver.

I waited.

"They did some tests on his lungs and I heard the doctor yell at him, 'Why didn't you come in sooner! What were you waiting for?' Then the doctor said 'Very aggressive. I'm sorry. Too late'."

"Oh, my God," I whispered. "Are you saying...?" I thought of Phil's coughing, his raspy voice.

Rámon nodded and squeezed out the word through his hand pressed over his lips. "Cancer." Tears slid down his cheeks. "They wanted him to check into the clinic, you know, but Phil told them he was going to finish this mission."

I sat back. "What do you want me to do?"

"You are a compassionate, gentle, loving woman, Tessica. If you could just show him some kindness, now and then. He never had a relationship that lasted with a woman."

"A relationship, Rámon?"

"No, no. Just some words of kindness. A man needs the gentle hand of a woman, whether we admit it or not. Culley is a better person than the man I used to know."

"Can I tell Culley about this?'"

"I made a promise to Phil that I wouldn't tell anyone about his sickness. I broke my promise once, with you, for his sake."

"What was Culley like back when you knew him?"

"More...arrogant."

I smiled. "I can believe that. So you don't want me to tell Culley or anyone else? Rámon, I want to help, but you've put me into a difficult position."

"*Si*. You can say no. I would understand."

"No."

"No?"

"I mean *no,* I'll do what I can." I thought of how Phil had treated Culley. "But don't expect too much."

I got up and went to the side of the boat. Something nagged at the back of my mind, behind the bad news about Phil and the uncomfortable commitment I'd just made. In the distance a small, uncharted islet barely peeked above the waves. No, that wasn't it.

Jellies!

There were fewer of them. Especially the great Nomura jellyfish, with a diameter of about six feet and a weight of about 400 pounds. The species had been discovered in 1921. Then, in the twenty-first century, jellies had become the dominant life form in the sea, eating the eggs of fish, the young fish fry, and competing for the zooplankton that other fish needed to live on. So why were there fewer jellies here, where the giant octopuses were seen to gather?

I went into the cabin. Phil was still asleep. I motioned to Mini, George and Brad to come on deck.

They followed me to the side of the boat. I waved at the water. "What do you see?"

The surface was empty.

Brad studied the islet "Are you going to give us a hint, Tessica? Does it have white sand and trees?"

"Wait a minute," George said, "where are all the jellies?"

"No jellies," I said. "Especially no giant Nomuras."

"Son of a bitch," Mini said softly. "You're saying that the giant octopuses are living on the Nomuras, aren't you, Tess."

"It's a possibility," I said.

"And a theory," George added.

"If jellyfish are the giant octopuses' source of food...." Brad started.

"They could cause another flip," George continued the thought, "back to the domination of fishes!"

"So," Brad said, "if there were a way to convince the Krakens to stop destroying human structures, maybe we could be friends."

"Octopus psychology," Mini said. "We're dealing with the smartest fish in the sea. If we could discourage them from laying their eggs on our ships and ocean structures, and reward them for laying in dens that *we* provide...."

"They could be a boon," I said, "to the fish and sea mammals that compete for food with the jellies."

"It sounds very promising," George said, "but there's still that little thorn in my mind."

"Which thorn is that?" Mini asked.

"What brought them into shallow water to begin with?" he said.

"Does it matter?" Mini asked. "Maybe dead zones."

Dead zones, I thought. The zones of pollution in the oceans. "Only jellies can live in dead zones," I told them.

"Well, what if these huge octopuses wiped out the dead-zone jellies," George said, "and the few fish left that die and drift down? They would have to come up to look for more jellies."

"Still," Brad said, "why would they lay their eggs in shallow water?"

"Perhaps the pollution at the Hadopelagic zone," Mini offered. "It could damage their eggs or the hatchlings."

"The Hadoe...what?" Brad asked.

"Hadopelagic," I told him. "It usually means below 6,000 feet."

"Oh." Brad tried again. "The Hadeo...oh, what the hell!" He fluttered his hands.

"Not hell." I chuckled. "The Greek Hades."

"But why aren't the males coming up?" George slammed a fist on the gunnel. We all jumped. "I keep telling you people that we need samples of the sediment and the water. We could get them right here." He jabbed a finger at the surface. "It's deep enough and close enough to Bikini."

Brad took a deep breath of ocean air and smiled. "I do believe that my Team Pacifica has just brought us leaps closer to solving the mystery of the Krakens. Bonuses all around! Well." He scratched his cheek. "Providing I can convince the government."

"Does that mean," George asked Brad, "that we no longer have to go to the Marshall Islands and the Bikini atoll?"

"Georgie," Brad said, "how are you going to convince the dynamic duo to stop here for the time it would take to bring up samples from 6,000 feet, let alone turn the boat around?"

"Well," George said, "well, if we tell them our plan to have divers build dens all over the Pacific Ocean, and...and maybe then the octopuses would no longer be a threat." George furrowed his brows. I think it sounded lame even to him.

Phil came out of the cabin looking haggard and sullen. His hands shook as he lit a cigarette. He looked at us, threw the match overboard and made his way to the stern to join Rámon. He sat down heavily and coughed.

"Here's your chance, Georgie." Brad nudged him in the direction of the stern.

"Uh." George nudged back. "Uh, maybe when Phil is in a better mood." He took a candy bar from his pocket, opened it and chewed. I saw the look of sheer pleasure on his face.

"Don't hold your breath," I told him.

I went to the stern and sat down. "I have something in my med-kit that can soothe your cough," I told Phil. "Can I get it for you?"

Phil gave me a suspicious look. "What do you want in return?"

Brad, Mini, and George watched us.

I shook my head. "You're still our shipmate. I'd like to help you to...to get over that cough. Can I get the medicine?"

His expression softened and he nodded.

I went to the cabin, took the cough medicine from my med-kit, a teaspoon from the drawer, and brought them to Phil. "Follow the directions on the bottle," I told him, "but don't overdo it." As he reached for the bottle and the spoon, I saw the pain patch stuck to his upper chest. He drank a teaspoonful of the cough medicine and extended the bottle to me.

"No, keep it." I forced a smile. "I hope it helps."

I went to rejoin Mini and Brad and George. Culley stood with them. George was on his way to the bridge for his watch.

"Hi, hon," I said and walked up to Culley.

He didn't smile. "Collaborating with the enemy?"

"Culley, the guy's coughing his lungs out. I just gave him some cough medicine, that's all."

"Couldn't he get it himself?"

"It was a simple act of kindness. I would've done it for anyone!"

Brad and Mini discreetly drifted away.

"I don't like it when you're jealous," I said. "You have no reason to be. How many times do I have to say that I'm not going anyplace without you?"

Culley lowered his head.

I kissed his forehead. "I love you so much, you big klutz."

He hugged me. "I just couldn't stand it if I lost you. That's all."

"I'm not *going* anywhere, hon. OK? Not without you."

Phil watched as Culley and I walked to the cabin.

Over coffee and beer, I told Culley about the theory we had developed on the giant octopuses. "What do you think?" I said, to draw him into our group.

"Sounds reasonable, but what do I know? You think the octopuses will lay their eggs in the dens that divers set up? Why should they?"

"Well, because the eggs they lay there won't be torched. It might take a while for them to get the idea."

"Trouble is, it's Phil and Rámon's call. And they've got orders to kill the ones we come across."

I couldn't tell Culley that Phil had terminal cancer. "Do you think Rámon would be open to our plan? I mean, instead of following orders and killing the octopuses? Phil and he are good friends. If Rámon believed in our plan, maybe he could convince Phil."

Culley stared at me. "I know you're not naive, Tess. Rámon would have to get new orders to change his mission. Is there something you're not telling me?"

"Yes."

When the time came that Phil could no longer function, a Navy helicopter would take him to the clinic in Pearl Harbor. At least he would be comfortable in his last days, if Phil were ever capable of being comfortable.

"There's something I *can't* tell you," I said, "but this much I can say. Phil won't be with us much longer."

"You mean with the expedition or with the living?"

"Both, Culley. He's very sick, and he's not going to recover."

Culley was about to drink, but he put his beer down. "The poor son of a bitch has cancer, doesn't he? I know the signs."

I nodded. "You said it. Not me."

"It can be cured."

"Not at this stage. He waited too long."

"You know...." Culley stared at his beer. "He once told me he couldn't wait for it to be over."

"Couldn't wait for what to be over?"

He looked up. "Life."

The boat suddenly lurched. Culley jumped up. "What the hell is George doing?'

I got up.

Culley started toward the door. The boat lurched again and he fell against the wall. I held onto the table.

"Stay here!" he said and went on deck.

I followed him. Phil and Rámon brushed past me and went into the cabin. Mini came out of the lab. We ran to the bridge as the boat listed to starboard.

Brad was on the bridge, bracing himself against a wall.

George was trying to steer the boat. "It's not working!" he cried and spun the wheel.

"Give it to me." Culley took the wheel and turned it. "The rudder," he said. "The rudder's not responding."

The boat drove toward the shallow islet as though a spirit from hell were guiding it. Culley cut the engines. It didn't matter. The boat still plunged ahead, pushed from behind in a zigzag motion.

I hung onto rails and ran toward the stern, followed by Culley, Mini, and Brad. George remained on the bridge.

Culley shoved me behind him as a great white tentacle rose over the stern and reached for us.

Rámon came out of the cabin and fired his machine gun, smashing the tentacle with bullets. It was ripped apart. Blue blood seeped from the stump. The octopus sank beneath the boat.

Phil pushed past us with a rocket launcher in hand.

"I think there's more than one," Mini said. "I saw the head of another one break the surface further out there." She pointed past the stern.

"Oh, fuck!" Brad said. "You mean they're cooperating?"

"They're capable of it," Mini said.

We grabbed the rails as the boat lurched forward again. I scanned the water.

Mini picked up a chunk of tentacle and stumbled back to the lab. "Whatever happens," she threw over her shoulder, "I want this sample."

"Culley!" I called and pointed at the islet. We were heading toward it.

"Christ," he said. "They'll drive us into the reefs."

"Launch *Nomad!*" Brad shouted.

"Brad, that's probably just what they want," I told him. "In the inflatable we'd be trapped."

We watched as *Reverence* approached the islet at a speed that would crash her into the reefs and rip apart her hull.

Phil and Rámon checked the water from the stern to the bow. The octopuses were well under the boat.

"Do you think," I asked Culley, "they're burning through the double hull?"

"It could be." He stared at the islet. We were approaching fast. "Come with me, Tess."

We made our way to the cabin.

Culley reached under his bunk, dragged out his personal bag, and unzipped it. He fished around inside and drew out a gun and a box of ammunition.

His hands shook as he loaded the gun. He slapped it into my palm. "It's on safety right now. Tess...." He looked at me the way a person looks at a vulnerable child he loves more than life. "Tess, if the worst happens, don't let them use their acid on you."

I was shaking badly. I almost dropped the gun. He took my hand and wrapped my fingers firmly around the weapon.

"What about *you?*" I asked.

He shook his head. "Just do what's best for you."

"Oh, Culley, no! It can't end this way."

"C'mon," he said and took my other hand. "You'll be safer on deck when the boat goes down."

Phil and Rámon still waited for the octopuses to show themselves, but the creatures weren't about to.

Mini came out of the lab. She covered her mouth and gasped when she saw the direction the boat was headed.

"What should we do?" George squeaked.

No one answered. I couldn't stop shaking. I held the gun loosely, not really wanting to admit its purpose.

"The dive gear." Culley ran to the wet room.

With the dive gear we could return to the boat and salvage whatever was still usable, if we were still alive. Was this a hunting trip for the octopuses? With no more jellies around, did they mean to eat us?

My stomach clenched and I thought I'd throw up. I couldn't remember ever being so scared in my life. I clung to the rail. "Oh Mom, Dad." I sobbed. "I'm sorry. Chris. Grow up well."

Brad looked calm and determined. "Help me launch *Nomad*," he called.

George, Brad, and I winched *Nomad* over the side. Brad held her close to *Reverence* with *Nomad's* bow line.

Mini looked frozen. her eyes were wide. her hands were over her mouth.

"Phil!" Culley shouted as he came on deck with our two dive bags. "Rámon! Grab some tanks."

"I want my life preserver," Mini said. "In case I go into the water. I can't swim!" She ran into the cabin.

"Mini!" I yelled. "Don't stay in there long."

"Hold on!" Brad shouted.

Reverence's hull scraped the islet's outer coral mounts with a screech like a death cry. We clung to the rails as the bow rose up out of the water. The boat listed to port.

"Get ready to jump!" Culley shouted and threw the dive bags into *Nomad*. Rámon and Phil slung their weapons over their shoulders and lowered four scuba tanks into *Nomad*.

I watched, my mouth open, as *Reverence* slid sideways and begin a slow roll.

"Jump!" Culley shouted.

"Mini!" I screamed. "Mini!" She was still in the cabin, probably strapping on her life preserver.

Culley grabbed my arm and we jumped into *Nomad*, followed by the others. "Mini!" I yelled. "Come on."

George looked around. "Where is she?"

"In the *cabin*," I told him.

"What? We have to go back for her."

No one answered him as *Reverence* rolled and the cabin went underwater.

"Oh, Mini," I whispered.

Phil started the motor and drove toward the beach.

I sobbed as I watched *Reverence* sink beneath the waves. Air bubbles burst at the disturbed surface. Then the water grew calm.

Mini....

A giant octopus raised its bumpy head and watched us with slitted eyes. It turned blue within seconds and became almost invisible against the water. But Phil and Rámon saw her. Before they could aim their rifles, she sank beneath the surface.

"It knows about weapons," Brad said.

We all kept watch for rising octopuses as Phil steered us between hills of coral.

George crawled to Phil. "Please," he said, and pulled on Phil's arm, "please go back for Mini. I'll *pay* you. How much do you want?"

Phil gave him a stony look and brushed off George's hand.

George stood up unsteadily in the slowly moving boat. "Then I'm going back for her!" he announced and jumped overboard. He immediately went under. Brad reached over the pontoon, grabbed George by his hair and pulled him up. Culley and Brad dragged George, who was sputtering and coughing, back into the boat.

"Did you forget you can't swim?" Brad asked George.

George wiped tears and water from his face. "Oh, but Mini!" He sobbed.

I began to shake and I started to cry. I was alive, but I had lost my best friend.

CHAPTER TWELVE

The islet was flat. Mangrove and coconut trees flourished in thick groves. Seagulls squawked but they stayed on the sand as Phil drove *Nomad* onto the beach. Red crabs scurried out of our path.

We dragged *Nomad* into deep sand, then sat among coconut trees to rest and take cover from the octopuses. The giants would have to expose themselves if they wanted to come ashore and destroy *Nomad*, or us. I had stuffed the gun Culley gave me into a neoprene bootie in my dive bag to keep it dry.

I picked up a coconut. I was thirsty.

George took it from my hand and rolled it like a bowling ball. "Don't think about eating the coconuts," he said listlessly. "We're too close to Bikini."

"Radiation?" I asked.

He nodded. "It's in the coconuts, especially in the milk. It's even in the hulls of sunken ships."

"Did any of you get off a mayday?" Phil asked and coughed. His brow was furrowed with pain.

George raised his hand like a school boy. "I did."

"Oh, look!" I said as a yellow scarf floated in with the waves.

"I'll get it," Brad trotted to the water's edge. He scooped up the scarf and came back, studying it.

"That's *Mini's*," I said.

He nodded and handed it to me.

"Can I have it?" George pleaded.

I gave it to him.

Phil laid down with a grunt and tucked his weapon at his side. He was breathing heavily. One hand was pressed against his chest.

Rámon sat next to him. "How you feel, amigo?"

Phil shook his head. "I never knew my body could betray me like this."

Uh, oh, I thought. His pain patches were lost. I scanned the northeastern sky. It was empty. With luck, a rescue helicopter or a boat from Pearl Harbor would arrive soon. "George," I said, "when you called in the mayday, did you tell them about the octopus attack?"

George shook his head. "Sorry, no. The mic was ripped off in my hand when the boat listed. I held onto it to stop myself from sliding."

"Oh," I said.

He took a soggy candy bar from his pocket and stared at it. "This is my last one." He flipped it into the sand.

A red crab approached the brightly wrapped candy bar. We watched as he grasped it in a claw and dragged it away.

"He'll be the fattest crab on the island," Brad remarked.

A small spider with black beads for eyes and full of fuzzy stuff scurried across my shoe. I shook him off and he jumped and landed in the grass.

"Havaika," George said.

If Mini were here, I thought, *she'd say something like "George, isn't that a Jewish dance?"* I pressed a hand to my lips.

"What's Havaika?" Brad asked.

"Jumping spider," George told him.

"That's nice!" I stood up, opened my dive bag and began throwing my gear into the sand. "I'm going back to *Reverence* to find her!"

Culley rubbed his forehead. Then he got up and opened his dive bag. He took out his underwater torch and the rest of his gear.

*****

Rámon put the rocket launcher and the machine gun back into *Nomad*. Brad and George helped him launch the small boat. Rámon followed us in *Nomad* as Culley and I swam the short distance to *Reverence*.

The water was clear and warm. Coral fish and small sharks cruised around hills of sea fans, fire and staghorn coral. The colors were dazzling. Visibility was about a hundred feet and the underwater horizon was an azure blue. An inquisitive green turtle circled us, then paddled away.

What a paradise this could be, I thought, under different circumstances.

Culley went to *Reverence's* bridge to see what he could salvage. I went to the cabin and looked through windows, afraid of what I'd see.

I screamed and almost dropped the mouthpiece when I saw her.

Mini floated in an air bubble against the window with a frozen, wide-eyed stare. I thought I was looking at death, when she suddenly pounded her fists against the window. "Tess! Tess!" she screamed through glass.

"Oh my God!" I mumbled around the mouthpiece. I made an "OK" sign to her and swam down quickly to look for the cabin door.

No. No! I pounded on the cabin.

With *Reverence* on her side, the door was jammed against coral. I swam back to the windows and chose one that was tilted lower than Mini's air bubble. I unbuckled my weight belt, sleeved off a five-pound weight and clamped my weight belt back on. I used the five pounder to repeatedly smash at the window. It finally shattered. I pounded out a jagged hole I could swim through, stuffed the five-pound weight under my wet-suit jacket, and pulled myself inside.

With the cabin filled with water, the pressure on both sides of the broken window was equal. I checked my depth gauge. Twenty three feet. OK. No matter how long Mini had been in that pressurized air bubble, it was too shallow for her to have to decompress. I swam up into the bubble and lifted my mask.

"Tess!" she screamed. "Tess. I was preparing to die." She cried out loud with her mouth open and hugged my shoulders.

"It's OK, Mini," I told her. "It's OK now. We thought we lost you."

The air was stale. I pressed the purge button on my regulator, pouring fresh air into the bubble.

"Now listen to me, Mini," I said as I unstrapped her life preserver and got it off her. She held onto me and I poured some air into my buoyancy compensator to keep us afloat.

"All you have to do is close your eyes," I said, "hold your nostrils closed, and hang onto me. Here." I gave her the second regulator we always carried. "And promise me you'll keep breathing as we go up to the surface."

"I'm so cold, Tess."

"I know, Mini, but we're alive. The rest is easy." *Oh shit!*

A giant octopus slid up to the other side of the window and watched us. Mini had her back turned to it.

The octopus wrapped its tentacles around the cabin and opened its huge beak. It scraped the broken window.

Mini turned and screamed.

The octopus began to widen the hole I'd made.

"Oh, God, Tess! They can fit through almost anything."

I tried to stay calm. Had we come this far only to be ripped apart by that beak and eaten alive?

Mini and I clung to each other. I had nothing to use as a weapon. If I thought I was frightened before, I didn't know what real fear felt like. I was paralyzed.

Suddenly the octopus jerked sideways and ejected a black pool of acid.

Culley! His torch blazed red as he swam away from the acid pool. He swung the torch against the tip of her extended tentacle.

The octopus jetted to the surface. Even underwater I heard the boom as the octopus exploded. Only the rocket launcher could've done that.

The acid pool dissipated in the littoral current and Culley came through the hole in the window and up into the bubble of air. He spat out his mouthpiece. "Is this a private party," he said to ease the tension, "or can anybody share your bubble?"

Culley gave Mini his mask so that she wouldn't panic, and I guided them to the surface. Rámon helped her into *Nomad*. "Thank you, Lord" He looked up and crossed himself.

Chunks of octopus sank around us.

"Mini!" George screamed from the beach. He waved his arms and ran toward the water as we approached. "Mini!" He slipped on a dried tube of coral and fell on his face.

*****

I gave Mini the woolen pants and shirt from my bag. Her arms and legs stuck out but it kept her warm. George sat next to her, looking like a pudgy child against her lanky frame.

Rámon sat cross-legged beside Phil, who kept an arm over his eyes, and moaned out raspy breaths.

"I hope a rescue boat or a helicopter comes soon," I whispered to Culley and scanned the sky.

"I hope," Culley answered, "an octopus doesn't get it."

Brad sat with us. "We'll wave them off," he said. "Wait a minute. I've got a better idea." He got up. "Help me with this."

Brad's plan was to spell OCTOPUS on the beach with rocks and branches and coconuts. I was skeptical, but Culley brought our flippers to help with the letters, and in the end, we had a fair, if eclectic facsimile of the word. We hoped it could be seen from the air.

As we walked back to Phil and Rámon, Rámon caught my eye and glanced at Phil.

"I'm going to sit with Phil," I told Culley.

"Do what you can for him."

"Thanks, hon."

I sat down next to Phil and took his hand. I was surprised when he grasped mine tightly. "A rescue boat should be here any time now," I said.

He nodded from under his arm, which was still draped across his eyes. He guided my hand to his chest and a bumpy tumor. "You feel that?" he said.

"Yes."

"They're all over, even in my ears. There's no hope for me."

"I know, Phil," I said. "What can I do for you?"

"Rámon says you have a gun in your dive bag."

My hand in his shook.

"I don't want to go to the clinic," Phil said, "or a hospital! I want it to end right *here*."

"Phil," we can't do that. They'll relieve your pain at the clinic."

"You don't have to do anything. Just leave me the gun."

"We can't do that either."

"Then what *can* you do for me?" He coughed and slammed a fist into the sand, then coughed again. "Oh, Christ!" He moaned. "I can't take this pain. Tess! I want release."

"We'll be rescued soon," I told him and scanned the sky.

"There's no rescue for me," he rasped, "except the gun."

I looked at Rámon.

There were tears in his eyes. He got up, went to my dive bag, and took out the gun. I watched him check to see that it was loaded. Then he took off the safety. No one said a word as he returned to Phil and stood over him.

Phil blinked up at Rámon. "I hope you're right about your God," he grated.

Rámon nodded. "I am right, *amigo*. He watches over you now and waits to take you in His arms."

The beat of a helicopter!

Rámon stuffed the gun into his belt and we ran to the beach.

"Rámon!" Phil called from where he lay.

A Navy helicopter lowered as it approached.

We pointed to the word in the sand and frantically waved our arms to warn them off as they lowered.

A white tentacle rose up from the surface and lashed out at the helicopter."

"No!" I screamed as the helicopter spun and slid into the waves. "Oh, no!"

Culley ran to *Nomad*, followed by Rámon, and took out the machine gun. The launcher was empty. He fired as the helicopter rose again in the grip of the tentacle and was smashed down onto the water's surface.

"Oh, God!" I whispered. "They're dead."

Culley lowered the machine gun. He was too far away to hit the octopus.

We stood silently and watched the tentacle smash the helicopter against the surface again, then drag it down below the frothing waves. The water calmed into ripples that lapped the beach. Rámon crossed himself. Culley put his arm around my shoulders as we all walked back.

"I wonder how many lives were lost?" I asked dully.

"There's usually two on board," Culley said sadly. "Maybe a doctor."

"Three people," I said. "They were trying to rescue us."

Culley nodded.

I went to Phil. "Did you see what happened?" I asked him.

"It's that idiot George's fault," he gasped. "He should've warned the base about the octopus."

I looked at Rámon.

"Rámon," Phil rasped, "help me, *amigo*. I can't stand it."

Rámon took the gun from his belt and looked at me.

I gripped Phil's hand and tried not to let mine shake.

"God will be with you, my friend," I said, though I had no idea if He would. As I closed my eyes and sat back, Rámon fired.

I felt Phil's body jerk. Then he was still. His hand slid from mine.

Rámon dropped the gun in the sand, turned, and walked away.

I took the gun and wiped it on my shirt, then put it in Phil's hand and pressed his limp fingers around it.

Culley came over and helped me up. I cried against his chest and he held me and took me away from the body.

*****

We buried Phil in a shallow grave that we dug out with shells and dive knives and our hands. We covered his grave with rocks but we all knew that the crabs and the seabirds would be at it as soon as we were gone from the islet.

Rámon uttered a eulogy over his friend's grave. He made a cross of palm branches, jammed it into the sand, and tied it with his belt.

Later that day, two attack helicopters approached. They bristled with weapons. One stayed high while the other one landed well into the islet. Somebody in the first `copter must have gotten off a message before the 'copter was destroyed. I silently thanked him or her.

We were glad to be rescued, but we walked solemnly to the helicopter, well aware of the price of our rescue.

"As far as we all know," Culley said before we reached the 'copter, "we left the gun with Phil to protect himself from the octopus when we went back to *Reverence* for salvage. Brad, you and George were waiting for us on the beach. You heard a shot. When We all nodded.

"Thank you, my friends," Rámon said. "May God forgive me for taking a life."

We boarded the helicopter. The pilot and rescue diver, both young men, welcomed us aboard, and to their credit, they never mentioned the lives that were lost in the first 'copter. But when I realized how young these boys were, and considered that the crew of the first 'copter were probably just as young, I bit my lip to hold back tears.

I watched the islet shrink as we lifted into the sky. The coconut and mangrove trees, the crabs and spiders, the cawing seabirds, were just a memory now, along with the lives that had been lost below us.

CHAPTER THIRTEEN

When the rescue helicopter set down on Pearl Harbor, we were inundated with invitations to news and talk shows, and an interview with the prestigious scientific journal *Mariana America*. A Vancouver production company wanted to buy the rights to a film about our adventures. They already had a title: *Acid Kraken*.

We took the opportunity the media afforded us to promote our message that killing every last giant octopus was not the way to resolve this threat.

*****

Three days after we landed, we were gathered in the green room of a news TV station before an interview, drinking coffee. No beer.

"This time around," Brad said, looking a little weary from our whirlwind celebrity agenda, "let's see if we can't get a word in about our need to borrow a research vessel from some benevolent foundation."

"Well," George said, "I've been thinking about that."

"And!" we all said.

"You'll see." He grinned evilly.

Mini, sitting next to him, put her hands around his neck. "Georgie! I'm going to throttle you!" She pretended to strangle him.

The door opened and a station worker's eyes widened as he looked in. "Uh...you're on," he told us and hurried away.

"Now see what you did, Georgie?" Mini said as the five of us walked onstage to cheers from journalists who had flown to Pearl Harbor for the occasion.

We took our seats behind the panel table onstage, and Brad, as our leader, introduced us.

I felt uneasy in front of this audience of professional news people. The lights were hot. The cameras were too close for comfort. Culley glanced around. I had a feeling that he wished he were somewhere else. Brad had a permanent smile on his face. Mini looked down more than up. But George beamed.

Fortunately, we were only here to answer questions and we didn't have to give talks on the giants.

"Miss Hoffman." A journalist stood up. He was a stout man with an air of assurance and a beard. He peered at me and I thought of a shark swimming in its natural element. "Why," he started, "is it so important that we keep hands off the giants? In what way do they benefit mankind?"

Benefit mankind! I thought. As though that were an animal's only excuse to survive. I felt myself stiffen. Culley took my hand under the table.

"Well," I said, "for one thing, the giants are already making a dent in the jellyfish population. This will allow more fish eggs and young fish to survive. It could result in a flip back to the domination of fish species."

"And also for the fishing industries?" he asked. "Would the replenishing of ocean fish species include those we prefer as food, such as the tuna?"

"That would naturally follow," I said, "although tuna are very slow breeders. We should keep hands off that species for a long time."

"There go my lunches." He chuckled and looked around. Finally, as others raised their hands, he sat down.

"Mr. Backer," a journalist called from the rear of the room, "as a marine ecologist, what's your take on the theory that this species has been around for millions of years and has nothing to do with radiation and oil spills?"

George sat up straight and clasped his hands. "Well, without further studies," he said in a tone deeper than his natural voice, "including the Mariana Trench, it's difficult to state with any authority just what exactly *is* the origin of this newly discovered species." He pushed his glasses further up his nose.

I squeezed Culley's hand and almost laughed.

"For that," George continued, "we're going to need another research vessel to continue our very important studies."

A journalist waved her arm.

George nodded benevolently toward her.

"Does the Pacifica Lab have another vessel that your team can use for a second scientific expedition?"

"Unfortunately...*no*," George responded. "Of course if a foundation would offer us the *use* of a research vessel, we would be pleased as punch to take them up on their offer." I saw him smile.

There were a few chuckles from the audience.

Another journalist waved and George magnanimously acknowledged him with a pointed finger.

"Sir," the man began, "do you have a particular foundation in mind?"

"Well," George said, "the Biosphere Society has a vessel that would suit our purposes very nicely. You must understand," he continued in his base tone, "that destroying the eggs of giants, and removing this possibly short-lived species from the ecosystem, would not only mean an increase in jellies, but oceans that would eventually consist of nothing more than jellies, and the Humbolt squid that prey upon them. Our future work is calculated to discover the needs of the giants, and to find a compatible way for giants and humans to co-exist." He coughed into his hand. "For the benefit of humans, of course."

It was a just a little bit sensational, but George made his point.

The audience murmured and softly applauded.

As the interview progressed, Culley gave the commercial diver's viewpoint on the feasibility of placing artificial reefs with dens in areas where the giants had been known to lay their eggs.

The stout, seasoned journalist stood again, without Culley acknowledging him, and said, "Mr. Ryan Culley, isn't it true that you were once jailed for stealing a car?"

I froze. Culley let go of my hand.

"I was sixteen," Culley told him, hunching forward on the table. "Just what does my police record have to do with giant octopuses?"

There was an uncomfortable silence in the audience and on the panel.

"I was simply curious," the journalist said, "about your credentials as a commercial diver who is qualified for such important work." He looked around at his colleagues and scratched his beard.

"I have my license." Culley's voice was tight.

"Let he who is without sin," Brad offered to the audience.

"True." The journalist nodded smugly and sat down. The bastard had made his point.

The rest of the meeting was tense, and Brad broke it up early.

The next day we watched an admiral on a TV news show from the lobby of the hotel where we were staying.

"They're scientists," he said, referring to our interview, "what do they know about the security of our country? All they know is what they see under a microscope." He shifted position and the brass on his uniform gleamed in the lights. "The Navy intends to destroy every damned last one of those mutant Krakens for the security of our nation."

The next day, journalists reported that our televised interviews had swayed public opinion into our court. There was even sympathy for Culley. I think his admittance to stealing a car at sixteen made some people examine their own checkered pasts.

We heard through the grapevine that the admiral got a call from the White House. He scheduled another interview and explained, "After careful consideration, the Navy has decided to destroy only those giant octopuses that have proven to be a threat to naval activities."

"That's a bite out of their collective asses," Brad remarked as we watched the interview on TV.

"They do a good job, boss," Culley said. "They've just got their fair share of hardasses, like any other institution."

"Like journalists," I added.

"Listen, Ryan," Brad said, "I speak for all of us when I say that stealing a car at sixteen means *nothing* to anyone with half a brain in his head. In fact, I think you made a connection with the other journalists when you admitted it. We all have skeletons in the closet." He fluttered a hand. "Some of us come out. Now if you were to steal at car at thirty-two years old, we might hold that against you. Especially if it were *my* car."

We all laughed. It was the last time the car incident was ever mentioned between the team.

I breathed a sigh of relief. It all seemed too good to be true.

It was.

*****

"Wish I were that pillow," I heard Culley say in my sleep.

I opened my eyes and squinted in the glare of afternoon sunlight. Culley sat beside me in the stern of R/V *Cousteau*. I realized I was hugging the pillow to my chest in the beach chair.

"Pervert," I said and rubbed my eyes.

He bent down and kissed me. "Time to go watch the nut cases." He pulled me out of the chair.

We were anchored off O'ahu, the location of the Pacific Naval Base. Stacks of artificial giant octopus dens were tied down in the stern. We planned to deploy them where the giants were known to lay eggs on docked ships and ocean structures.

I held Culley's hand as we walked to the bridge. The boat was a sixty-foot research vessel. She'd been loaned to us by Sea Worthy Conservation, funded by

The Biosphere Society, after our interview and George's outstanding bit of diplomacy. *Cousteau* was a good boat. She even had a shark cage on board.

I think the five of us were glad to be back at sea. Rámon had been called to the Naval Base and reassigned. An inquiry into Phil's death concluded that it was a suicide, after his physician testified that he was dying of cancer. They buried him in the National Memorial Cemetery of the Pacific in Honolulu, with a military funeral honors ceremony.

The five of us gathered on the bridge to watch a crimson-robed priest from The Church of the Hands of God's Vengeance on a TV-mode screen.

"And first God destroyed the sinful world with a *flood*," the fiery-eyed preacher announced. He jabbed the air with a Bible as though it were a weapon. "Now He shows His wrath at a sinful world that turns its face from Him who *loves us*. And He has sent forth his minions in the form of Krakens to *destroy* those men of evil, the scientists!"

I gasped.

His voice shook with passion. "For they turn their backs on our Lord Jesus Christ. Prepare, my brethren." He came close to the camera. His thick black brows and fierce eyes filled the screen. I found myself leaning back. "Prepare for The End as the Lord releases His wrath against a sinful world. Be steadfast in your belief, my brothers. For only true believers will escape His wrath. Blessed be the Lamb of God."

"He's wearing eye liner," Mini remarked.

Brad shut off the TV and we sat quietly with our thoughts. I chewed a nail and felt numb from the onslaught of rage.

"Do you...." George cleared his throat. "I mean does anybody think these lunatics will really make war on scientists?"

"They already killed two geneticists in Arkansas," Mini reminded him.

"Oh, yeah," George shrugged. He looked like a turtle pulling in his head. He reached into his pocket and pulled out a candy bar. "There's no real proof of it, though."

"I'd guess," Culley said, "that a research vessel would be a prime target for those nut cases."

We were prepared for attacks by the giants with the rocket launcher. We had rifles, a gun, and Culley's Mark 3 underwater gun. We felt pretty secure. But now we might have to use these weapons against humans. It was not a pleasant thought. A worse thought was that they might use their weapons against us. Why this destructiveness in the name of religion?

"Where do these lunatics get their funding?" I asked.

"World-Wide Church of the Deranged." Brad fingered a tooth on his shark necklace. "We just got the military off our asses. Now *this*."

I heard a helicopter approach. We went on deck and watched a Navy 'copter fly by. It turned and circled us. We waved to it. The pilot waved back, and the 'copter continued east.

"Probably on patrol," Culley said. "They've had reports of Somali pirates in the area."

I'd read somewhere that the pirates were much like the Mafia, with separate branches and their own code of conduct. "I've heard," I said, "that many of them are the grandsons of fishermen."

George nodded. "They lost their livelihood a long time ago when international ships dumped nuclear and toxic waste in their waters, and then they even buried it along the coasts. Can you believe that?"

"Why not?" I said.

"The tsunamis dug it up and spread it," Brad added.

"You think there are Somali pirates in the Pacific?" I said.

"Could be," Culley answered. "I hate to worry you guys, but I heard reports of hijacked fishing and cargo ships. The Navy's keeping an eye out."

I sighed. These were no romantic Hollywood pirates, but bold, young, impoverished men who were willing to risk it all for a chance to strike it rich.

*****

The next day dawned warm and clear, the sort of weather that brings tourists to the Hawaiian Islands. The sea was green, with streaks of blue, and white foam. I watched fish move beneath it, over a blur of coral reefs. It was the kind of day that makes me want to roam the seascape, to watch the myriad of fantastic sea creatures in that seductive world beneath the waves.

I went into the water with Culley, but it was definitely not a fun dive.

We were deploying the dens offshore from the Pearl Harbor Navel Base, and hoping this experiment would prove successful. Mini told us how far apart to place the dens to prevent conflicts between brooding females. The shark cage was on the bottom, in case we were attacked by giants.

The giants had already sunk two skiffs by burning holes in their hulls. One giant burned through the light, outer hull of a submarine. Before she could burn the inner, pressure hull, she was blown out of the water. It was sad, but boats had to defend themselves.

Brad lowered one of the dens from the deck. Culley and I followed the line down to the hundred-foot bottom, below the storm-wave zone.

The den was concave, with a three by four-foot opening, and perforated to allow water to aerate the eggs. It was painted blue and had a crinkled surface to resemble rocks, an octopus' preferred hideout. A line attached beneath the den to a lead weight would allow the den to sway with currents. A roof line ran up to a marker buoy on the surface. We were trying hard to help this giant species survive, but Culley and I both carried torches.

"Oh my God!" I whispered into the mask mic.

On the underwater horizon, about seventy feet away, a large female giant, white as death and twice as big, slithered toward us.

We couldn't surface. This was a decompression dive.

"Brad!" Culley called into his mic, "there's a giant headed our way."

"Oh, shit!" Brad exclaimed. "Can you guys get into the shark cage?"

"She's between us and the cage," Culley told him.

"Can you come up?" Brad asked.

"No," Culley said. "Get the rocket launcher and the machine gun on deck."

"What are you going to do?" Brad asked.

"Depends on what she does," Culley said. "We'll hide for now. Send down two tanks." He took my hand. "C'mon, Tess."

"Where are we going?"

"We'll hide out and see what she does."

The two tanks came down on a line and plunked to the bottom, raising silt. The giant moved closer to us.

"Ryan." I grasped his hand tighter and felt my heart pound. I was breathing too fast.

"Easy, Tess. Take it easy. I won't let anything happen to you."

I gripped his hand as we searched the coral bed and found a breach to hide in. From here we could torch the giant's tentacles if she came too close.

She loomed over a coral mount, probing with a tentacle into fissures. We settled on the bottom and faced her.

"Culley!" I said as the octopus jetted closer. I squeezed his hand harder.

"I know, Tess. Don't worry. We've got our torches, and God knows, I've got your hand."

I was shaking but I loosened my grip.

"When this is over," he said, "I'll buy you lunch at that Jewish deli you found. I'll even try a knish."

"OK," I said shakily. "I'll leave the tip."

"That's my lady."

We unhooked our torches as the giant studied us with slitted eyes. Her skin flashed red in our lights.

"Get ready to make your torch hot," Culley said. Fish darted away as the giant approached. A gray reef shark swam by to inspect us. He probably wasn't aware that the octopus was a living creature. She whipped out a tentacle and wrapped it around him. His struggles raised sand. She dragged him under her body to where her beak was located, and blood mixed with water.

"The poor thing," I said.

"Yeah, but better the poor thing than us."

We watched silently as she devoured her gruesome meal. Blood and chunks of the shark drifted around her. Fish came back to grab the pieces.

"Stay here, Tess."

"Wait! Where are you going?"

"The tanks."

I let go of his hand and he swam toward the tanks and purposely kicked up sand with his fins. He was shrouded in mist. The giant ignored him as he brought back the tanks.

She finished her meal and watched us. She knew very well where we were and probably what we were.

Culley was so calm and steady as we faced the creature. His courage was like a soothing hand over my heart. "I love you, Ryan," I said.

"You do?"

"I do."

"Ah, I forgot the ring."

The giant turned from us and slithered to the den.

"Look at that!" I whispered.

She stroked the den with tentacles, which have taste buds on the suckers, then probed the interior. She pushed at the den and it swayed on its foundation.

I watched, mesmerized, as she turned upside down, her tentacles hanging around her. White eggs, like large frosted teardrops, emerged from her siphon. She weaved them into strands by their floating strings, then glued them to the interior roof with a gentle touch that belied her size.

"I wish Mini were here to see this!" I said.

"Oh, yeah, I'm sure she'd be thrilled to be here. Brad!" he called into the mic.

"I'm here, Culley. What's *happening* down there?"

"Tell Mini that the giant is giving birth!" I said.

"I think," Culley told Brad, "Tess wants to be the godmother. We're coming up to our decompression stop. Lift the cage. This mother's too busy to bother us. Anyway, she just ate a shark for breakfast."

CHAPTER FOURTEEN

That evening we celebrated the first success of our experiment with three bottles of champagne Brad had saved for a special occasion.

Mini, who loved to tell jokes, sat on the other side of Culley and bombarded us with them.

"Mini!" George finally said, "I never knew you had such a dirty mouth."

"Oh, go fucales yourself," Mini responded. "In a kelp bed!" She threw back her head and laughed. I saw her nudge Culley. She drank again.

"Just don't get the crabs!" Brad added, and laughed until tears streaked his cheeks. He pounded his fist on the table and drank more champagne.

I watched Mini spill her drink. "Mini, your drink."

"Oh," she exclaimed, "I'll put a head on it." She poured champagne into her glass until it spilled onto her hand. "That oughta do it!"

I watched the room slowly spin. "Crabs in the bed. That's so *funny!*" I told Culley.

George giggled and gulped champagne. "Crabs in the pot! That's even better."

"Oh, go fucales a crab!" I said to no one and laughed.

"I think it's time for my lady to hit the sack," Culley said.

I leaned over and nibbled his ear. " Let's go to bed, Ryan. I want to make love in a bed of sea...I mean, a seaweed of bed." I put my hand on his thigh.

He lifted it to the table. "Not tonight, kid."

"Why? You want a contract?" I imitated what he'd told me back in my apartment.

"It's not that."

"Then what?" I felt a stab of fear. "You want to make love to somebody else?" I looked at Mini, who was listening.

"He's your guy," she said.

Brad stood up unsteadily with his glass and a bottle. "Let's all go on deck to finish this party," he said to George and Mini, "and leave these two to their sinful devices." He staggered into the john and slammed the door. A minute later he came back out. "It's *dark* on deck," he announced.

The three of them made it out the door, stumbling over each other's feet.

"Don't fall overboard!" Culley called.

I got up and pulled Culley out of his chair. "Let's go to bunk." I giggled.

"Sure, kid."

I kissed his lips as he undressed me. "I love you, my honey bee," I whispered as I stood naked.

"That's good." He took my pajamas from a drawer and helped me into them.

"Why do I need these?" I asked as he buttoned them.

"You'd be cold without them." He picked me up, carried me to my bunk, laid me down and covered me with my blanket.

"Aren't you coming?" I asked.

"I just might." He sat on the edge of my bunk and tucked me in. "Now close your eyes and think sweet thoughts."

"But I want to make love."

"That's the champagne talking."

"Champagne doesn't make love."

"Oh yeah, it does."

I felt hurt. "Are you tired of me?" Tears welled up. "That's it," I said, "you're tired of me."

"Cut it out, Tess."

"I know. It's Mini, isn't it? She's very pretty."

"Dammit, Tess, don't bait me! Sure, she's pretty. So what?" He wiped tears from my eyes with his sleeve. "How many times do I have to tell you that *you're* my lady."

"You promise?"

He sighed. "I promise. Now go to sleep."

Suddenly I felt drowsy. The bunk was so warm; the pillow so soft. I put a hand on Culley's thigh and he lifted it to his arm.

"Where's Ice?" I said. At home he slept on my bed. "I miss Ice!"

"I'm sure he misses you too. You can tell him all about the giant octopuses when we get home."

"OK."

"Sweet dreams, kid." He kissed me on the cheek.

"You too, kid." I yawned. "Don't go make love to Mini."

"I won't."

I smiled at him. "'My love's like a red, red rose'."

"Sometimes with a thorn in my side," I heard him say as I closed my eyes and drifted off to sleep.

*****

I awoke the next morning and saw Culley asleep in his bunk. The others were gone. Culley's blanket had slipped off. I got up, covered him with it, and gently tucked it around his shoulders. He looked so handsome and innocent in sleep, I had to smile.

Mini came out of the john brushing her hair. "Oh, morning, Tess."

"Morning."

She pointed at Culley with her brush. "You know, I woke up about three o'clock and I went out on deck to get some fresh air. My head felt like a rock band was giving a concert in there. Your guy was on deck. He was keeping an eye on things while we all slept off the party." She took a red scarf from her pants pocket, shook it out, and tied back her hair. "If you ever get tired of him, send him my way."

"In about a hundred years."

"I'll wait." She went to the closet and took out her sandals. "What's this?" she said.

"What?"

She reached into the closet and came out with my green dress. It was as clean and beautiful as the day I bought it.

"That's my dress!" I said. "Culley must have found it on *Reverence* after it sank. Or maybe it was floating in the water."

Culley was still asleep.

"Surprise him some day," Mini said, "maybe on a special occasion, and wear it."

I nodded and looked at him. "You cutie," I whispered.

Mini put the dress away and sat at the table. There were boxes of cereal, a container of soy milk, fruit, bowls, and silverware. "Want some?"

I shook my head. My stomach was still queasy from all the champagne.

She poured cereal into a bowl. "We're going to lower the ROV and get some footage of the giant while she lays eggs. It usually takes a few days. I'm anxious to see how a giant does it."

"You don't think the ROV will be intrusive?"

She stopped chewing. "I don't think so. They're highly intelligent, but obviously non-technological." She shrugged. "I don't think she'll have a clue as to what it is."

Culley woke up and stretched. "Hey, Mini. How you feeling, Tess?"

I sat on his bunk, took his hand and kissed it. "Like a very lucky lady."

*****

We gathered on the bridge to watch as Culley guided the ROV toward the den.

"There she is," Brad said when the vehicle's camera focused on the octopus. Her tentacles were wrapped around the den. As the ROV got closer, I saw that eggs still emerged from her siphon. She continued to weave them into strands by the strings attached to each egg, and glued them to the den's interior roof. She gently caressed the strands to aerate the eggs, though the current already kept them swaying within their nursery.

Mini watched intently and took notes.

"What's that?" I said and pointed to a movement at the edge of the camera's frame.

Culley turned the ROV in that direction. Another giant female octopus approached the den. This one was huge.

"Uh, oh," Mini said with her pen poised.

The new female swooped down to the den, wrapped her tentacles around the laying female and yanked. The laying female fought back. She stopped the flow of eggs from her siphon and spread tentacles to guard her eggs. The attacking giant covered the other female with her larger body. Blood mixed with water. We weren't sure which octopus was bleeding until the attacking octopus dragged the other female out of her den and began to rip her apart with her beak.

I wanted to look away, but that was not the scientific method. In our efforts to gain knowledge, there were times when we had to look life in the face and not flinch.

"The poor thing," I said.

George nodded. "Survival of the most brutal."

Culley sat next to me and put his arm around my shoulders as the dying octopus lowered her tentacles and drifted down to the bottom. The new female tore the eggs from their holdfast beneath the roof. The eggs spread across their dead mother like strands of broken pearls.

Mini sat back and stared at the screen. "Well, boys and girls, this barbaric ritual proves that our artificial dens are at a premium for brooding giant octopuses."

"It just might be the proof we need," Brad offered, "that this species, wherever the hell it came from, and we humans, can co-exist without having our ships used for nurseries."

We watched silently as the new female turned upside down and began laying her own eggs in the den. Below her, the remains of the dead octopus were ripped apart and eaten by hordes of hungry fish and reef sharks. Somehow, they knew better than to eat the acid-coated eggs. Maybe it was their odor. Dolphins swooped down into the frame of the camera and played with pieces of tentacles, rolling and wrapping them around their mouths before eating them.

"When you think about it," George said, "*brutal* is how our own species competed and dominated the planet." He fished around in his pocket, but then realized he had no candy bars with him. His expression became strained.

CHAPTER FIFTEEN

"I've been more than very patient, haven't I?" George looked around. "Well, *haven't* I?"

We sat in the cabin three weeks after deploying that first den. The experiment had proven more successful than we could have hoped. Twenty-one out of the thirty dens we set up were occupied by brooding female giants. Six had been taken over by moray eels and lobsters. We wondered why the other three were empty until Culley and I went down to inspect them. Baby octopuses had made their homes in the safety of the three dens, with the current bringing in plankton through the perforations for them to eat.

Later that day, we gathered around the ROV screen on the bridge.

"Those lobsters and that moray eel are sitting on an octopus dish," George said and pointed at the screen, "if they only knew."

"Octopuses eat lobsters," Mini told us. "They'll probably welcome a moray eel for dinner too."

"Hmmm, yummy," Brad said.

"My mother's Italian friend used to cook eels," George said. "I still remember how the pieces flopped around in the frying pan."

I looked at Mini.

"You *ate* that?" Mini asked George.

"It was tasty," George said. "It tasted like chicken."

"Oh, give me a fucking break!" Brad exclaimed. "If it tasted like chicken, why didn't you just *eat* chicken?"

"Why don't you just eat crow!" George got up and left the bridge.

"That wasn't very nice, Bradford," Mini said and went to the open door.

Brad sighed. "Tell him I'm sorry."

"*You* tell him." She left the door open as she went on deck.

Brad got up and followed her. "Oh, Georgie," I heard him call. "The next time we make port, I'll buy you a dish of eels. In fact, I'll try some myself. Yuch!" I heard Brad say under his breath.

"OK." I heard George call.

With the data we sent back to the Pacifica Lab, the federal government agreed to fund the building of artificial reefs with numerous dens, placed far apart, like apartment rooms, where the giants could safely brood their eggs with space enough between them. The reefs would attract fish, which would be a food source for the mothers, if they decided to eat again after their eggs hatched.

"So?" George said, "when do I get to take samples of the water, the sediments, and the rocks in an oceanic trench? We *still* don't know why the giant males haven't come into shallow water, or why the females did in the first place. And I've been patient."

Mini looked at Brad. "He's been patient, boss, especially now that he's run out of candy bars."

Brad looked at me and Culley.

"He's been patient." I nodded.

Culley scratched his chin. "You guys know that there are still reports of attacks by giant octopuses. You haven't tamed them all. And Somali pirates have expanded their operations. They're in the Pacific now." He looked around. His gaze rested on me. "They don't always take prisoners, and when they do, especially women...." He let it hang there.

"Then there are those religious nut cases." Brad sighed. "There are more dangers above the water than below it." He stood up and stretched.

We waited.

He went to the door and turned. "You said it yourself, Culley, we have some extremely awesome weapons on board, and this is still a scientific expedition. Set your course, George." He yawned. "It's time for my afternoon nap." He looked at our serious faces and raised his brows. "Wake me up if we're attacked by a giant female." He went out the door.

"Did I call them extremely awesome weapons?" Culley asked.

*****

"The Mariana Trench?" I said to George. "Can the ROV take the pressure?"

"George," Mini said as she, George, and I sat on the bridge, "did you have to pick on the deepest known point in the oceans?"

"Well," George responded, "actually the Arctic Ocean is closer to the center of the earth."

"We all *know* that," I said," but it's only because of the shape of the earth. But what if the ROV crumbles under that kind of pressure? You'll have to answer to Sea Worthy and the Biosphere Society."

"Well, what's science if it's not bold?" George answered.

"True, "Mini said, "but not usually with equipment on *loan!* What do you expect to find at seven miles down?"

George grinned. "I have a theory."

"It had better be a good one." Mini told him." Your reputation in the scientific community will be dog shit if you destroy an expensive ROV out of recklessness."

"Then so be it!" George said bravely and slammed his fist on the table. "I give my all for science."

Mini turned to me. "I think he made more sense when he was on a permanent sugar high."

*****

George, at the helm, set our course for the Mariana Trench, east of the Mariana Islands in the Western Pacific. He seemed more self-assured these days, since Brad had agreed to follow his plan. I noticed that he didn't eat as many candy bars either. But he still remained secretive about his theory. It was his power, and he was enjoying it.

We passed an old oil platform in the distance, abandoned now, since the world had mostly turned to greener forms of energy. The platform stood like a skeletal monument to a time when humans depended on oil, and spills created dead zones in the oceans that would last for centuries. Some scientists believed that these zones would never support life again. We were passing over a dead zone from an old spill that had occurred long ago from the distant platform.

I leaned on the rail with Culley beside me. The day was warm and humid. Storm clouds gathered on the western horizon. My shirt stuck to my back and my long hair kept my neck hot. I'd have to ask Mini if I could borrow a scarf. I watched a school of dolphins ride the bow waves and call to each other in a language I hoped we would one day crack.

"Sometimes I wish I could run with them," I said.

"It's the sense of freedom," Culley answered. "It feels that way riding a motorcycle, too."

He had his arm around my shoulders. I didn't tell him that it made my back even hotter. "Will you teach me to ride?" I asked, "when we get back?"

"It's a dangerous sport, Tess."

"But you ride."

"OK, I'll teach you to ride." He nodded at the platform. "I'll bet there's eggs on those columns."

"Maybe not such a bad thing," I said. "I've seen less and less jellyfish in these waters. You know, hon, I think that nature has sublime ways to heal herself, even with all the damage we've done."

He kissed my forehead. "Maybe our kids will have a better world."

"How many do you want?"

"Oh, a baker's dozen."

"Then you'd better marry a baker."

"Two," he said. "How about two to replace us?"

"That's what I was thinking. A boy and a girl."

"So you want them designed?"

"Only so that it's a boy and a girl." I smiled. "And that they both look like you."

"How about we skip the last part and let it be a surprise?"

I leaned my head on his shoulder. "OK, a boy, a girl, and surprises. As long as one doesn't fly away."

"More likely she'll swim away with the dolphins."

Brad strolled over. "Is this a private conversation?"

I shook my head. "I was saying that I see less and less jellies, especially the giant Nomuras."

"Compliments of the Krakens?" Brad asked.

"I can't think of another cause. I've already noticed more fish too."

Mini came out of the cabin. "Can I join the party?"

"Did you bring the champagne?" Brad asked. "Culley." He leaned forward to look at Culley, who was on my other side. "I never properly thanked you for being the designated driver while the rest of us indulged."

"You're welcome, boss." Culley smirked. "But next party, choose a different driver."

Brad reached in front of me to shake Culley's hand. I backed a step and glanced at Mini. It was good to see Culley and Brad acknowledge each other's friendship.

Mini winked at me.

"I think he's a keeper," Brad told me.

"Considering the bait," Culley put his arm around me and squeezed, "I was

76

hooked and sunk."

I turned to Mini. "I feel like a fish."

But she was staring at the platform. "What's that? There's a ship moving behind that platform."

Culley grasped the rail. "That's a fishing trawler."

"What's it doing in this dead zone?" I asked.

"We'd better find out." Culley went to the bridge.

We followed.

He grabbed the binoculars and studied the ship. "It's approaching full speed," he said. "That's the fucking mother ship! It's a Chinese trawler. There's two skiffs in front of her headed our way."

Brad got on the radio and called the Naval Station at Pearl Harbor "Mayday. Mayday. Mayday. This is R/V *Cousteau*. I think we're being attacked by a hijacked fishing trawler. Over."

Brad took the helm and headed us away from the skiffs at full speed.

The rest of us went with Culley to bring the weapons on deck. He took the rocket launcher.

"Oh my God," I said as I watched the skiffs approach. "Oh my God."

"Tess!" Culley said, "you and Mini hide out in the cabin."

I stood frozen as the skiffs raced toward us.

"Take these." Culley gave me and Mini two rifles. "Don't hesitate to use them if it comes to that. *Go,* Tess."

"I'll stay here," I told him. "I can back you up."

"Do you know what they'd do to a woman? Now go!"

"What would they do to a man? I'm staying."

"Tess, don't fight me on this. Just go."

Mini took my arm. "C'mon, Tess."

"What about *me?*" George asked, wide-eyed.

"Culley shoved a rifle into his hands. "Shoot if they get here first." He pointed to the returning Navy helicopter. It was a race between the skiffs and the helicopter.

"They're pirates," Mini said shakily as we made out four black men in one skiff; four more in the other. Their heads were wrapped in white and checkered scarves.

"They're wearing the *Koofi,*" Mini said.

"Goddammit, go!" Culley ordered us. The look in his eyes scared me. "No matter what happens, don't come out."

"Can't I go too," George whined.

"You stay here," Culley shouted, "and help defend the boat!"

Brad ran out on deck and took a rifle. "A Navy warship's on its way." He stared at the approaching skiffs. "Shit! Those are Somali pirates."

George sobbed and crouched below the rail.

"Take the wheel," Brad told him.

George crawled to the bridge, dragging the rifle.

Mini and I went into the cabin. We stayed low and watched from a window.

"Oh, God, Mini, I'm so scared. I'm scared for Ryan, too."

"He knows how to handle himself, Tess. He'll do the best thing for all of us. These hijackers...they, they just take hostages and the boat for ransom."

"Mini." My throat felt tight. My stomach was clenched. "If they're attacked,

I heard they shoot the hostages as a warning to governments not to interfere."

"I know," she said. I felt her hand shake in mine. "I know. I hope I don't throw up or pee myself."

I saw Culley brace the rocket launcher on the rail.

Machine gun fire strafed the side of the boat and he fell back.

"Culley!" I screamed.

Grappling hooks swung over the stern. Brad ran there and tried to unhook one, but it was taut. The pirates were already boarding!

Culley got up and grabbed the launcher. Before he could aim, another round of machine gun fire over the rail kept him and Brad low.

I watched Culley hunch down and run to the stern.

"Oh, Culley!" I cried as he aimed over the stern and fired.

I heard an explosion. Water and debris flew up past our boat.

"I hit a skiff!" Culley called to Brad.

The helicopter was close, but so was the mother ship. It fired on the helicopter but missed. The helicopter swung wide and away.

Three pirates, naked to the waist except for the *Koofis* wrapped around their heads and faces, and bandoliers of ammunition strung across their chests, leaped aboard, holding rifles.

"Oh, No!" I picked up my rifle and aimed through the glass, but I couldn't get a clear shot. Culley and Brad were in the way. Culley's launcher was empty. One pirate strode toward him with his rifle pointed. He looked like a gangly teenager. Culley raised his hands, but I saw the look of defiance on his face. He glanced up at the receding helicopter. Brad held his rifle pointed down.

An older man, thin and dark, with a clipped white beard, was helped on board. He looked around. "Abdul," he told one of the youths, "see who's at the helm." His voice was raspy, with a thick Somalian accent. "And be careful!" He turned to Brad, "Fire at me, and my friend kills your friend."

One of the two young pirates pulled the rifle from Brad's hands.

"Too late," I said. "Mini, we'd better hide under the bunks."

Mini nodded and crawled under her bunk. I got under mine.

"Hussein," I heard a pirate say, "the others in the skiff are all dead! Let me kill at least one of these heathens and send him to hell!"

"Oh, no. No!" I whispered.

"Kill one if you must," Hussein, the older man, answered. "But understand that his ransom will be your pay."

"Then I will get no pay?" the young pirate asked.

"That is why you will do nothing without my orders."

I breathed a sigh of relief.

I couldn't see what was happening on deck but I heard Hussein say "Get on your radio, and tell them that if they send a warship, you are all dead."

The engines were cut.

Oh, God, I silently prayed. *Please. Save us.*

I heard the cabin door swing open. I tried to slow my breathing, afraid I would be heard. My fear seemed so palpable, I thought they'd know I was here.

George was sobbing. I only saw feet, but there was Culley, and then Brad was brought in.

"This is the one you have to watch." I heard Hussein say. "What is your name?"

"Culley. What's yours?"

"I would kill you now, Culley, for destroying the skiff and killing four of my soldiers, but you are worth a ransom. Even that garbage there is worth some money." I saw him raise a foot and kick forward.

George fell with a sob.

"Since when do *soldiers* board a private vessel for ransom?" Culley said.

I heard a smack. I almost cried out, but Culley didn't.

Oh, Culley, shut up! I thought.

"Get up, garbage," a pirate said to George and kicked him again.

If one of them bent down, he would see me or Mini. Sweat soaked my shirt. I felt it drip down my sides. I realized I was grasping the rifle and slowly let it go. It could scrape the bare floor and make a sound in my shaking hand.

George saw me and got quickly to his feet.

"I've got a deal for you, soldier," Culley said. "Send your troops out on deck with their weapons, and you and me have it out like two men, bare knuckles."

I realized that Culley was baiting him. If he could get the others on deck, Mini and I could come out with our rifles.

"I do not deal with despoilers," Hussein said.

Dammit! I thought.

"Your country knew very well that nuclear waste was dumped in our waters and even buried on our shores."

I had a cramp in my left calf from the twisted position I was in, but I dared not stretch my leg.

"What sort of boat is this?" Hussein asked.

"It used to be a pleasure boat," Brad told him.

"Until now," Culley added. "You won't get much for it on the black market."

"A pleasure boat?" Hussein said, "with a laboratory?"

"Previous owner," Culley told him.

My mouth was as dry as the dust I lay in. I realized that I had to pee, but I was afraid they'd smell the urine.

God, if you let us live through this, I'll never ask for another thing. Then the irony struck me. I had never believed in a compassionate god who watched over us.

"You hear that, my soldiers?" Hussein said. "This is a research vessel that Allah has sent to us. There will be a large ransom for this one."

"So the money," Culley said, "will go to the Somalian poor?"

Dammit, Culley! I thought. *It didn't work. Back off!*

"Take him onto the deck," Hussein said, "before I kill him myself! Tie him where the sun can beat down on his bare head. Perhaps that will take some of the arrogance out of him. If he begs for water, give him a drink from the sea."

Two of them took Culley outside.

I closed my eyes. Tears slid down my cheeks and wet the dusty floor.

CHAPTER SIXTEEN

R/V *Cousteau* was underway, but without the rumble of engines. She was being towed. Brad and George sat on bunks. The pirates ate dinner at the table. They held their rifles steady on the floor with their feet pressed over them.

"Aren't you going to feed us?" George asked.

"Why feed the dead?" A young pirate chuckled.

"You don't get ransoms for the dead," Brad said.

"Hussein knows what this boat is," The young pirate said. "She's worth much more money than I have ever seen. Now shut up. We want to eat."

I had peed myself. I hoped my pants would soak up the odor.

*****

By nightfall I was thirsty. I wondered how Culley felt after being out there all afternoon in the sun.

Flashes of lightning lit the floor. Distant thunder grew louder as the storm approached. The boat rocked in waves. I held onto the bunk straps overhead.

"She'll be swamped if you tow her in this storm," I heard Brad say.

"Abdul," Hussein said, "come with me to the bridge. Nadim, Yasar, give these two something to eat."

They left the cabin.

I put a hand on the rifle. *What would Culley do in my situation?* He would be strong. He would do the best thing for all of us and let the chips fall where they may.

I waited for Nadim and Yasar to fill two plates and bring Brad and George to the table. I saw that their hands were tied behind their backs.

"Here," one said, "eat it with your mouth in the plate, like the faithless dogs that you are."

The engines rumbled to life and the boat steadied.

I took a deep breath, ordered my heart not to leave my chest, rolled out from under the bunk and up to a sitting position. "Back up!" I ordered and aimed the rifle at the two pirates. "Get your hands up!"

Mini came out and raised her rifle awkwardly.

I stood up and slid the pirates' rifles away with a foot. "Get down on the floor!" The rifle shook in my hands but I steadied it. "Now!"

Brad and George remained quiet. I think they knew that Mini and I had to concentrate.

"You heard her," Mini said. "Get on your bellies before I blow off your heads."

They looked at each other and got to their knees. "Yasar," Nadim said, "they are only women. Why should we listen to them?"

"Because bullets have no gender," Brad told them.

"On your bellies," George said, "you pieces of garbage!"

They laid down flat on the floor, their hands extended. I think they listened because this time the order came from men.

I grabbed a knife from the table and cut Brad and George loose.

"Oh, thank you, Tess." George rubbed his wrists.

"Give me your rifle, Mini," Brad said.

She did.

"Now tie their hands behind their backs, Mini," Brad told her, "and use those *Koofis* to stuff their mouths. We don't want them calling out to Hussein if he comes back. George, take one of their rifles."

Mini began tying the hands of one pirate. "You're a disgrace to your race!" she told him.

"I do not need a traitor to tell me who I am," the boy answered.

"I'm going on deck to Culley." I took the knife and two rifles. But as I reached the door, I saw Hussein walking toward the cabin. "Hussein's coming!" I whispered. "Abdul must be at the helm."

Mini tied the other pirate's hands.

George stuffed their headdresses into their mouths. "Chew on *that*, you murderers!"

A bolt of lightning struck close and thunder cracked the night sky.

Brad shut off the cabin lights. "Stay quiet," he told us.

"Yasar? Nadim!" Hussein called as he opened the door. What happened to the lights? Was it the lightning?""

Brad threw on the lights and the three of them aimed at Hussein.

He looked from me to Mini. "So," he said to Yasar and Nadim, "these women have subdued you like children."

"Would you mind putting your rifle on the floor?" Brad said sarcastically.

Hussein unslung his rifle and laid it down.

I went on deck and ran to Culley. Rain pelted me and lightning struck close to the boat. I felt my hair rise on my neck.

"Tess! What happened?"

"We got them, Culley. We *got* them. All but Abdul, the one steering the boat." I cut the ropes that bound him. "Are you OK?"

"Sure." He rubbed his wrists. "What's a little thirst like I've been on a desert for a week?"

I handed him a rifle. "Compliments of 'just a woman'!"

He threw me a look. "I'll get Abdul."

"*We'll* get him."

We moved carefully to the bridge.

Culley threw open the door.

Abdul's rifle was laid on the console beside him as he steered the boat.

"Get away from the helm!" Culley ordered.

Abdul drew in a quick breath and grabbed the mic.

"Put it down!" Culley aimed.

"Put it down, Abdul," I ordered. "He'll kill you!"

"The hostages are loose!" he cried into the mic and grabbed his rifle.

Culley fired. I screamed as blood spurted from Abdul's chest. He jerked back and dropped the rifle as he slid to the floor. He was still. His eyes were closed. Blood spread around him.

"Take the helm, Tess. Hard to starboard. Full speed."

I stood there, staring at Abdul.

"Tess! You want to help? Then take the wheel. I had to do it."

"I know." I pushed Abdul's rifle aside with my foot and turned the boat to starboard. "I'm not blaming you. it's just that...he was only a kid."

"A kid with a loaded rifle!" Culley dragged Abdul onto the deck. A smear of blood marked their path.

The mother ship was a black hulk, trimmed with lights, not far off to port. Lightning flashed and lit *Cousteau.*

A few minutes later Culley came back with a bottle of water in one hand, a rifle in the other. "Here." He handed me the bottle. "Let me take over."

The mother ship was turning.

"She's coming after us," Culley said.

The radio crackled. "This is Captain Mustapha. Was that you, Abdul? Abdul! Who am I speaking to?" he demanded.

"This is R/V *Cousteau,*" Culley answered. "We have your soldiers in custody. If you try to board us, we *will* kill them. Now back off!"

But the mother ship turned its bow toward us.

"They're probably out of skiffs," Culley said. "They'll try to ram us. Tess, get into your life vest. Tell the others."

"I'll bring yours." I ran through pouring rain back to the cabin.

Brad, Mini, and George were already in life vests.

"What's happening?" Brad asked.

I grabbed a life vest. "Culley had to kill Abdul," but Abdul radioed the trawler first. They're going to ram us."

Hussein lowered his head. Yasar and Nadim looked at each other and their lips quivered. I knew that Arab men were expressive in grief.

"You have killed Hussein's son!" Yasar cried.

"God," I said. "I'm sorry, Hussein. I really am." I got into my life vest. "But your son didn't give us a choice."

"Then he died bravely," Hussein said. "Now he is with Allah."

I grabbed a blanket off a bunk, and another life vest for Culley.

I went on deck. Rain washed blood from Abdul's slender body. I covered him with the blanket.

The trawler had gained on us.

I brought Culley the life vest. "Here, hon. I'll take the wheel." I walked around the blood stain.

We slammed through waves. The trawler loomed like a nightmare behind us.

"You think they'll ram us," I said, "with their own people on board?"

"These are the nut cases who bring their coffins to the front lines."

With each stroke of lightning, the mother ship appeared closer.

"It's time to launch *Nomad,*" Culley said.

"What about the three pirates?"

"They stay on board as insurance so maybe the bastards won't sink our boat."

Culley radioed the mother ship. "Ram *Cousteau* and you kill your own soldiers. My crew's abandoning ship. There's an American warship on the way. Sink our boat and they'll blow you out of the fucking water. Go ahead! Be my guest!"

Brad came onto the bridge. His captain's hat was gone. His blonde hair was plastered to his forehead.

"I'm thinking," Culley told him, "we launch *Nomad* and head for the platform."

"That's what I'm thinking," Brad said. "Great minds...."

A radio transmission came through: "This is the USS *Barack*. Are you under attack? Over."

"Affirmative," Culley answered. The mother ship is a Chinese trawler. They intend to ram us. We're about to abandon ship. Over."

"Give me your coordinates. Over."

I left the bridge with Brad.

Lightning flashed and thunder rolled as we loaded *Nomad* with blankets, rain slickers, survival suits, water bottles, dive gear, the rifles, which we'd sleeved inside plastic bags, a compass, flares, and a signal light. We were loaded to the pontoons as we launched her.

We had strapped life vests on the three pirates in the cabin as best we could, but left their hands tied.

We climbed into *Nomad* and lowered her down to the water.

Culley started the motor and we held on as *Nomad* slammed through waves. We put on our rain slickers and zippered them up, but water splashed over the pontoons and we were all soaked, and cold. We left the bow and stern lights off so the mother ship couldn't see us. Culley started the bilge pump.

Mini had the compass. She turned on its small light and held it under her slicker.

"How's it look, Mini?" Culley asked over his shoulder.

"We're pretty much on course for the platform. I think."

"When we get further away from the pirate ship," Brad said, "we can turn on the signal light to look for the platform."

"Uh, guys?" George said.

There was silence.

"What, George?" I asked to acknowledge him.

"I...I want to apologize for being such a wimp. I'll try harder."

"You mean if the inflatable gets boarded?" Brad asked.

"I mean...whatever happens. We're not out of the woods yet."

Mini wiped water from her face. "Woods sounds nice."

Behind us *Cousteau* and the mother ship were lit by flashes of lightning. The storm was moving northeast. Culley slowed down and water no longer splashed over the pontoons.

"If *Cousteau* is sunk," Brad said, "there isn't a society on this earth that will loan us a fucking *rowboat* anymore."

George pointed. "Look!"

I saw the lights of a big ship approaching the trawler from the northeast.

"The SS *Barack*," Culley said.

Brad flashed our signal light but the ship continued on her course.

I was shivering. I took a blanket and held on as I crawled to Culley on my hands and knees and wrapped it around his legs.

"Thanks, kid."

"You're welcome, hon." I kissed his cheek with trembling lips. "How bad can it be if we're together?"

His shoulders were shaking. "Ah, this is nothing compared to the time I killed that grizzly with a butter knife."

I wanted to laugh but I was shaking too hard. I wrapped a blanket around my own legs and feet.

The bilge pump kept the water below the floorboards, but the boat was wet and rain still pelted us. Thunder receded and lightning flashes lit clouds further and further to the northeast.

"A star," I said as the clouds parted.

"I wish I wish," Brad said. "I wish that fucking Navy ship would see us!"

But the ship moved away from us, heading toward the mother ship and *Cousteau*.

"Follow her, Culley," I said.

"I told them we'd wait at the platform," he answered. "We might not be able to climb up to its deck, but at least *Barack* will know where we are. We don't want to be in the line of fire in this inner tube."

Streaks of red lit the night as the trawler fired on the approaching warship. An explosion!

I no longer saw the lights of the trawler. "Oh my God," I whispered.

"They have orders to kill pirates on sight," Culley said. He turned on the bow and stern lights, but the low inflatable was lost between waves as we headed to the oil platform.

*****

The storm moved on. The sun rose in a warming blaze of light.

The lower deck of the platform was too high for us to climb up, but George found some breaks in the wall of the deck and looped our anchor line around them.

I wanted to check out the columns that held up the platform for possible dens before we boarded *Barack*.

Culley and I suited up, took torches, and went over the side of *Nomad*.

Hundreds of fishes swam beneath the platform. In "the big blue," as sea goers refer to the open ocean, there are precious few places for fish to find shelter. Even a mat of floating kelp attracts them until it rots and sinks.

I watched a juvenile blue shark hover while a school of cleaner wrasse nibbled parasites off his skin.

A splash at the surface, beyond the deck, and the paddling legs of a seabird.

"Uh, oh," I said into my face mask as the shark swam up to the bird. I thought he'd eat the bird, but instead he rolled to his side and the seabird peck off the more stubborn parasites.

Culley and I looked at each other and laughed into our masks.

We followed the columns down to search for dens. This was prime real estate for mother giant octopuses.

At seventy feet we found an empty burned-out den.

We also found the mother!

Culley and I unhooked our torches. The octopus was surrounded by swarms of hatchlings, about ten inches long.

"My God, Culley," I said, "she survived the birth of the babies! They're growing."

"Looks like she's taking care of them, too."

"I've never seen -- "

A few of the babies jetted toward us. I think out of curiosity. They no longer had their brown coating. Without it, the acid layer had probably sloughed off, too. By now, they'd probably developed acid sacs like mom's for defense and killing prey.

I prepared to light my torch. The mother flashed. The babies flashed back in short streaks. They turned and swooped under her spread tentacles. She made no aggressive moves toward us, but in our lights, different colors rippled like neon across her huge body. I had a feeling that she was attempting to communicate with us. I was certain she knew what the torches could do. But how? Did these giants learn by communicating with the giants we had already encountered? Whales communicate around the oceans by sound, but an octopus? And something as specific as a torch that can burn them?

"This is getting curioser and curioser," I said. "I think this species is in communication with one another! I think...."

"That she's trying to communicate with us?"

"There seems to be a pattern to the flashes," I told him.

"I felt it, too."

"Wait until I tell Mini and George what we've seen."

"I'm glad you were the first marine biologist to see it," Culley said.

"Thanks, hon. I wish we had the camera. It's back on *Cousteau.*"

"Hope we still have *Cousteau.*"

We surfaced and Culley remained face down to keep an eye on the octopus.

"Mini!" I said as she helped me over the pontoon.

"What?"

"You're not going to believe this!"

"Try us," Brad said.

"Start the motor," I told him as I saw the *SS Barack* approach.

"Is Culley practicing how to play dead?" Brad asked.

"He's keeping an eye on a mother giant until we're ready to leave. Start the motor."

"Mother fucker!" Brad exclaimed. "There's a giant under the boat?"

I nodded.

"She could probably swallow us whole!" George exclaimed.

Brad turned on the motor as Culley lifted himself into the boat.

"That's a bit of an exaggeration," Mini told George.

We headed for *Barack,* which had *Cousteau* in tow, while I told Mini, Brad, and George what we'd seen.

"That's incredible," Mini said. "We have to go back after we board *Cousteau.*"

"And the hatchlings, Mini," I said, "they jetted back to their mother when she flashed at them."

"But how could she know about the torches?" George said.

"You didn't light them?" Mini asked.

I shook my head and smiled at Mini and George.

"I think," Brad threw over his shoulder as he steered, "we should Christen this new species the Tessica Hoffman Giant Octopus. What say you all?"

"I'm for it," Culley said.

Mini and George nodded, but I saw the hurt look on Mini's face. After all, she was the cephalopod expert, not me.

"Thanks, Brad," I said, "but I'd like to elaborate on it. What say you all to the Tessica Hoffman, Minerva Johnson, George Backer Giant Octopus," I said.

"I say," Brad answered, "that we'll need a scroll to announce the name of our new species. But, say I, it sounds OK to me." He fluttered a hand. "How about just surnames, though, to keep from running out of ink when we print it?"

"OK," I said, "then the last revision is Hoffman, Johnson, Backer Giant octopus."

I hugged Mini and George.

"Hey," Culley said, "what am I, chopped liver?"

We pulled him into our group hug.

"You're my knish," I said and kissed his cheek.

"And your Nathan's hotdog!" Brad threw in from the wheel.

"Oh, yum!" George said, "a Nathan's Coney Island hotdog. I'm hungry!"

"We're *all* hungry," Mini told him. "All we have left to eat are our own words."

I looked from Mini to George. "Were you guys drinking champagne while Culley and I were under?"

"And if you were," Culley said, "did you save us any?"

"Somebody get the man a beer," Brad said.

We all laughed. Somehow, laughter eased the tension of the terrifying experience we'd been through with the pirates, and cemented our group into a cohesive whole.

CHAPTER SEVENTEEN

Once aboard *Cousteau,* we contacted Pacifica Lab with our findings. The lab sent the results to scientists around the world. They would, of course, test our conclusions and try to break them down. At this point, it was still a working hypothesis. If the scientific community could find holes in it, we'd have to re-evaluate our results and we *still* knew nothing about the males of the species.

"There have to be giant males, no, Mini?" I asked.

We were anchored off the oil platform. Mini steered the ROV under the deck to search for the mother giant and her babies. "There have to be," she said. "Octopuses can lay unfertilized eggs, but they don't hatch." After searching the four columns, she leaned back in her chair. "Well, she's gone, and the kids, too."

"I wonder where she takes them?" I asked.

"If she keeps them with her," Mini replied, "I think she'd take them to a protected reef with a good source of food." She reeled in the ROV.

"There was a good source of food right under the platform," I told her.

"It's possible that she left because of our presence," Mini replied.

"I know this sounds like a wild idea," I said, "but is it possible that this species communicates with one another with flashes of different colors?"

"Well, most octopus species do," Mini said. It's not unusual."

I leaned forward in the chair. "I'm thinking language, Mini. I'm thinking not just emotions, as when they flash red for anger, but syntax."

She gave me a quizzical look. "Grammatical arranging of words into sentences?"

"I know. It's a giant leap from single words, if you'll excuse the pun. But how do you explain this last giant's recognition of our underwater torches?"

"Were they turned on?"

"No. They weren't." I sat back. "Yet she called in her babies."

"Well...." Mini twirled a lock of her hair. "Well, suppose she knew that the torches weren't organic, like you and Culley, and she saw them as a threat."

"Mini, our tanks aren't organic."

"Did the babies flash colors back to her?"

I nodded.

"Wow. Still, Tess, we know that chimps have language-ready brains. It probably developed before our two species split. But octopuses? That's a very different brain."

"But a highly intelligent one that can learn from other octopuses."

"Yes, that's been proven," Mini admitted.

"And they also have a form of hands."

Mini twirled a lock of her hair. "It's going to be a very controversial subject in the scientific community, with your name attached to it. I'd hate to see you ridiculed."

"What did George say? 'What's science if it's not bold'."

Mini slid me a look. "Consider the source of the statement."

We went into the cabin. Culley had our regulators apart on the table to overhaul them. Brad was lying on his bunk. It was close to three p.m. George was reading a scientific journal. "Did you see her?" he asked.

Mini shook her head and sat down. "She's gone. And she took the kids with her."

I poured myself a cup of coffee. "Anybody?" I held up the coffee pot.

They shook their heads.

"Culley," I said, "a cold beer?"

He shook his head. "Not while I'm working on our regulators. On the off chance it could spill.

I sat at the table with my coffee. "You know, hon..." I said to Culley.

He looked up and smiled. "What do I know?"

"I've been thinking that the giants communicate with language."

George put down the journal.

"The next time we come across a giant," I told Culley, "I'd like to go down without our torches."

"And *that*," Brad said, "is what scientists refer to as 'test to destruction'."

"What if you take your Mark 3 gun," I told Culley, "and see if she recognizes it as a weapon."

"And if she doesn't?" Culley said too softly.

"Then we'll know that the species has a language. Do you realize what this means?" I looked around. "We might be able to communicate with another species."

Mini shook her head. "Tess, even if they *do* have a language of sorts, how can we decode a language based on different colors?"

"Universal grammar," George said. He came to the table and sat down. "The theory goes that all human languages have a common structural basis."

"That's human, George," Mini said, "and others don't agree with the theory."

George strummed his fingers on the table and smiled at me. "Still, it's an intriguing idea." he lifted his brows.

"You'd have to get animal researchers interested in doing the work," Mini told him, "and it's a hell of a lot safer to watch the words that chimps bang out on special keyboards."

I stared into the opaque liquid of my coffee. "But the way that mother giant called in the hatchlings when we showed our torches...." I looked up. "And then the babies flashing back to her. How did she *know* it was a danger to the hatchlings?"

Mini put a hand on my shoulder. "I'll help you any way I can, Tess. But it's going to be a long road to get recognition from animal researchers, cryptologists -- "

"I'll help, too," Culley said, "but we better make out our wills before a dive like that. If an octopus can let go of a tentacle to get away from an enemy, I don't think the Mark 3 will stop her."

"Can I be the beneficiary?" Brad said.

"No, you can't," I told him. "I'm leaving everything to Ice."

I watched Culley work on my regulator. His fingers are long and dexterous. The back of his hands are criss-crossed with veins. What evolutionary developments lay behind our incredible human skills? And who's to say with finality that we're the only species capable of abstract thought?

George picked up a part from a regulator and studied it.

Culley looked at him

He laid it gently on the table.

"Suppose," I said to Culley, "you hide the gun inside your buoyancy compensator, and we approach her empty-handed."

"Tell you what." He looked up. "How about we hide the torches inside our BCs too. Just as backups."

"Why don't you hide your lunch there, too?" Brad asked.

"Go to sleep, boss," I told him. "All right, Culley. It'll show us if she can recognize any weapon, or only torches, or the fact that empty human hands are not a threat. That alone can tell us if they communicate, and on such a specific level as stringing words together."

"Ryan," Brad said, "will you please talk some sense into your girlfriend? Just because she subdued two buccaneers, she thinks she's superwoman."

"Take your nap," Culley said. "I'll be right beside her on a dive like that."

"Did I tell you," Brad said to Culley, "that you're on the payroll?"

Culley glanced at me and raised his brows. "Thanks, boss. What's my salary?"

"We'll negotiate that," Brad said.

"How about my title?"

"Certified commercial diver and dive master."

"You hear that, Tess? From now on *I'm* the boss on dives."

"Don't hold your breath," I said.

Culley chuckled as he worked on my regulator. *Don't hold your breath* is a diving mantra.

*****

Culley went to the wet room to store the regulators in our dive bags.

He came back and opened the door to the cabin. "Hey, Tess, there's a dead Nomura jellie floating around the stern. You want to have a look?"

"Yes!"

Brad woke up. "What?"

"Dead Nomura," I said, on my way out the door.

"Who's dead?" he asked, still half asleep.

We all went to the stern.

The jellie was in shreds right down to his inner nerve net. What remained of his umbrella-like aboral surface was blackened along the torn edges.

"Something big's been chewing on him," Culley said. "Tess, you want me to being him in?"

"I just need samples," I said.

"I'll get suited up." Culley went to the wet room.

"Bet we'll find acid burns in those blackened areas," George said.

I peered over the side. "I hope he was alone when the giant got him."

"Alone?" Mini asked.

"When jellyfish are killed," I told her, "their last act is to release eggs or sperm, though some jellies are both sexes."

"Hermaphrodites," George said.

"Which gives a new meaning to the term 'go fuck yourself'," Brad added.

Mini shook her head. "Oy vey," she said in Yiddish and grinned at me. "I'll get some specimen jars for Culley."

She went into the lab.

Culley came on deck in his wet suit, carrying his fins and mask. A bug bag was clipped to his weight belt. I love the way he looks in a tight, black wet suit.

"Watch the tentacles," I told him.

"Yeah, they can still sting." He lifted a hand. "Gloves."

Mini came back and put the specimen jars into his bug bag.

"Watch those hands," I told her.

"Oh, damn," she said, "and I was just about to tear off his wet suit and rape him.

"Oh, let me," Brad said.

"I'm getting the fuck out of here," Culley said and went over the side.

"Before you get fucked." Brad waggled his head.

I told Culley which areas to cut from the dead Nomura, and he filled the jars.

"Let's go!" George cried and pointed to starboard.

A giant had raised her head above the surface.

"Get out, Culley!" I yelled. "A giant!" He had no weapons with him.

Brad ran to the bridge to start the engines. Mini followed and stood by the open door of the bridge.

I reached down the ladder as Culley approached it. The giant was jetting toward the Nomura.

Culley took off his fins and slapped them into my hands, then he climbed the ladder and rolled onto the deck.

"Go!" Mini shouted to Brad. "He's on board."

The engines came to life with a comforting roar and the boat plowed forward.

The giant reached the Nomura and dragged it under.

George's hands were clasped to his throat. "I guess...." He caught his breath. "I guess she just didn't want her lunch stolen."

*****

I studied the jellie samples under the microscope and did some tests. The blackened areas were acid burns, all right. But there was something else.

I went to the cabin. With the helm set for a computerized course to the Mariana Trench, the team was gathered there.

"The jellie was a male," I told them as I entered the cabin. "But the gonads are larger than usual." I looked at Brad. "No comments from the boss man."

He fluttered a hand.

"So," I continued, "I suspect that predation by the giants has caused a quantum leap in the Nomura's evolution. If they produce more eggs and sperm, the species has a better chance of surviving the onslaught of the giants."

"I have a feeling," George said, "that if we humans don't interfere, nature will balance the ocean ecology again. She's good at that."

"Consider this," Culley said, "that giant could've stayed underwater and picked me off like a grape on a vine."

I took Culley's hand as a sudden fear flashed through me.

"Is it possible," Brad said, "that the giants no longer see us as a threat? I mean with all the artificial reefs being laid by humans in their favorite haunts?"

"We're not even their natural prey," Mini said.

"Besides which," George added, "we humans are just a mere morsel to a giant."

"Are you hungry again?" Mini asked George.

He shrugged. "I could go for a morsel."

CHAPTER EIGHTEEN

Cousteau was sea-anchored between the Mariana Trench, seven miles down, into a black seascape less explored than the surface of Mars, and the cloudless sky above. Around us, only open sea. We hung like a speck in God's Great Eye. I hoped He wouldn't blink.

George operated the ROV. He sent it plummeting down into the trench. The rest of us gathered around the screen and held our breath as the vehicle encountered crushing pressure. Its video camera recorded the reckless dive. George was hell-bent on reaching the bottom, but at four miles down, the tether line ran out and the vehicle came to a bouncing stop. it hung in open water.

Four of us gave a sigh of relief. The fifth, George, said "Dammit!"

Mini patted him on the shoulder. "Let us know if you find anything interesting. I'm going to have lunch now."

"Oh," George said, "bring me back something."

"Like what?" she asked.

"Anything sweet."

"I'll sprinkle sugar on your sandwich."

"OK. Two sandwiches. What have you got to put inside?"

"Rats' assholes," Mini replied and left the bridge.

"She's cruel." George shook his head. "But I love her."

"I think, George," I replied, "that in her way, Mini loves you too."

"You think so? She's a fascinating woman."

"Oh, yes" I said, "and very beautiful." What I was really thinking was that all Mini needed in her relationship with George was a whip.

Culley and I went to the stern and sat down to enjoy the warm sun on our faces. I watched an albatross circle and caw. The wind brought a sting of salty air. With Culley by my side, holding my hand, I felt as though this were my natural environment.

Mini looked out from the cabin's open door. "You guys want anything?"

"Oh, thanks, Mini," I said. "A cup of coffee?"

"Black, with sugar?"

"Yes,"

"Like me."

Culley and I laughed.

"Like you?" I said. "It should have lots more spice."

"OK. Sugar in George's sandwich and chili in Tess' coffee. What's your poison, Culley. A beer?"

"And no egg," he replied.

"You got it."

"Thanks," he called.

"Welcome." She smiled and closed the door.

I knew that Mini's "welcome" meant more than an answer to Culley's *Thank you*. He was now an integral part of our group, valued for his many skills, his diving ability, and his quiet courage. When the chips were down, it was Culley and not Brad, who gave the orders that we followed.

"I'm so proud of you." I said.

"Ah, shucks." He squeezed my hand.

Mini came on deck with the coffee and a can of beer. As she walked toward us, I realized again what a stately beauty my best friend is. Her black skin caught blue highlights in the sun. She wore a yellow silk scarf knotted in her tied-back hair. She moved with such grace.

"Mini," I said as she approached, "you look like the Nubian Goddess of the Fast Food Altar."

"Thank you, my pale subject." She handed Culley the beer. "I didn't open it," she said, "so you'd know there's no egg in it. De black maid know how to take orders an' please de white folk."

"You know how to give them, too, Mini, when it comes to George."

"You think I'm too hard on him?"

"Are you aware that he loves you?" I asked.

"Well, I love the little guy, too, in my own cruel way."

Culley gave her one of his more devilish smiles.

She handed me the coffee.

"You know, Tess," she said, "if you ever get tired of him, throw him my way."

Culley smirked. "I always wanted a harem of my own."

"Two women don't make a harem!" I pulled my hand away.

"Thanks," he said, "I needed that hand to open the beer. Anyway, two women are a start." He opened the beer.

"How would you like your air hose snipped on our next dive?" I asked him.

"Uh, oh," Mini said, "I'd better leave before she decides to snip more than your air hose."

"Come here quick!" George called from the bridge door. "Quick!"

Brad came out of the cabin. "What?"

We all ran to the bridge.

"Look!" George pointed to the screen. "Look at that!"

I looked and my jaw dropped.

"What the hell is *that*?" Culley said.

Mini and Brad were speechless as we gathered around the ROV screen.

There, floating in the sea, at four miles down, was an island. I don't know how else to describe it. A huge ring, thick with mussels, bi-valves, crabs, strange small lobsters, clams, shrimp, cold-water tube worms, all clinging to a *lake* that was so briny, the empty center of it lapped the "shore" like waves on a beach.

"My God," I said. "I've heard of this. Two scientists in a deep submersible saw one decades ago. But no one's seen one since."

"Considering that we've only explored three percent of the deep sea floor," George said, "I'm not very surprised."

"Is this what you were looking for?" I asked him.

He nodded. "Watch!" He steered the ROV to the empty center of the ring. He tried to lower it, but the briny water just bounced the ROV back up.

"Jesus Christ," Brad said.

"It's a living raft!" I moved closer to the screen. "This is incredible." The video camera recorded the surreal scene. "Are you getting still shots too?"

George nodded."

"I thought I'd seen a lot of weird stuff on dives," Culley said.

"You ain't seen nothing yet!" George announced. "Uh, if I'm right." He guided the ROV below the living raft. Then he tilted the vehicle up and shined its lights on the underside of the raft.

Mini gasped. "It's the males!" She pointed at swarms of small, charcoal-colored octopuses, from two to three feet long, that crowded the raft. "That's the same species as the female giants!"

"Oh, my God," I whispered. "But they're so much smaller, and dark."

"The Pillow," Mini said.

"The pillow what?" George asked.

"The pillow octopus," Mini told him. "The female is a hundred times larger than the male. This species might be the deep-sea version."

"How do you know they're males?" Brad asked.

"Look at their third tentacle to the right," Mini explained. "See, it has no suckers. It's modified to pass packets of spermatozoa to the female."

"That's how they mate?" Brad asked.

"That's how it's done, boss. Now tell us how you'd rather get root canal than mate that way."

"Did I say anything?" Brad remarked. "But you must admit, Minerva, it's more like a Christmas present than mating."

"Whatever," Mini said.

Some of the octopuses were moving along the raft, upside down, and plucking mollusks off the underside like fruit off tangled vines.

George stood up. "Ladies and gentlemen, may I introduce you to the male Hoffman, Johnson, Backer Giant Octopus?"

We laughed and clapped for George. I hugged him, then Mini joined in, Then Brad. I grabbed Culley by his shirt collar and pulled him in.

"I'm out of champagne!" Brad said.

We sat down and grinned at each other.

"George," Mini said, "go for a sample!"

"A living octopus?" George asked. "Won't he die on the way up?"

"Not if you bring him up slowly enough," she told him.

George bit his lip as he concentrated and guided the ROV toward the swarm. He extended the suction sampler. The tube was smaller than the octopuses.

"Go for it, George," Mini said. "They can fit into the tube. They don't have bones."

"I know," George said. "I know, but I don't want to hurt them."

The octopuses spread out, away from the approaching ROV.

"Oh, here, give me that," Brad said. He took over the controls and scooped an octopus quickly into a tube. Then he scooped another one into the second sampler. "Mini, take over and bring them up."

Black acid spread around the ROV, but it didn't damage the glass samplers.

Mini sat at the controls. "This will take hours. Tess?"

"Yes?"

"Could you bring me a couple of sandwiches?"

"Sure. Sprinkled with sugar?"

"Yeah," George said. "Sugar on mine, please. I want to stay here."

I left the bridge with Culley and Brad.

"Two with, two without," I called back.

"Yes!" they both answered.

Culley and I made the sandwiches.

"You know, hon," I said, "we're running out of food."

"Fuel, too."

"We'll make it to the Mariana Islands, though, won't we?"

He nodded. "Then it's home to California and your first love."

"My first...oh, you mean Ice. I miss him."

"I know. It won't be long." Culley sprinkled sugar on George's sandwiches. "Got to keep the guy happy."

We brought the sandwiches, and coffee, to the bridge.

The day grew dark before we had the two octopuses on the boat and into separate tanks. They looked like miniature giant females, except for their charcoal color and their third modified right arms.

Mini set the tanks as close as possible to deep-sea conditions, but it was just a fair approximation of their native habitat. We didn't know how the change in pressure would affect them on a long-term basis.

George defrosted some shrimps for them. Mini brushed the shrimps against their suckers, which have taste buds, but neither octopus would accept the food.

*****

The next morning Mini came into the cabin looking glum. "Well, one of them died last night, and the other guy looks like he's got one tentacle in the grave, and the other seven on banana peels."

"Suppose we put him back into his natural element," George said, "and give him a chance?"

I nodded agreement. So did Brad and Culley.

"Let's do it," Mini said, "though there's very little chance that he'll find the raft again. In fact, I don't believe he'll live."

Mini took the live octopus to the side of the boat in a glass jar, unscrewed it and let him slide out into the water. He lay on the surface for a while, then sluggishly jetted away.

"Good luck," George called as the octopus dived.

Mini froze the dead octopus for future study. George contacted the Pacifica Lab with his findings.

"I took some sediment samples with the ROV," Mini told George. "You want to study them?"

"Absolutely!" George said. "How did you get bottom samples?"

"The ROV passed a sea mount on the way up," Mini said. "I scooped up some samples for you."

"I could kiss you!"

She stooped down and George kissed her on the cheek.

*****

We set a course for the Mariana Archipelago, west of the trench. After we refueled and took on provisions, it was home to Northern California and the Pacifica Lab. We had enough data to keep us busy for months.

The mood on board was relaxed. The weather was a balmy eighty degrees, with rain showers that kept the air fresh.

Islands appeared on the western horizon as we approached the Marianas. We all looked forward to R&R. We had earned it.

Culley was at the wheel when it happened.

CHAPTER NINETEEN

A bar of swift, dark water rode the surface, a bare half a foot high, headed toward our stern. Culley swung the boat around to put the bow into the fast-running wave. *Cousteau* lifted and slammed down as the wave raced past us.

"Tsunami!" George cried.

"Oh my God," I said. "It's headed for the Mariana Islands!"

Brad got on the radio and contacted the Pacific Tsunami Warning Center. We held on as another bar of water tore past us.

"That's the second wave." I chewed a nail. "They're probably moving at five hundred miles an hour."

The deep-ocean tsunami monitoring-sensors would pick up the swells, but we were probably further out at sea and could warn the islands sooner. The Mariana Trench is a subduction zone, where two of the planet's tectonic plates meet. Earthquakes there can trigger huge tsunami waves.

"What the hell is *that?*" Brad said and pointed off the stern.

A school of giant female octopuses was headed our way.

"Uh, oh." George backed a step. "Uh, oh."

We held on as Culley headed *Cousteau,* full speed, toward the open sea. Another swell slammed the bow and lifted the approaching giants behind us.

"That's the third wave," I said. I wasn't sure if I were more worried about us or the islands.

"They know," Mini said as the giants receded behind our speeding boat. "They *know* that a tsunami's approaching and they're headed away from the islands."

"How could they know?" I asked.

"In Stromboli, off Sicily," she said, "the octopuses around the active volcano there flee whenever it's ready to erupt."

"Infrasound," George commented.

Culley slowed the boat. "We have to conserve fuel."

"George," I said, "can you tell by these waves how big the tsunami will be?"

He shook his head. "The sensors still aren't a hundred percent accurate, either."

"But I think the giants' sensors are," Mini said. She stared toward the octopuses and the islands beyond. "I'm afraid this one will be tragically big."

"God help them." I thought of videos I'd seen of tsunamis that hit Southern California and Indonesia and Japan and Alaska years ago and took terrible tolls in lives. "God help them."

The school of giants was catching up now that Culley had slowed the boat. All we had were the rifles and Culley's mark 3 underwater gun. There were no more rockets for the launcher. We had felt safe, knowing we could outrun any octopus attack. But now, with little fuel left, and the tsunami targeting the islands, who could the authorities spare to help one boat if tragically, hundreds, or even thousands, were hurt and killed in the tsunami?

"If Rámon were here," I said, "he'd say a prayer for all of us."

"God knows we need it," Mini said as the school of octopuses came closer. "Look at the up-side."

"And that would be?" Brad asked.

"If we could monitor the giants," Mini said, "in active volcanic and earthquake zones -- "

"They could predict eruptions and tsunamis," George interrupted, "better than our seismic systems!"

"If they don't eat the divers monitoring them," Culley said. He pressed his lips. "We're low on fuel, boss. If we're going to abandon ship, we'd better do it soon."

Brad was already searching the nautical map. He shook his head. "There's no place to hide. I see only one alternative," he told Culley.

Culley nodded. "Break through them."

"What do you think, Mini?" I asked.

"Octopuses don't have a lot of endurance," she said. "It's their copper-based blood. These guys might not be in the mood for a fight while they're still fleeing a tsunami."

"Culley," Brad said, "turn the boat around to face them and keep the engines idling. "If they make an aggressive move, slam through them. George, get the rifles and load them, and get Culley's Mark 3 gun and the other gun. Tess, you know how to use a rifle. You take one of them. Mini, use your expertise to keep us alerted on the Krakens' behavior. If you perceive signs of aggression, don't be shy about giving us orders. If I see another wave approaching," he told Culley, "I'll let you know to turn the bow into it."

Culley nodded. "Sounds good, boss."

Brad went to the stern. Mini headed for the bow as Culley turned the boat to face the octopuses. George left to get the weapons.

Somehow, knowing that we had a plan, and that we were all taking action, calmed me. I felt my tense shoulder muscles relax, but all my senses were on high alert. *Is this how a soldier feels,* I wondered, *just before a battle?*

George came back and handed me a rifle. "Be careful," he said, "it's loaded."

"Did you bring the boxes of ammunition?" I asked him.

"Uh, I'll get them." He left the bridge.

I went on deck and checked that the rifle was really loaded, then I took off the safety.

"I hope it won't be a massacre," I told Mini as I went to the bow.

She threw me a tense look. "Of them or us?"

Culley came to the bow with his Mark 3. Brad followed with a rifle.

"Just remember," Culley said to me, "priority one is taking care of my lady."

"You remember that, too, about my guy." I gave him a quick kiss on his cheek.

George came back with the boxes of ammunition. He looked over the bow. "Uh, I'll go steer the boat." He hurried back to the bridge and closed the door.

We all kept an eye on the open sea behind us for signs of another wave.

The white hatchlings approached first, probably pushed ahead by the adults for the hatchlings' own safety. They ranged from two to three feet long, except for the charcoal-colored males, who were barely inches long. The brown juvenile mucus coating was gone from all of them.

"You think they have their acid sacs?" I asked Mini as hundreds of hatchlings jetted past the boat.

"It's safe to assume so," she said.

"Well, that was easy," Brad said.

The rest wasn't.

Thirty or more giants flashed rainbow colors as they curved across our bow. The hatchlings flashed back, turned and headed for our boat.

"They're communicating, all right," Mini said, "and don't ask me about syntax right now. OK, Tess?"

"OK."

I don't know if the giants were after us as food, though I doubted it, or wanted to claim the boat as something solid against the force of the waves they'd encountered. Tsunamis extend to the ocean floor and tear apart coral and everything else in their paths.

"I'm going back to the helm," Brad said. "I don't want George falling over his feet if we have to break through the giants."

He handed Mini his rifle. "Just point and shoot, if it comes to that."

Mini nodded and held the rifle awkwardly.

"Don't point it at anything you don't want to kill," Culley told her.

The giants closest to us jetted toward the boat. Mini and I raised our rifles and aimed. Culley pointed the Mark 3.

"Wait!" Mini lowered her rifle as the giants swerved away.

"It sure looks like they know about weapons," Culley said.

Mini nodded. "You were right, Tess."

"Don't forget *communicating*," I added.

The hatchlings swarmed around the hull, then began to climb it, pulling themselves up with their suction cups.

"Brad!" I yelled up to the bridge.

"I see them," he said through an open window.

"Keep the boat idling," Culley called to Brad. "You don't want them burning through the propellers or the shafts."

"That wouldn't be good," Brad yelled back. "Mini, what's your take on our guests?"

"I think the adults want to protect the youngsters from more tsunami waves."

"Should we let them come aboard?" Brad called.

"My gut feeling is yes," Mini said. "We can always hose them off the boat and hose off any acid they might secrete."

"It's still a scientific expedition," I told Brad.

"As long as we're not the subjects," he answered. "OK, guys, come onto the bridge. What the fuck. What's life without a little excitement now and then!"

George sat at the controls of the ROV, watching the few adults that were underwater. He looked guilty as we came in. "Uh, Brad wants me to make sure none of them tries to burn a hole in the hull."

"That's good, George," I said.

He smiled.

Baby octopuses swarmed across the bow, flashing at each other like little frosted light bulbs with legs. One female climbed a window and scraped at the glass with her small beak. I spread my hand across the inner window and she slithered to it and tried to probe my hand through the glass. A tiny dark male, looking more like a spider than an octopus, followed her up the glass.

The school of adult females began flashing in the most beautiful array of colors.

George stood up. "Roy G Biv!" he exclaimed.

Mini sighed. "What tongues are you speaking in this time, George?"

"Don't you get it, Mini?" George answered. "The adults are telling the hatchlings to come back into the water. They're going to dive deep, probably back to the dens!"

"Who the hell is Roy G Biv?" Brad asked. "And do I want to meet him?"

"It's the underwater colors," Culley said as the hatchlings slithered to the gunnels, climbed them and began plopping back into the water. "It's how instructors teach new divers about the color loss underwater."

"*See,*" George said to Mini.

"First you lose red," Culley continued, "then orange, then yellow." He counted on his fingers. "Then green goes, then blue, indigo, and finally at a hundred feet, where the artificial reefs were placed, you're down to violet."

"Roy G Biv," George said again.

I looked at Mini.

"It's *still* not syntax," she said.

I stared at the misty islands on the horizon and wondered what was happening there. "George," I said, "would you turn on the screen to TV mode?"

He turned it on and tuned to a Guam channel in the Mariana Islands.

"Oh, God." I sat down.

A woman reporter in a helicopter over Guam screamed into the mic: "It's coming ashore! It's the first wave coming ashore! Estimates range from forty to, to sixty feet high. It's -- it's a *monster*. Oh, the people. There are *people* on the beach!"

"Why aren't they running?" Mini said and sat next to me.

"It's happened before," I told her. "They just don't see it as a threat until it's too late."

"Boats are being washed ashore," the reporter said. "It's spreading out. The wave is spreading...buses, cars. I, I can see people running...oh, disappearing under the wave...houses being washed away. This is a tragedy." Her voice shook. "I...what is there to say? May God be with them."

We watched silently as the wave smashed through fields, tearing down barns, dragging boats and vehicles like battering rams. A school bus crashed to its side. The seething wave washed over it.

I pressed a hand to my mouth. My eyes burned with tears. "Oh, my God," I muttered.

"Beneath us," the reporter said shakily, "beneath us people are being swept away. Families. This monster is moving so fast. Nothing can survive this!" She began to cry. "Oh, no. Here comes the second wave."

Culley got up and went to a window. I followed him. I saw tears slide down his face. I put an arm around his waist and we stared at the distant islands, looking so calm, like frozen blue waves themselves in the misty distance.

Brad shut off the TV mode. "We don't need to see any more."

We were a solemn group as we headed toward Guam.

Brad was still at the wheel. "We'll see what we can do to help."

The octopuses disappeared beneath the stirred water. George stayed at the ROV controls to watch the giants and make sure they didn't attempt to glue eggs to the hull.

They didn't.

CHAPTER TWENTY

As the tsunami waves receded, they scoured the land and dragged everything loose with them. White hulls of overturned boats drifted by like dead whales. The debris field spread out and George, at the helm, avoided the ruins of what must have been a thriving village just hours ago.

I dreaded to see bodies, but soon they floated by. Culley and Brad launched *Nomad* to search for survivors. Mini and I scanned the sea with binoculars for people in the water or clinging to debris. I was on the starboard side. Mini was on the port side.

Other private boats joined in the search.

"They're sending supplies and a hospital ship from Pearl Harbor!" George called from the bridge.

"That's good," I called back and watched a helicopter fly low over the water. The 'copter hovered and a rescue diver jumped out. I trained my binoculars on him as he swam to a man who waved and held onto a wooden beam. The diver plucked him out of the water and they were both hauled up into the helicopter. I lowered the binoculars and sighed. The only good thing to come out of this horror was to see how people were rushing to help the victims. I lifted the binoculars again and continued to scan the surface.

There! Two people. *Was one a child?* They clung to a small, overturned sailboat. "George," I yelled and pointed to them.

"I'll tell Brad and Culley," George called back.

Seconds later *Nomad* turned in the direction of the sailboat. *Hurry!* I thought. We had taken out all our blankets and jackets, and our medkits. The cabin was set up as a first-aid station. I watched Culley jump into the water, swim to the child and bring her to *Nomad*. Brad reached over and pulled her into the boat. Culley swam back for the other person, either an older child or an adult, and brought him to the boat.

It's strange how tangled our emotions can become. I felt relief that Culley and Brad had saved two people, but overriding the relief was a terrible sense of the loss of lives.

"George!" I heard Mini call, "there's a survivor thrashing in the water!"

A minute later, *Nomad* took off and made a turn that sprayed white foam. It headed across our bow and disappeared from my sight.

"He's going under!" Mini yelled.

"Mini!" I called, "did they get to him?"

"Culley's diving," she called back. There was a pause, then she shouted "Yes! He's got him. He brought him up by his hair!"

Another success. But as the afternoon wore on, they weren't all successes. A hospital ship from the northern Mariana Islands, which had escaped the brunt of the waves, took aboard survivors, and the bodies, from other boats that cruised the inland waters, searching, searching...into the night.

The surface was lit with lights that swept and searched. Every so often, one would pick out a person who frantically waved, or one who floated, face down. The inevitable media helicopters and boats crisscrossed sky and sea, searching for a story, while the world waited for news of the Great Tsunami Disaster.

Night closed over us and Culley and Brad came aboard. They looked weary as we winched up *Nomad* with the motorized launcher.

We anchored *Cousteau* and we all went into the cabin. Mini and I made a quick supper of salad, and dinners we defrosted and heated up.

Culley stared at his dish, then pushed it away. "I can't look at meat right now." He went to lie down on his bunk. I sat quietly beside him and took his hand. He closed his eyes, and started to fall asleep, but jumped and opened his eyes. I gently kissed his hand.

Brad, too, left the table and went to his bunk.

George began to eat, then put down his fork. Mini stared out a window with her chin resting on one hand.

Outside, boat lights flashed as they swept the surface. Voices, calling to each other, were carried clearly across the water's flat surface.

We listened.

Debris bumped our boat all through the night. A sleepless night, not only for the five of us. In my mind's eye, the devastation played out over and over, until from sheer emotional exhaustion, sleep overtook the images I had seen and weaved them into a nightmare of dreams.

*****

The next morning, we saw the extent of the devastation. Mini and I scanned the surface again with binoculars, but survivors had either all been picked up in this area, or...I hated to consider the other possibility. A dead oxen floated by off the stern.

I trained my binoculars on the island. It was green, hilly country as far in as I could see. A few trees still stood along the beach, but there were no structures, just debris. The sea was calm and blue, but the radio warned that more earthquakes were possible, with more waves.

"We'll head northwest, around the island," Brad said as we sat at the cabin table over coffee. "We need to find a refueling station. We're not going home or anywhere else on fumes."

"We might not make it to a port," Culley said.

We had planned on refueling at Mount Santa Rosa, and taking on provisions. That was no longer an option.

We listened as planes roared by, probably from Anderson Air Force Base, an American base northwest of us on Guam.

Mini and George went on deck to watch the rescue boats and helicopters.

I thought of the man-made devastation that had occurred here during World War II, in the last century. Afterwards, Guam had become a serene tropical island that attracted tourists. The earth throws up a sea mount that breaks the water's surface, and we humans brand it with blood from our lust for territory, and leave our money on it as tourists, with our desire to find paradise. I thought of a line from a poem: *A being darkly wise, and rudely great.*

This time it was nature doing her thing, grinding the tectonic plates that we all float on. Who could we blame when we knew the forces at work between the moving plates beneath the sea, and we *still* got in the way?

I realized that Culley was staring at me.

"Are you OK, Tess?" he asked.

I nodded. "I was just thinking. That's all."

George threw open the door. "Come out here, quick," he said hoarsely. He looked pale.

We ran on deck.

A school of giant octopuses had surfaced. One jetted to the dead oxen and dragged it beneath the surface. Others searched the surface. Two planes roared by low in the sky, but the giants slid under as one fired.

"Dammit!" Mini said. "Just when we convinced people not to kill them."

"I hope the giants aren't going after the living," I said as I watched the oxen's blood smear the surface. I chewed a nail.

Culley took my hand and lowered it. "They've all been rescued by now."

The planes circled, but the giants remained underwater.

"Oh, no," Mini exclaimed as a group of white juvenile octopuses jetted across the surface, attracted to a bright red beach umbrella that floated like a large Nomura jellyfish. They wrapped their tentacles around it and pulled. Each one tried to claim it for her own. Small dark males crawled across the females' heads and slithered onto the umbrella. A giant female surfaced as the two planes came roaring back.

We tried to wave the planes away, but they just dipped their wings to wave back. The giant female flashed red, but the juveniles were too busy playing.

The giant disappeared beneath the surface as the two planes swooped low and opened fire.

"Oh, shit!" Brad said and hit the rail with a fist.

The umbrella and the playing juveniles were torn apart. Shreds of the octopuses and the red umbrella floated together.

A giant female surfaced as the planes began their turn, then she dipped back under.

"They *just* couldn't leave it alone," I said.

George sighed. "We never can."

"I'm going for the weapons." Culley went into the cabin.

The planes came back, dipped their wings and left, headed toward the air force base.

The adult female rose again, watched us with slitted eyes, then jetted toward us.

"Here she comes," Mini said as the giant turned bright red.

"And she's pissed as hell," Brad added. "Culley! Don't stop for a beer."

Culley came on deck and handed me a rifle. We raised them and pointed at the female. She paused.

"George," Culley said, "launch the ROV and see if there's any more of them down there. She might be a decoy while the rest go for our hull. Son of a bitch!" He hit the rail. "They just couldn't leave it alone."

George ran to the bridge.

The female went to the shreds of the umbrella and the remains of the juveniles. Her skin vibrated with flashes of violet and blue.

"Keep the rifles out of sight," Mini said. "Let's see what she does."

We did.

She stroked the dead juveniles. I lowered my head and thought of what George had said when we found the burned seagulls. *Pain is pain, and death is death, no matter the species.* There had been too much of it here.

"There's more of them underwater," George called from the bridge door, "but they're just hanging out."

Culley and I kept the rifles out of the giant's sight.

She slid beneath the surface.

Mini trotted to the bridge door. "What're they doing, George." I saw her nod. She turned to us. "They've left."

"I wonder for where?" Brad said.

"Anywhere they please," Culley answered. "With no law on the island, they'll have the run of the place if they want it.

CHAPTER TWENTY ONE

We were dead in the water. *Cousteau* had hardly made it past Mount Santa Rosa when the engines sputtered and died. As we suspected, there was no help. Guam's coast had been shattered and while ships raced to the area to help, there were much greater concerns than for five fools who had run out of fuel.

Brad came off the bridge shaking his head. "I contacted both refueling services," he told us as we stood on the deck and watched boats slowly cruise past debris, searching. "They're too busy refueling rescue boats. We're on our own, boys and girls. Anybody have a brilliant idea?"

"I don't know if it's brilliant," Culley said, "but we can leave the boat anchored here, take *Nomad* and try to make it to Anderson Air Force Base. If *Nomad* runs out, we can hike it the rest of the way."

"I suppose," Mini said, "if there's help for us anywhere, we'll find it at the base."

"What say you all?" Brad asked.

I looked around. "I say yay."

"Minerva, what say you?" Brad said.

"Unless someone's got a brillianter idea, then yay," she answered.

"And last, but not the least of us." Brad looked at George and smirked. "I'll bet there's a candy machine at the air force base." He lifted his brows.

"My kingdom for a Hershey bar," George said.

We laughed for the first time in a long while. Mini slapped George's shoulder. "As you like it!" she said.

*****

We wore casual clothes, hiking boots, and hats. We stuffed the last of the food inside our backpacks along with matches, a mirror, water bottles, water purification pills, tissues, sunblock, soap, towels, a flashlight. We took rolled blankets, jackets, the two rifles, ammunition, and the Mark 3 gun. We didn't know what we'd encounter on land with the breakdown of law.

We skirted the island and headed northwest, hoping to make it to the air force base. But *Nomad's* motor sputtered and we drove to the nearest land, somewhere near Mount Santa Rosa.

When we reached the beach, Culley and Brad dragged *Nomad* ashore, and anchored her in the white sand. Culley took some thingamajig out of the raised motor so no one could start it.

The beach was silent except for wavelets that sizzled up to the high-water mark, and slid gently back down.

Native people and Japanese and American tourists sat and stared at the sea. Their faces were either expressionless with shock, or had the long look I'd seen in photos of soldiers returning from the front. Children played silently in the sand.

Three men and a woman strode across the beach with bulging shoulder bags. They approached the children first and handed each of them a package wrapped in tinfoil and a container of milk. Then they continued on to the adults and handed out packages and bottles of water.

I saw a child open her package. She reached in and stuffed food into her mouth. My lips quivered. This was the silence of hell.

Where once there had been a wharf, there were pilings and a floating roof. Where once there had been angular white houses with families inside, now people moved silently between hills of scattered wood and plaster and broken roofs. Houses that still stood were damaged. Sand above the high-water mark was water-logged.

The cliffs on the beach came down to deep water and were impassable. We headed inland to flatter terrain to continue northwest, toward the base.

Brad tried to contact the base with his Q-Tree, but the hills made it impossible for the signal to get through.

We were silent as we entered a destroyed village. Overturned vehicles lay strewn across the road. I cannot describe the stench of death, except to say that it was overpowering. I retched, and a bitter taste of bile rose in my throat.

Two men with white masks covering their noses and mouths, and plastic gloves on their hands, picked up a naked, muddy body and dumped it into a black, plastic bag. I gasped and turned away. I couldn't tell if the body were a man or a woman, as though Death made no distinction.

Culley got between me and the scene. "C'mon, Tess."

Out of respect, we slung our loaded rifles over our shoulders. *We come in peace.* Where we had expected lawlessness, we found only silence. People carried the dead from their houses and from overturned vehicles. I realized that what had seemed like indifference in the way they threw the bodies into bags and quickly zippered them, was the fear that the dead would kill the living with a plague.

Photographs of people were tacked on walls and trees. The messages, in English, were pleas to call the telephone numbers scrawled beneath the smiling faces, if the person were found. These were acts of desperation. The phone and electrical lines were down.

I heard a child cry.

There, on the front steps of a flattened house, a boy, perhaps a year old, muddied and naked, cried and rocked back and forth. His hair was thick and black, clumped with dried mud. His eyes were large, dark, and appealing. His skin beneath the mud was a warm, light brown.

That horrible smell was strong here. I gently picked up the child and talked to him as we continued walking.

We stopped away from the house and the odor surrounding it. Mini took a towel from her backpack. The boy hugged me around the neck and I crooned softly to him as Mini wiped him off.

George looked worn out. He sat down heavily and took out a candy bar. The child watched him bite into it and reached out with a tiny hand. George studied the candy bar wistfully, then flipped it to Culley, who broke off pieces and fed them to the child.

Brad leaned against a broken wall and absently fingered his necklace as he stared at the sky. Culley unhooked his water bottle, squatted beside the boy and helped him drink. The boy took long gulps and coughed between them. Then he grasped me again. I held him against my chest and rocked him. Culley took a banana from his backpack and peeled it. When the boy saw it, he grabbed it and began chewing.

We rested while he ate. A young, native woman walked by, paused and smiled sadly at us. I smiled back. She continued on to whatever was her quest.

We took turns holding the child as we walked, but for some reason, he kept reaching out to me. I walked beside Culley as he held him, and the boy quieted and finally fell asleep on Culley's shoulder.

"The poor kid's exhausted," Culley said.

"You know how to hold a baby."

"Told you, Tess, I'm the oldest of five. You should see me change a diaper, faster than an Indianapolis race team changing a tire." He patted the boy's back.

"Be careful, Tess," Mini said, "he's going to want a large family."

"He said a baker's dozen," I told her.

"Baker?" George said. "That's what my name, Backer, means in German."

"I suppose," Brad said, "that somewhere in your ancestry, you had a baker or two?" He raised his brows. "Go figure."

We had only made a few miles when the sun lowered over the hills of Guam. The child had awakened in Culley's arms and squirmed to be set down. Culley did and the child squatted and peed, then he defecated.

"All right, Mister Faster Than an Indie Race Team," I said, "Now what?"

Culley smirked. He took tissues and a towel from his backpack and wiped the boy's tuckus with the tissues. Then he ripped the towel in half, made a diaper out of one half, put it on the boy and tied the two ends together. "Does it meet with your approval?" he asked me.

"He'll make a good mother," Brad said.

"No better than *you*," Culley muttered.

"What did he say?" Brad asked.

"He was talking in tongues," Mini said.

Culley dumped out his backpack and cut holes in the bottom. "For the kid," he told us. He lined the inside of the backpack with a soft towel, and strapped it on his back. Mini lifted the child into it and let his legs dangle through the two holes. With the straps to hold him in place, it made a fair carrier. The rest of us put Culley's stuff into our backpacks. Brad took the Mark 3 gun.

It was dark when we reached a stream.

"I'd like to wash the mud off him," I told Culley. "There are beneficial bacteria in the soil, but there are also harmful ones."

"Well, don't wash off the beneficial ones with the nasties," George said and laughed.

I took the last two towels, a bar of soap, and gave the boy a sponge bath. He screamed his head off and Culley had to hold him. The water was cold, but the air was still warm and we dried him off quickly.

"Got a feeling," Culley said, "he's not going to be a diver."

"Not a cold-water diver, anyway," I said.

It was too dark to continue our trek. We camped for the night and ate a cold supper around a small fire. I fed the child some whole wheat bread, a piece of shredded chicken breast, and some peas from a can. He made a face at the peas and spat them out.

"So what are we going to call the little rug rat?" Brad asked, "since it seems he's now a part of our dysfunctional family."

"I know!" George said. "Champ."

"Champ?" I made a face.

"For his ancestry," George told me. "He's a member of the ancient Chamorro people. They settled Guam four thousand years ago."

"What say you all?" Brad asked.

"Sounds good to me," Culley said.

"Me too," I said. "That's three yays."

Mini shrugged. "Yay, but I'm glad he's not a girl."

"Boss?" I asked.

"Yay." He fluttered a hand.

"The yays have it," I said.

I laid down on my spread blanket with an arm around sleepy Champ. "George," I said, "do you think there's crawly things in the grass?"

"I'm not familiar with Guam's fauna," he answered sleepily and yawned, "but considering the climate and the flora, and Guam's proximity to other islands, I'd venture to say that the island's been colonized by crawly things."

"Yuch!" Mini said.

Culley wrapped my blanket around me and Champ, who was nuzzled against my breasts. "Lucky kid," he whispered and tucked in my feet. "There, that'll keep away the crawly things." He leaned down and kissed my cheek, then he kissed Champ's head. "Get a good night's sleep," he told me. "We're in for a long hike to the base tomorrow."

"Goodnight, hon." I yawned.

I was asleep when Champ suddenly jumped and screamed. Culley walked over. He opened the blanket and shined a flashlight. There were no crawly things inside the blanket and I wondered what nightmares the child was enduring. He finally quieted to sobs and I held him close.

We all went back to sleep, but a good night's rest was not to be.

Somewhere around midnight I heard screams. I thought it was Champ again. I sat up and realized the screams came from the direction of the beach.

"Another tsunami?" Brad said.

"We haven't felt the rumbling of an earthquake," George replied. He threw off his blanket and stood up. "But if it is, we're too far inland to be affected."

"Those people on the beach aren't." Culley shook out his boots and put them on.

"Wait a minute," Mini said. "I hope it's not what I'm thinking."

"What're you thinking?" I asked.

"I didn't want to scare you guys." She got up, "I've been wondering about the giants. You know, they're perfectly capable of coming ashore."

More screams from the beach.

"The giants small cousins have been known to steal bait from fishermen, then slither back into the water."

"What are you saying, Mini?" I asked. "Are you saying that the giants might've gotten a taste for human flesh after the tsunami?"

"Either that, or a thirst for revenge for what the planes did to their offspring."

"Or both," Brad said.

Culley picked up a rifle and a flashlight, and stared toward the beach. "In Bangladesh, the tigers ate so many bodies after tornadoes that now they attack the living."

"OK," I'm convinced," Brad said and got into his boots.

So did I.

"Maybe," Culley said to Brad, "we can drive them back into the sea by showing them our weapons. I'm going to have a look." He headed toward the beach.

"Wait for me!" I called, took the other rifle, a flashlight, and trotted after him. "Mini, would you watch Champ?"

"Dammit, Tess, *stay here,*" Culley said. "Brad's coming with me."

Brad's light shined behind us.

Mini and George, with no weapons left, stayed with Champ.

"Be careful!" Mini called. "If it's *them*, it could be that school we ran into."

I strode past Culley, threw him a look, and headed for the beach.

There were more screams.

He caught up. "What do I have to do to keep you safe? Sit on you?"

We strode together.

"What do *I* have to do," I shot back, "to prove I don't need your orders to take care of myself?"

Brad caught up with the Mark 3 in hand and we strode toward the beach together.

"There they are!" Brad said and pointed with the rifle.

The moon cast light over the water and backlit the great, lumpy heads of giants that had come ashore and were slithering into the silent, destroyed village. A young girl ran into the woods. "Run!" she screeched and waved toward the giants. "The Krakens!" She disappeared between trees.

"My God," I whispered. The giants towered above the houses that still stood, and the hills of debris. Their heads were probably thirty feet off the ground.

"It's the whole damn school," Culley said as more giants lifted themselves out of the water. "Probably thirty of them with the juveniles. Shut off your flashlights!"

We did.

"They don't appear to be chasing people," I said.

"I'd venture," Brad added, "that they're headed for the air force base."

"They'll be blown to pieces," Culley said.

Brad climbed the ladder of a damaged house.

"What're you doing?" I called.

"Maybe," Brad said, "I can contact the air force base from this roof."

The giants were flashing to each other in repetitive patterns of various colors as they advanced.

"I wonder...." I said to Culley, "I wonder if those flashes are a form of morse code with lights instead of clicks?"

"You mean each pattern is a letter?"

"Or a word."

"I got the air force base!" Brad called. "They're sending a helicopter to pick us up!"

"OK, that's great," Culley told him. "Now get the fuck off the roof! They're *coming.*"

Brad did, and we trotted back toward the camp.

The giants were hampered in their march through the village and the trees beyond. We easily outran them and kept track of their advance by the flashes of colors between trees. I prayed that the helicopter would arrive before the giants made it to our camp. Through the fear, a notion nagged at the back of my mind. Could we crack this language, as alien as anything we'd find someday when we contacted life forms in other star systems? Linguists had ways of deciphering patterns even if they didn't know the language.

I heard the beat of a helicopter. We kept our flashlights turned off and stayed dark. The crew could track us with their infra-reds.

The giants were getting the hang of sliding between trees and were approaching faster.

"Do you think they know we're here?" I said through hard breaths as we trotted between trees lit only by the moon.

"It doesn't matter," Culley said, "they're gaining on us."

Brad turned on his Q-Tree and contacted the helicopter. "Head for our camp," he told them through breaths, "there's a kid there."

The 'copter flew overhead and continued on. The giants were too close to us for the helicopter to fire at them. Part of me was glad.

But we weren't going to make it to the camp in time! The 'copter crew knew it. They came back and hovered above us. With the stars as backdrop, I saw the rescue basket being lowered. It bounced to the ground.

"Get in," Culley told me.

I did. "Can't we all go?"

He shook his head. "One at a time."

I held on as the basket lifted quickly. I saw the giants below in the light of the moon. They were close!

I rolled out of the basket into the 'copter, helped by a crewman. He slid the basket over the side. It dropped quickly and bounced. "C'mon, Culley," I whispered. "C'mon!" But I wasn't surprised when Brad was lifted. The helicopter gained height as the giants caught up under it. It was too high to drop the basket again.

"Oh, Culley." If I hadn't gone with him and Brad, he'd be in the helicopter now.

The 'copter took off toward the camp.

"What about Culley?" I asked the crewman who had helped me inside, a young man whose face was half hidden by his helmet.

"We have to get the others while we can, ma'am," he said.

I looked down at flashing giants as the 'copter swooped toward our camp. "Oh, Culley."

"He's resourceful," Brad said. "If anybody can outwit those bitches, he can."

The crewman looked at Brad.

We reached our camp and George came up first in the basket, clutching Champ, who was crying. I took him in my arms. My own tears were silent.

"Where's Culley?" George asked.

"The giants caught up." I said. My voice was choked.

"They couldn't bring him up," Brad said.

Mini came aboard from the basket and asked the same question.

"Can't we please go back for him?" I pleaded with the crewman.

"We'll search, ma'am, but we can't take a chance on getting too low. We lost a crew that way."

"I know," I said.

"I'm sorry," he told me, "but even if we find him, we can't lower the basket. If a Kraken yanks on it, it could bring down the 'copter."

We circled, far above the giants, too far to use the infra-reds.

Suddenly Champ's crying got on my nerves. We had done so much to save him, and all he did was cry!

I realized how foolish that thought was and rocked him. Below, I saw the lights of the Anderson Air Force Base grow closer.

But my mind was filled with what we had left behind.

CHAPTER TWENTY TWO

The American Anderson Air Force Base was an urban sprawl of modern buildings, lights, helicopters being loaded with provisions, others lifting into the sky. On their way to help the tsunami survivors, I surmised. Towers loomed above rows of planes on asphalt runways. Uniformed men and women strode to and from buildings. I stared at neat, residential houses, and all of this within the primal hands of the black woods and the surrounding dark ocean.

Brad had told the helicopter crew that we thought the giants were headed for the base to get revenge for their dead offspring.

James, one of the crewman, took off his helmet and rubbed his knuckles through his blonde crew cut. "Well, then, we'll blow them to hell," he told Brad. "I have to report this." He strode toward one of the buildings.

Brad followed.

"Brad!" I called. "Try to convince them not to fire on the giants...unless they're aggressive."

He waved a hand. "That's what I *intend* to do, Tessica."

If anybody could talk fast and give a convincing argument, it was Brad.

"Maybe I can help," George said. "I can offer some real science to back up Brad's soapbox act. Like for instance, if they destroy these giants, others might attack civilian populations. Hey, wait for me!" He trotted after Brad and James.

Mini took Champ from my arms. He had fallen asleep. "Why don't you try to get some rest?"

"I don't think so." I looked southeast, where the 'copter had picked us up. And left Culley. I laid a hand over my trembling lips. "Why does he always have to play the hero? Can't he let somebody else do it for a change?"

"It's his nature, Tess. I think it's part of the reason you love him, no?"

"I guess." I stared back at the woods. "But he doesn't make it easy. Mini. Oh, I wanted to tell you. I think the giants are using a language based on patterns for each letter, or word, like morse code." I shrugged. "You can take it from there, if you like. I'm just too tired to care anymore."

"Don't give up hope, Tess." She put a hand on my arm. "You told me yourself, Culley's a hard man to kill."

The alarm system sounded. A young Chamorro woman in uniform pulled up in a jeep. "Get in, please." Her expression was strained. "We're under attack. Please get in."

We did.

She looked around and idled the jeep. We were well inside the base, on an asphalt pad, with a clear view all around.

Champ woke up and started crying again. Mini tried to soothe him but he hit her with his tiny fists and screamed louder.

I was just too weary to deal with him. I watched uniformed men and women jump into armed military vehicles. Helicopters hovered above. Their lights swept the giants, who had stopped among trees, just beyond the perimeter of the base.

"I wonder what the giants have in mind?" Mini said and rocked Champ.

I felt numb, not caring if the giants were communicating, or had a plan, or were blown into the deepest circle of hell. Brad and George must have convinced the commander to order his troops to hold fire. It seemed to be a standoff.

The giants stopped flashing and camouflaged themselves to look like wide patches of dark grass and rocky outcroppings, and even fallen logs.

"How long can they live out of water?" I asked Mini.

"Usually about a half hour. But with these guys, I just don't know. I wonder what they want?"

I shrugged.

"What's that?" the driver said.

A great, flat piece of asphalt moved toward the jeep.

"Go!" Mini shouted to the driver. "It's a giant! *Go.*"

"Hurry!" I whispered.

The woman put the jeep into gear.

Too late!

The giant raised up over the jeep. I screamed. A caustic smell invaded my lungs. I tried to jump out of the jeep but the giant laid her wet, briny body over me. I clawed frantically to squeeze free of her. She pressed down harder.

They can't fire! I thought. *The base can't fire! We're too close. We're dead.*

Champ screamed.

I felt the giant's beak against my back. *Oh, God. No!* I was dizzy with terror. I squeezed my eyes shut and waited for the beak to open, to rip into my back and tear me apart. *God! Let it be quick.* "Oh, Culley!"

But the giant lifted off my back and I saw light again. Champ was still screaming.

"No!" I heard Mini cry. "Oh, don't! He's just a baby."

"Mini!" I looked up and gasped. The giant had Champ wrapped in a tentacle with only his head and shoulders showing. She lifted him high, too high for the base to fire on her. If they hit her, she would drop Champ.

"No!" Mini stood up on the jeep's front seat and pulled at the tentacle that held Champ.

Lights from all over the base swung and targeted the giant and screaming Champ. She stood like a white, lit tower, holding the baby aloft.

Mini jumped off the jeep. The driver still sat behind the wheel, her eyes wide.

"Oh, Mini," I said, "what are we going to do?" I realized I was squeezing her arm and let go.

The giant began to flash. Her companions, still at the perimeter of the base, flashed back. She slithered toward them, holding Champ high off the ground.

Mini, the driver, and I, ran after her.

We stopped when she reached her companions. She lowered Champ gently to the grass. Mini, with her long strides, reached him first and scooped him up.

One giant threw something ragged and white with her tentacle. It plopped onto the asphalt. Shreds of red fabric were stuck to its wet surface.

"What -- ?" I started.

"Damn," Mini said sadly, "it's the remains of a juvenile who was killed at the floating beach umbrella. They don't need words to describe their sorrow. These guys are leaps and bounds smarter than any octopuses I've ever studied. I wouldn't doubt that they have language."

The giants flashed purple as they turned and lumbered west, toward Uruno Beach and the dark arms of the sea.

"Don't fire!" I yelled toward the base. "They're leaving." I waved my arms. "Don't fire! They might attack!"

"I'll radio it in." The driver ran to her jeep and jumped in.

"Give me the baby," I told Mini.

I walked back with Champ held close. He sobbed and I felt his small body trembling.

"You know what I'm thinking?" Mini said.

"I think so," I answered.

"They showed us what the planes did to *their* children, and that in spite of it, they were not about to strike back."

"It was a real display of tolerance," I said. "I wonder...."

"Suppose we drop off Champ, borrow a jeep, and go and look for him, Tess."

"OK."

*****

We dropped Champ off at the base's medical clinic to be checked out and cared for.

The only way we could borrow a jeep was with a driver. Anna, the Chamorro woman, was behind the wheel. Mini, Brad, George, and I rode with her into the black woods.

I was physically exhausted, but mentally wired as I strained to catch sight of Culley in the bouncing headlights. Anna blew the horn every so often, to alert Culley if he were in the vicinity. We listened, silent, for the sound of a human voice calling beyond the soft whine of the engine and the murmur and clicks and growls of nocturnal forest creatures. The air was sweet with the scent of wild flowers and grass. The jeep ground over rocks and ruts. I held on as we guided Anna to our camp.

When we got there, we sorted through our backpacks and looked around for any clues Culley might have left for us to follow. Brad took a small lantern from his backpack, turned it on, and hung it from a branch.

"Wait a minute," George said, "Culley's backpack is missing." He looked around. "The one with the holes in it."

"Then he made it back to camp!" I said.

"And he took some provisions," George said. "Maybe so he'd have stuff if the giants blocked his path to the air force base.

"Culley!" Brad shouted into the night. An animal's soft growl was the only response. "Culley! I *told* him to carry a Q-Tree." He kicked a stone. "He's so fucking old fucking fashioned!"

Anna glanced at Brad and put a hand to her mouth. She went to the jeep and got on the radio. I heard her call the base to request a search and rescue helicopter. She shut off the engine and left the jeep. "Now that we know the

Krakens are gone," she said in her gentle tone, "the 'copter will be able to search." She smiled at me.

I managed a wan smile, but my stomach felt tight. My legs were trembling with exhaustion. I sat down and leaned back against a tree. "I feel sick," I said.

The lantern swayed in the breeze, throwing harsh light and black shadows. I thought I saw the shape of a man approaching. *No,* I thought, *it's only the slender trunk of a tree.*

Mini sat next to me and took my hand.

"I shouldn't have insisted on going along," I said miserably. "It's all my fault."

"C'mon now, Tess," she said, "how could you possibly have known?"

"Yeah, she should of known! Next time listen to me."

It was Culley's voice!

I was on my feet in a flash.

Culley stood, lit from behind by the lantern, leaning on one leg, his thumbs hooked in his pants pockets, the backpack over his shoulder.

"Oh," I said. "Oh!" I ran to him and threw my arms around his neck. We almost fell. He steadied us and I sobbed and buried my head against his sweaty chest.

Mini's grin was so broad, it seemed to split her face in the lantern light.

George danced on his toes and wrung his hands. His pudgy body jiggled with delight. "That's *him*," he told Anna, who was smiling sedately. "That's Ryan Culley!"

She nodded.

Brad came over. "Nice to have you home." He smirked. "Although to tell you the truth, Ryan, if we didn't find you, I could've taken you off the payroll."

I slapped Brad's chest. His plastic shark teeth rattled.

Anna's eyes widened.

"What happened, Culley?" Mini hugged him. "Were you too tough for the mollusks to chew?"

"Hey!" I said. "I want to see light between you two."

"You're not going to believe this." Culley shook his head. "I think they couldn't agree on what to do with a human."

"Oh, give me a break!" Mini said.

"Dissent among the mollusks," Brad added. "I can't wait to hear the rest of this civil war." He slapped his hip as though he were drawing a gun. "Tentacles at eight feet!"

Anna looked from one to the other of us. She went to the jeep and got on the radio. I heard her call off the search. "Yes," she said, "He just walked into camp. ...I *think* he's all right." She lowered her voice. "They're sort of a strange group, you know?"

We piled into the jeep.

"Home, James," Brad told Anna.

She glanced back. "*Anna,*" she said.

"'Home is where'," George announced from the front seat and spread his arms, "'when you have to go there, they have to take you in'."

Anna kept her eyes glued to the road.

I leaned against Culley and chuckled. He put his arm around me and his head against mine. I suddenly felt exhaustion overwhelm me.

"So?" Mini said, "*Details*, Culley. Details. Start at the beginning, and don't stop until you come to the end."

Culley rubbed his eyes sleepily. "I think there was a gap between the kids and the grownups."

"The *giants* had a generation gap?" Mini said. "Culley, are you dreaming?"

"Not yet." He kissed my head and sighed sleepily. "Well, one of them pulled the rifle from my hand and flung it into the trees."

"Oh, Ryan," I said.

"Then what happened?" Brad asked.

"A smaller giant, I think she was a juvenile, came toward me." He rubbed his forehead. "I was about ready to kiss my ass goodbye."

"Oh, let me." Brad waved a hand.

"Do you want to hear this?" Culley told him.

"I'm all ears," Brad said.

"You're all mouth!" Culley responded.

"Culley," I whispered soothingly.

"Point taken," Brad said. "Proceed."

"The big giants blocked her path and started flashing," Culley continued.

"What colors?" Mini asked.

"Looked like the whole damn rainbow. They put on quite a show."

"So," George said, "then what did the juvenile do?"

"She left the party." Culley gestured west. "Took off toward Uruno Beach."

"Were there other juveniles?" I asked.

He nodded. "They grouped together and followed her. But she was the biggest. "I'll tell you, Mini, they're a hell of a lot smarter than we think."

"They followed the ring leader," Mini said. "Sounds like the family's breaking up into separate tribes."

"Chimpanzees and other species do it," I said. "Sometimes they come back and make war on their former troops."

"So," George said. "you think these guys will make war on their own parents?"

"It's a big ocean," Mini answered, "maybe there's room for all."

"Not if they make war on humans," Culley said.

We sat quietly. We humans are always amazed at the intelligence in the animal world, as though we have sole property to brains. I thought of a scientist who saw a female chimp chew the end of a branch into a sharp point, and use it to spear bush babies, a small mammal that hides in tree boles. Chimps love meat, just like their cousins.

The scientist was criticized for calling it a weapon. "Chimps don't make weapons!" she was told. "Only humans are capable of doing that." There's something to be proud of. "And," they told the scientist, "female chimps don't hunt!"

What, I wondered, will they say when linguists crack dolphin language, and the language of the giants?

Anna was in no hurry to get back to the base now that we had Culley. The soft rocking of the jeep as it lumbered over ruts was putting Culley and me to sleep.

"I love you so much, Ryan," I whispered and nuzzled against him.

He touched my lips with his. Then we kissed.

"Oh, *please,* not here!" Brad waved a hand. "I need a hot meal, not hot employees."

I felt Culley's body stiffen.

"It's OK, hon," I whispered. "That's just Brad."

I saw Anna's shoulders bunch up as she drove, and felt sorry for her. We were a strange group, after all, but a happy one.

One thing nagged as I fell asleep. Orphaned elephants have been known to run in packs and kill animals that elephants don't normally kill. Would the juveniles really become rogues and make war on humans? God knows, they had cause.

CHAPTER TWENTY THREE

I jumped in my sleep as the jeep jerked to a stop. The roar of planes and the beat of helicopters were a continuous drone overhead. We were parked in the driveway of a dark residential house on the base.

The first veils of dawn lit a gray sea. Roiling clouds were caught in the dull light. The air felt cold and wet. I shivered and rubbed my arms as I got out of the jeep. A patter of rain spotted the asphalt driveway and rivulets dripped down my face.

"She's really tired," Culley told Anna, and put an arm around my shoulders to brace me.

Anna nodded and unlocked the front door with a click. She turned on the lights and I hurried inside, followed by Culley, Mini, Brad, and George. Anna turned up the thermostat. The warm smell of heat as it rose from vents was relaxing.

"Thank you, Anna," I said as she went to the door.

"That goes for all of us," Brad added.

"You're very welcome," Anna said. "Someone will bring you breakfast." She smiled, went out, and gently closed the door.

"Breakfast?" George said. "What happened to supper?" He sat at the table.

"It flew away, George." Mini sat next to him.

Culley pulled up a chair beside me and laid his head down over his crossed arms on the table.

Lightning flashed and thunder reverberated like tolling bells. Rain drummed on the roof and poured down the windows. A sudden wind shook trees in a strangle hold. Loose leaves tapped the windows as though they wanted respite from the storm.

Culley sighed. "It's good to be indoors."

I rubbed his wet back.

"It feels like heaven itself is crying tonight," Mini said.

The door opened and a tall, thin man, wearing a loose, black rain slicker, his face hidden beneath the hood, came in with a bulging, white bag in his arms, and closed the door. "It's the devil's night," he said in a hollow voice and went to the counter. He laid out food with white, bony fingers.

I peered at his face, but couldn't make it out under the hood, except for pale, gaunt cheeks. Something about his manner made me tense up, as though an inner wisdom were setting off alarm bells.

"Thanks," Culley told him without raising his head.

"You're welcome to stay and eat with us," Brad said. "There's enough food there for an army."

"My time here is limited. I'm on duty," the man said.

Culley sat up. "How are the survivors doing?" I saw his jaw tighten as he looked at the man.

"I think the Lord showed his wrath at this island," the man said.

"Now why would He do that?" Brad asked.

"Battles," the man said forlornly. "Battles and death."

"It started with the Spanish-American War in 1898," George told us. He threw the man a fearful glance. "It ended with World War II."

Thunder rolled like cannon fire across the sky. I jumped. Lightning flashed in dark woods through the bare, rectangular windows. Wind moaned and whipped palm trees into the cries of tortured souls.

The man went to the door. " It's time." He opened the door and was gone. Thunder rattled the windows.

George's eyes grew wide as he stared at the ceiling. Rain drummed like a roll call. "It's...it's good to be indoors," he said.

I jumped as the door opened again.

A tall man hurried inside carrying a bulging white bag. "Wow, what a night!" He pushed back his hood. He was black, with strong bone structure and eyes that drew you in. "Hi, guys, I'm First Airman Elijah Jones." He glanced at Mini and his cheeks broadened with a shy smile.

Mini smiled back.

"I, uh, I brought you guys breakfast." He saw the food spread out on the counter. "Oh, no. Don't tell me somebody else got the same order to bring you food?"

Brad nodded.

"Just another snafu." Jones laughed and plunked his bag on the table. "Well, now you have lunch, too. Compliments of Commander Jackson F. Lee."

"Uh," Brad started, "thank him for us."

"Do you want to stay and eat with us, airman?" Mini asked. "Lord knows there's enough food."

I caught the slight Southern dialect Mini put to her words to make a connection with Jones.

"Why thank you, ma'am," Jones said, "but I can't stay. Everybody's pitching in to help the tsunami victims."

"That's real good." Mini smiled coyly.

Jones stared at her for a moment. "Oh, enjoy your meal. I mean, *meals*." He laughed and went to the door. He looked back at Mini with his hand on the knob. "Maybe another time?"

Mini nodded and fluttered her eyelashes. "Another time."

You vamp! I thought and held back a chuckle.

Jones hummed a tune as he went out into the rain.

Thunder shook the night like a gasp from hell, and the storm finally moved on.

*****

After we ate we were all ready for a good day's sleep. With four bedrooms, Culley and I claimed one.

I fell asleep, exhausted, huddled against him, until the warm afternoon sun on my face woke me up.

The base was finally quiet. I felt safe here, after the trauma of the night. I didn't want to get up. I didn't want to take a shower or go to the kitchen for lunch with the others. I didn't want to face the day. Culley's arm was around my waist. I put my hand over his. Here, we were safe from everything, from life, with all its hazards. This one small space, this bedroom, was sanctuary.

Culley kissed my cheek. "I think the rooster is crowing."

"It's a nightingale. I'm scared, Ryan."

"I know. You were shaking in your sleep. Bad dream?"

"I don't remember. I don't want to remember."

"You'll feel better, Tess, when you get up and get active. I've been through this sort of thing after bad times." He brushed back my hair and kissed my cheek. "I'll be right here with you."

"You *say* that, and then somehow we end up parted, and you end up in trouble."

"Yeah. Sorry."

"Oh, don't be. It's not your fault. It's your nature." I turned to face him. "Ryan, you always sacrifice for other people's safety. It's very noble, but it's hard on the ones who love you."

"It's not too easy when the woman you love won't let you protect her, either."

I smiled. "We're a pair, though, aren't we?"

"Forever, Tess."

We kissed.

"What did you think of that guy last night?" I asked.

"I can't make head or tail of him."

"I wouldn't be surprised if he had a tail, and horns."

"It was probably just a snafu."

"What's a snafu?" I asked.

"Situation normal, all fucked up."

We laughed. The anxiety that had accompanied waking up dissipated with Culley's gentle love.

He kissed my lips. "I don't know if it was a nightingale," he said, "but the cock is crowing."

"You pervert."

He ran his hand across my breast and stroked my hip. "What do you say to a little hanky panky?"

I felt fire rising in me. "I say yay."

He kissed my lips and my neck and down to my breast.

"Oh, Ryan." I held his head in both hands. I lifted my leg over his hip and felt the swelling of his penis as he pressed against me. I pushed back until he was inside me.

"Tessie," he breathed and rolled on top of me.

"What?" I lifted my legs around his hips and felt him push in deeper. I could tell he was already coming, but then, so was I.

I dug my nails into his sides and arched my back against him. "Oh, God, Ryan!"

What sweet bliss as we clung to each other and rocked and the orgasm rolled through my body.

I finished first, but I continued to move against him until he relaxed and lay across me, breathing hard. I kissed his cheek.

"Maybe you were right about staying here," he said.

"No, hon. It's time to face the day, whatever it brings."

I jumped as someone knocked on the door. "Get off!" I pushed him and threw the covers over myself.

"Roll call," Brad said from behind the door. "We've got places to go and things to do, and the coffee's instant."

We showered and ate breakfast, which was really a late lunch, took our backpacks and went out to wait for the jeep that would drive us back to *Nomad*, if she were still beached where we left her, and to R/V *Cousteau*, if she were also where we left her anchored.

I squinted in the sunlight. Small, innocuous clouds drifted, as though the fury of the night had never occurred. The air was fresh, scrubbed clean by the storm. Only wet palm fronds that lay across the asphalt bore witness to the night of the storm.

I wasn't too surprised when Airman Elijah Jones drove up in a jeep. He gave us a broad smile. "Need a lift?"

Mini smiled back. Her hair was tied with a beautiful gold colored, embroidered silk scarf that blew in the breeze.

"Wearing your Sunday best?" I said.

"It's Sunday," she whispered between teeth as she grinned at Jones, "when I say it is."

"Do you guys mind," I asked, "if we stop off at the clinic first? I'd like to say goodbye to Champ."

"No hurry," Brad said. "They're fueling *Cousteau* with a service boat."

"Champ's at daycare with the other kids," Jones told us and checked his watch. "Can do."

*****

Brad remained outside to contact the service boat on his Q-Tree and find out if they had finished refueling *Cousteau*.

Mini remained in the jeep with Jones.

A young, slender blonde woman greeted Culley, George, and me at the entrance to the daycare center.

"Come in," she said. "Champ will be happy to see you. My name's Gloria."

We gave our names as we entered.

The brightly colored room held cribs, low tables, and an abundance of toys. Soft music emanated from somewhere. Tropical fish swam in an aquarium in one corner. But some of the toddlers played silently by themselves. Others mingled and babbled.

Champ sat at a low table with three other toddlers, intent on drawing a picture on a big piece of paper. His pudgy little hand gripped the crayon awkwardly.

"You can tell which are the children of the tsunami," Gloria said and went to the table. "Champ?" she said softly.

He looked up. When he saw me, his dark, round eyes widened. He slid off the chair and sobbed as he waddled to me. I scooped him up. "Champie!" I hugged him and kissed his cheek. He clung to me.

George took Champ's hand and shook it. "Hi, Champie. Remember me?"

Champ slapped George's hand and squeezed me harder.

"Sorry about that, George," I said.

"No, that's OK." There was a bowl of cookies on a high shelf. "Can I have a cookie or two?" George asked Gloria.

She nodded. "Help yourself."

He did.

Culley rubbed Champ's back. "How's he doing?" he asked Gloria.

She shook her head. "It's going to be a long road. There's a lot of anger and fear in that little body." She looked at the silent children. "And he's just one of many."

"Where will he end up?" Culley asked.

"We're hoping he'll be adopted, eventually, but not yet. Not with all the problems he has. We have a therapist who comes in and works with the children."

"Ah, baby," I said to Champ. I sat down in a rocking chair and rocked him. "Everything's all right, little Champie." I loved having his small body pressed against my chest.

"If only it was all right," Culley said. He went to the aquarium and studied the fishes.

Champ needed me, but I needed him, too, I realized. I wanted to protect him from all the miseries that life can throw at us. I wondered who his parents had been, and if they had loved him well.

Minutes passed by. I realized that Champ was asleep.

Mini, Brad, and Jones came in. Jones pointed to his watch and raised his brows questioningly.

I nodded, got up and gave Champ back to Gloria with a sigh. She tucked him into a crib. His little body jerked. He cried, then he sucked his thumb and went back to sleep.

I wiped tears. Champ was one of the youngest of the tsunami victims. Suddenly I hated nature for the things she did to her children. *That's dumb*, I thought, *when we're the ones who get in the way*. "Thanks, Gloria," I said.

"You're welcome. Come and see him anytime. He really likes you."

I shrugged. "I'll try."

Culley threw an arm around my shoulders as we walked out. "They'll help him," he said. "They know how to heal those kinds of wounds."

My throat was choked. I just nodded as we went to the jeep.

Mini climbed into the front seat. George tried to sit next to her and she slid closer to the door to block him. George looked hurt as he squeezed into the back seat. I knew he liked Mini, but it was a relationship that I didn't think could go beyond a deep friendship.

Four of us in the back seat was one too many. I sat on Culley's lap.

Considering the bouncing of the jeep, it was an interesting ride to the beach.

I heard hammering and the whine of power tools as we drove through the destroyed village. There was a pleasant smell of wood dust in the air. People moved quickly as they loaded debris into trucks. One crew repaired a damaged foundation. Another was busy nailing together a wooden frame for a new house. In the end, life has an insatiable appetite to prevail.

Nomad was right where we left her, with a container of fuel by the stern.

"Compliments of the base," Jones said.

He and Mini went off by themselves while the rest of us checked *Nomad*. She was intact, and all our stuff was there.

Mini and Jones strolled back, talking and holding hands. He was even taller than she, I realized. *What a handsome couple.*

Mini walked Jones to his jeep.

"I get shore leave in three weeks," I heard him tell her.

"Keep in touch, Jones." She gave him a quick kiss on his cheek.

He put a hand to his cheek. "Why'd you go and do that? Now I can't wash my face until we meet again."

They both laughed.

"Well, that was quick," I told Culley.

"I think those two were born to meet," he said.

Mini trotted back to us, then turned and waved as Jones pulled away. "Hope I didn't keep you guys waiting?"

"Naw," I said. "He's really cute."

"You think?" She watched the jeep disappear into the town. "I guess he's all right."

George gave her a sullen look.

"I'm jealous," Brad told Mini and plunked his captain's hat, from *Nomad,* onto his mop of blonde hair. I detected sadness beneath his flip attitude. I looked at Culley, with his long brown hair blowing in the sea breeze. He connected the gas tank to *Nomad's* motor with deft fingers, his lean body braced, one foot in the inflatable, one in the sand. I smiled.

He looked up, saw me, and winked.

I winked back.

I wondered how Culley would respond if I told him I wanted to adopt Champ? I knew instinctively this was not the right time to talk about it. When we were back home, and into our normal routine, I would tell him how I felt.

I looked at *Cousteau*, fueled now and waiting, and wondered what was *normal routine?* Culley, my colleagues, the boat, had become home. Could I go back to apartment living and the Lab? Could Culley go back to living in his RV? Somehow I didn't think so. I could take Ice on board, but what about Champ? We were like a family of gypsies, traveling everywhere together and belonging nowhere.

CHAPTER TWENTY FOUR

Once on board *Cousteau,* we rummaged around and found that everything there was also intact. Brad had given the base a list of provisions and they were stocked and untouched. It gave me an added respect for the people of Guam.

The base had left a basket of fruit and chocolates on the table with a note that read: To The Crew of Cousteau. From the airmen and airwomen of Anderson Air Force Base.

I took a peach and bit into the sweet, juicy meat. "Is Pacifica Lab paying for the food and fuel?" I asked Brad.

"Oh yeah, big time. Considering the data my team is bringing back, it's a small price."

George came into the cabin with some papers in hand. "Well," he said and sat down, "the report is in on the preliminary work I did on Mini's samples."

"The ones from the Trench?" Mini asked.

George nodded. "Toxicity." He took a chocolate, unwrapped it and chewed. "The samples showed a high level of pollutants. The oxygen level in the water samples is too low to support marine life."

"It can be reversed, though, can't it?" I asked.

"It can," George said. "But first people would have to stop using fertilizers, and industries would have to install emissions controls." He handed me the report and unwrapped another chocolate. "Then the dead zones would begin to disappear." He popped the chocolate into his mouth.

"I'll go over it later," I said and extended the report to Culley. "You want to see it, hon?"

"I'll let you guys interpret it for me." He took a banana from the basket and peeled it.

"Mini?" I asked, and extended the report to her.

She took it and set it aside. "I'll look at it later."

"So the female giants," I said, "they *knew* better than to lay their eggs in these dead zones, and they came into shallow water?"

"It would probably be hard for them to breathe, too." Mini said. "They would know that low oxygen levels would kill their eggs. And if *that* didn't do it, the pollutants would."

"And the abundant jellies in shallow water," I said, "would be an added attraction." I chewed the peach.

Brad sat back. "Well, then, that sums it up, doesn't it?" He looked around and twiddled his thumbs. "My team has solved the mystery of the Krakens. Congrats to all."

"I'm not sure where I fit in," Culley said, "but you're welcome, boss."

"The discoveries you made on dives, my man," Brad told him. "They contributed to the whole. Well!" He looked smug as he stood up. "Home, James! I'm off to the helm, and home, and Harley." He left the cabin.

"Who's Harley?" I asked.

"Brad's love," Mini said.

"Oh." I stared at the closed door. "He never mentioned him."

"There are things, " Culley said, "that a guy like Brad might not want to talk about." He chewed the banana. "You know, the bravest guy I ever knew, a commercial diver who worked with hazardous material. He was gay."

"The Spartans," George said. "It was part of their culture for warriors to form strong male bonds." He unwrapped another chocolate. "When they went into battle, which was their favorite pastime, they would fight fiercely to protect their lovers." He popped the chocolate into his mouth.

"I didn't know Brad had a lover," I said. "Then we'll all be happy to get home."

I thought of home, of my family, of Ice's beautiful white fur, his dazzling blue eyes. I was anxious to see my other guy too. "Mini?"

She looked up from reading the report. "Will you and Jones be able to meet when he's on leave?"

"He'll let me know." She hunched forward. "What do you guys think of him. Really?"

George lowered his head. "He's OK," he mumbled.

"Culley?" Mini said. "As a man, what do you think?"

"My gut feeling is that he's a good man. Beyond that, I couldn't say."

Mini smiled. "Tess?"

"I don't know him, but I liked what I saw."

"Me too," she said.

George unwrapped another chocolate and stuffed it into his mouth.

Mini kicked her chair back as she stood up. She grabbed the basket, strode to the closet and slammed it down on a shelf. Then she slammed the closet door.

George got up with his head lowered. "I'll be in the lab." He swept the thinning hair over his bald spot and walked out.

Brad came into the cabin. "What's up with George? He walked past the lab, then turned around and went in."

"He's lonely," I said.

"Join the club," Brad replied. "Ryan, I think we have a problem with the engines. She's running sluggish."

"I'll have a look." Culley left the cabin.

"The helm's on auto-pilot." Brad sat down. "Where's the basket?"

Mini went to the closet, brought it back, and put it on the table.

"Where are all the chocolates?" Brad asked.

"Three guesses!" Mini answered.

Brad took a piece of coconut from a bag in the basket. "First thing," he said and studied the coconut, "when we get home, I'm having dinner at Armand's."

"Who's Armand?" I asked.

"Not who," Brad said, "What. It's the finest French restaurant on the entire west coast." He put down the coconut. "I'm sick to death of raw, healthy food."

"Do George a favor," Mini said, "take him with you."

"Three's a crowd," Brad answered. "But, I'll ask Harley Davidson."

"What?" I said.

"Not what. Who," Brad answered. "Harley's parents, John and Mary Davidson, thought it would be great fun to name their first son something different."

Mini and I looked at each other.

"I call him kickstart for short." Brad chewed a mouthful of dry coconut.

"Does he ride?" Mini asked.

"A motorcycle?" Brad said. "Oh, no. He's afraid of them. But we both like to bowl."

A while later, Culley came in, wiping his hands on a rag. "The engines are OK," he told Brad. "I'll check out the bridge."

I felt a bump from the bottom of the boat. I held onto the edge of the table and looked at Culley.

He ran onto the deck. We followed. George came out of the lab holding a sample bottle. "What was that?"

We checked the surface around the boat.

"Wait a minute!" Mini said. "It's a giant!"

George ran to the bridge, followed by Brad. "I'm launching the ROV," George called back. "I'll see what's going on under there."

Culley looked over the stern. "I better get suited up." He headed for the wet room.

"No, wait!" I said. "Let's see what's under there first."

He paused. "OK."

Culley, Mini, and I went to the bridge.

"Come here. Look at this!" Brad said.

We gathered around the ROV screen as George maneuvered the vehicle under the hull.

"Holy shit!" Mini exclaimed.

A group of about twenty juvenile female giants clung to the hull. Small, charcoal males held onto the females. There was a motion at the edge of the screen. George swung the ROV in that direction. Three females had their tentacles wrapped around the body of a White Shark. He slammed his tail against the hull.

"The poor thing," I said as he twisted and thrashed in an effort to shake off his tormentors. Blood spread around him as the giants dug into his flesh with their beaks. The shark rolled, then breached and slammed back into the water, flinging off one female.

Others let go of the hull and attacked the shark. One female ripped his gills open.

"Oh," George exclaimed. "They know just where to attack."

The shark's body twitched as he floated to the surface.

I turned from the screen. "I can't watch this."

"Me either." Culley left the bridge.

I went on deck. Blood pinked the waves. The shark's tail lifted out of the water and splashed down.

Culley trotted back holding a rifle. He leaned over the bow, took aim and fired. The shark's tail slammed the water. Then he sank. The juveniles hung back, watching the boat. After a while, they jetted down after him.

Culley and I went back to the bridge. George maneuvered the ROV to follow the still body of the White Shark as it sank. The juveniles gathered around the shark for their meal.

"Let's get the hell out of here," Brad said, "before they finish their feast and hitch a ride again." He went to the helm.

George stared out a window. "Just when we thought it was safe to go back into the water."

"Brad," Mini said, "I think you should alert the naval base at Pearl Harbor, and the Anderson Base. I doubt if we're the only boat they've hitched on, and that these are the only rogue juveniles." She stared at the ROV screen. "What's the hell's going to happen if a person goes for a swim off a boat, or falls in?"

"Point taken," Brad said and unhooked the radio mic.

George studied the juveniles with the ROV. Culley, Mini, and I went on deck.

Culley stared grimly at the sea.

"What are you thinking, hon?" I asked and put an arm around his waist.

"I'm thinking these rogues can disable a running boat and climb aboard."

"Or an oil platform or a bridge," I said. It seems we're right back where we started."

"Not quite," Mini said. "The adults are no longer killing humans, or burning out dens on ocean structures and ships. That's a big plus."

"But they can't control the kids," Culley said.

"And when the kids are fifty feet long...." Mini stared into the water.

I chewed a nail and realized I hadn't done that in quite a while. I studied my hands. My nails were growing. Culley smiled at me.

George came on the deck looking pale. "I checked the hull with the ROV now that, you know, the juveniles are feeding."

"And?" Culley asked.

"They started to burn the hull." He put a hand to his throat. "It's not damaged, but the burn marks are visible. "We're very lucky," he whispered.

"That they prefer White Sharks to humans?" Mini asked.

George nodded. "And that a shark came along when it did."

"Stealth hunters," Culley said.

We looked at him.

"These giants can hang out a few fathoms down," he continued, "and wait for a ship. When one comes along, they clamp onto the hull. They can board it anytime they want to or sink it. *Jesus.* We better have a guard posted, twenty-four, seven. Brad!" He went to the bridge.

"Why do I get the feeling," I said, "that we're not going home just yet? Mini, do you have any thoughts on how these rogues can be stopped?"

"You know what?" George said.

"What?" Mini asked him.

"Well, in Africa, poachers used to shoot adult elephants for their tusks. It left a lot of orphan babies and kid elephants. They came together in juvenile gangs and went on rampages. They killed hippos and rhinoceroses."

"I'm sure there's a connection here," Mini said.

I leaned against the rail and scanned the water. It was empty, but all I was seeing was the sky of a very alien, violent world.

"When the people at animal sanctuaries gathered the orphans," George continued, "and took them to where the adult males hung out, the males taught them how to be elephants."

"They stopped killing other animals?" I asked.

George nodded.

"So you're proposing," Mini said, "that we take the juveniles back to the giant communities?"

"The artificial dens," George said.

Mini looked at me. "Sounds like herding cats."

"No," George commented. "Cats are loners. Well, except for lions. But the juvenile giants are social animals."

I smiled. "The Judas goat, George?"

"That's it! We capture one, the biggest one, I would think, and the rest will follow."

"But these aren't orphans," I pointed out. "*They* abandoned the adults."

"What do you do with juvenile delinquents?" Mini said thoughtfully.

"You bring them home, "George said, "where their mothers can teach them how to be octopuses."

"But how do you bring octopuses home?" I asked George.

"Well, if we can capture the largest one," George said.

"Yes," Mini added, "she'll probably be the ring leader."

"These giants are communicating with each other," George said, "and I think -- "

"The others will follow!" Mini said.

"That's all well and good," I told them, "but how do you capture a giant-sized octopus?"

"You lure her into the shark cage," George said.

"With what?" I asked. Inner alarm bells began to go off.

"The only thing we have that she'll go after," Mini said and looked at George.

"Not a *human?*" I asked.

"Well, Tess -- " Mini started.

"Oh, no," I interrupted. "Culley's *not* going into the shark cage with a giant. Just forget it!"

"He'd bring his torch," Mini said. "Of course," George said, "only if he's willing to do it. And well, we'd cover him with the rifles. The giants are afraid of rifles."

"Don't even mention this insane plan to Culley," I told them. My heart was already pounding. "You know goddamn well he'll do it, for the sake of keeping people safe in their boats." I slammed a fist on the rail. "No! I won't allow it."

Mini bit her lip. "Do you have a better plan?" she said softly.

"Just bait the cage," I retorted.

"But you see, Tess," George said, coming closer to me, "you see, we need to catch the right giant, you know, the ring leader. And somebody has to open and close the cage door."

"Well, it's not going to be Culley!" I told them. "Maybe the adults will come after the juveniles themselves."

Mini shook her head. "All the reports that came in said the mothers are staying close to their dens. They're hunting and taking care of themselves, and the young, but they don't leave the community except to hunt. You two are the only divers. I'd do it if I could, but..."

"You'll get him killed!" I said.

"He'll have his torch and his Mark 3 gun," George said.

"Tess." Mini put a hand on my shoulder.

I shrugged it off.

"Listen. Culley's a dive master," she said. "He's qualified to teach me how to dive. *I'll* do it."

"He won't teach you to clear your mask," I told her, "when he hears your plan."

"I'd do it, too," George said.

"Well why *don't* you?" I asked him.

"I have a punctured eardrum. My father...." He shrugged. "My father hit me so hard when I was a kid, he punctured it."

"I'm sorry, George," Mini said.

"You'll get him killed," I repeated. dully.

They glanced at each other.

I turned and strode to the cabin. I slammed the door behind me and leaned my back against it. Sobs shook my body. I went to my bunk, laid down and curled up under the blanket, facing the blank wall.

I fell asleep, I think as a sort of an escape, and dreamed I was in a room with a snake. It kept talking to me but I was afraid it would attack me. Then Ice came into the room and chased the snake.

"Tess?"

I woke up and turned. "Culley?"

He sat on the edge of the bunk.

"Oh, Culley!" I sat up and hugged him. "Please don't do it!"

I heard him sigh.

"Teach Mini how to dive. She and George hatched this insane plan."

"You know better than that, Tessie."

"I just *found* you." I wiped tears. You once asked me to leave this dangerous expedition. OK. If you promise me you won't go into the cage with a giant, I'll go home and wait for you. OK?"

He lowered his head. "Brad hired me on as the dive master and a commercial diver. This is my *job,* Tess. It's a point of honor."

"Ryan, why do you always have to play the hero, forever sacrificing to save somebody else's ass."

"I'm no hero. But this is something I have to do. Believe me, Tess, I'm not thrilled about it. But if we succeed, and the juveniles stop attacking ships, the Navy and the Coast Guard just might continue the work I do and stop other rogues."

"But...but what if she releases acid while you're in the cage with her? Did you even *think* about that? It's not just her beak, you know, or, or her tentacles, or the other giants waiting outside the cage." I wiped my eyes on my sleeve. "Did you ask Brad? What did Brad say?"

"He said it could save lives, but only if I want to do it."

"And of course you *want* to!"

He shook his lowered head. "I told you, I'm not thrilled."

"But you'll *do* it. What about me?"

"What was that poem you once read to me?" he said. "'I could not love thee dear, so much, loved I not honor more'."

"I'm sick of doing work to serve mankind. We planned our future together, Ryan. We even decided on how many children we wanted. Now you're going to throw it all away."

"I hope not."

I pushed him aside and got up. "Go! Get yourself killed. There are plenty more fish in the ocean."

"I'm sorry, Tess."

"So am I."

I left the cabin and went into the lab. I threw myself into studying the rest of the Nomura samples. It was obvious that the jellyfish were under attack by the giants. But then, so was I.

CHAPTER TWENTY FIVE

Cousteau was sea-anchored, waiting for the juveniles to return. I spent most of my free time in the lab or sitting on a beach chair in the stern, watching the sea. Watching and waiting....

Culley brought my meals. I didn't say much to him. I hardly touched the food. I preferred to sleep. Sleep was my only reprieve from fear, although sometimes even in sleep I was haunted by helpless animals I tried to protect from snakes, and crocodiles with open mouths; metaphors, I think, for danger and death. One dream woke me up shaking. A tall man in a black slicker swung a scythe in white, skeletal hands as he cut down scurrying animals.

Mini came to sit next to me on the second day. I didn't talk and she finally got up and left.

On the morning of the third day, the bulbous head of a giant broke the surface. Smaller ones emerged behind her. They watched the boat through their slitted eyes.

I had tried to disconnect myself from Culley, but the queasy feeling in my stomach, the way my breath shuddered in my throat, told me I hadn't succeeded.

Culley came on deck. "Tess?"

I looked at him.

"I'll be careful."

"You'll be dead."

He shrugged and went into the wet room to suit up and get his tank.

Mini, Brad, and George were winching the shark cage over the rail.

Culley came out ready to dive. His Mark 3 underwater gun hung in a holster. He had a torch in hand.

I got up, went to him and kissed him. "Good luck," I said.

He smiled. "Thanks, Tess. That makes it a lot easier."

I wanted to say *I love you,* but my throat was too choked up. I just nodded.

Mini, Brad, and George were busy with the shark cage. Culley watched the giants.

The plan came to me very suddenly.

I slipped into the wet room and quickly got suited up and put a tank on my back. I grabbed my fins, fitted my full-face mask, strapped on my knife, took a torch, and opened the door a crack.

"About five feet down," Culley was telling the others as they lowered the cage into the water. "Here goes nothing." He went over the side.

I got my fins on, walked backwards to the gunnel and followed Culley into the water. I heard Mini scream "Tess! No!" Then water swirled over my head.

Culley was already in the shark cage with the door closed. The latch was a contraption he and George had devised. No octopus could unravel its mystery and make an escape. The bars of the cage were so close that even a juvenile giant couldn't squeeze through.

"Ryan," Brad called through the communication systems in our masks, "Tessica's in the water with you!"

Culley swung around. "Tess! Get the hell out of here."

"Don't hold your breath," I told him.

The largest juvenile approached thee cage and tried to get a tentacle inside, but it would only go through about a foot. *The ring leader,* I thought. Twenty or so white juveniles spread out and watched. Small males clung to them.

A few of the females moved cautiously toward me. I made my torch hot and they drew back.

I remembered to breathe as Culley opened the door. I swam closer and stayed toward the back of the cage, holding onto a bar, my torch in hand.

The ring leader watched me, then decided on the human without the fire.

I swam to the top of the cage to be closer as she jetted into the cage.

Culley took out his Mark 3 and moved around her to the door. She flattened against the bars, her eyes on the gun.

"C'mon, Ryan, get out!" I said and shut off my torch as I swam down to the door.

The gang hung back. They knew very well what this alien fire and the weapon in the human's hand could do.

I saw the ROV glide toward the gang, probably to intimidate them. *Good work, George.* I thought.

Culley was coming out. I reached down to pull him through the door when the ring leader struck.

She whipped out a tentacle. It smashed into Culley's chest and sent the Mark 3 bouncing into the bars.

"Culley!" I screamed. I pulled him out and slammed the door. He was limp. Blood dripped from his mouth.

"He's hurt!" I shouted into my mask.

The air sensor alarm on his mask began to blink.

"He's not breathing," I screamed and dragged him slowly to the surface. He was in danger of an air embolism if the pressure in his lungs built up and wasn't released as we rose. That alone could kill him.

The ring leader squirted acid from the cage but it only spread beneath us.

Brad was in the water, clinging to the ladder. He grabbed Culley's arm and pulled him up. Mini's hands were underwater, her fingers spread. She clutched Culley's other arm and they dragged him on board.

He's not breathing!" I screamed again.

I was halfway up the ladder when I felt a tentacle wrap around my leg and yank. It dragged me back under.

The ROV sped toward us and slammed the octopus in her left eye. She let go and released acid. I swam for my life, feeling the burning substance around my legs like a pool of fire. She was between me and the ladder. A line with a weight to hold it down splashed into the water in front of me. I wrapped the line around my wrists as the gang approached, and held on as I was hoisted up.

A tentacle lashed out. It missed me and hit the boat. I heard a rifle shot and the tentacle quickly sank.

Brad dragged me over the gunnel. I flopped onto the deck.

"George, go!" Brad yelled toward the open door of the bridge. "Go! Before they come aboard."

The boat leaped forward, dragging the shark cage alongside. The juveniles followed.

Mini was administering artificial respiration to Culley. Brad ran to the cabin. I pulled off my fins and tank. I hardly noticed the burn in my legs, worse now with the hot sun on them as I stumbled to Culley's side.

"Is he breathing?" I shouted and released my weight belt and threw aside my mask.

"I'm not sure," Mini said.

Brad slammed open the cabin door with the respirator in hand and ran to Culley.

"Ryan!" I whispered. "Oh God." I saw blood on his lips before Brad put the respirator mask over his face.

I felt dizzy. The clouds seemed to move in circles. The ship lurched as though it were in high seas, though I knew the sea was calm.

"George!" Brad called. "Get on the horn and call the Coast Guard at Pearl Harbor. Tell them we need a medical 'copter, ASAP! And don't outrun the giants. We want them to keep up."

I felt myself sway. My mouth was slack.

Mini grabbed my arm. "Put your head down," she said softly, and pushed on my back.

I did, and the dizziness went away.

"Is he breathing?" I sobbed.

"He's breathing with the respirator," Brad told me.

"Oh, Ryan." I leaned over him. "Baby, don't leave me. Please!" I kissed his forehead. "I need you."

"Keep talking to him, Tess," Mini said. "I've heard that it helps."

I realized my legs were burning. "Mini! Help me out of this wet suit! There's acid."

"Oh, shit!" Mini unzipped my booties. They shredded as she yanked them off. She hurriedly pulled off the pants. I saw the rashes on my calves. My feet, too, were streaked with red.

"I'll get the hose," Mini said.

She came back with it and opened the nozzle. The water was cold. It hurt, but it washed off the diluted acid.

"Get out of the jacket," she said. "I'll bring you some warm clothes." She went to the cabin and returned with my woolen shirt and pants, a towel, and a pair of socks. I watched Culley as she dried my legs, my hair, and helped me into the warm clothes. She couldn't wipe away all my tears.

Brad put a blood pressure cuff around Culley's arm. He read it and let out a breath.

I didn't ask. I didn't want to know.

"Culley?" I whispered. "It's Tess, baby. It's your Tessica." I took the towel and gently wiped his wet hair. "I'm here with you, hon."

I heard the beat of a helicopter. Then it came into view. George cut the boat's engines as the 'copter hovered overhead. A Coastguard woman was lowered to the deck in a basket. She took off her helmet and shook out dark hair. "Do you know you're surrounded by giant octopuses?" she said casually.

Her face was narrow, with a broad, thin mouth.

"We know! Take care of him," I gestured toward Culley.

"That's what I'm here for, lady." She took a cervical collar from the basket and strapped it on Culley's neck. "Help me slide him onto the litter." She lifted a board from the basket and we slid Culley onto it. Then we lifted him carefully into the basket.

"What happened to him?" the woman asked as she strapped him in. "He looks bad."

"Just get him to a hospital!" I said.

"That's what I'm here for." She signaled to the 'copter and I watched Culley's face, afraid it was for the last time, as the basket lifted and he moved away from me.

An octopus flung a tentacle over the rail and began to pull herself up.

"What the hell?" the woman said.

Brad slammed the tentacle with the butt end of his rifle. The tentacle slid back into the water.

The basket was lowered again, empty.

"Good luck," the woman said and climbed in. "You're going to need it." She signaled the 'copter and the basket was lifted.

"Good riddance!" Brad said.

Another tentacle slid over the gunnel.

"George!" Brad called. "Go."

The boat gained speed. The tentacle slid off, and the gang followed their ring leader.

I watched the helicopter until it disappeared into the sky.

"Culley," I whispered. "I'm with you, baby. I'm with you." I turned to Brad. "I want to go to the hospital and stay with him."

"Of course, you can if you want to."

"What does *that* mean?" I asked.

Brad looked weary. "It means that you're our only diver, Tess. We were supposed to have Phil and Rámon as our SEAL team. You know how *that* worked out. I'm not sure we'll need a diver, but if we don't get these giants back to their community, it will all have been for naught." He squinted into the sky.

"Including Culley's sacrifice," I said.

"Including Culley's sacrifice."

"You always win, don't you?"

"When you do the right thing," he said, "you usually win."

I entered the bridge and sat down heavily. I felt numb. George was still at the helm. I stared out a window.

George cleared his throat. I glanced at him and saw tears in his eyes. "Are you, uh," he started, "are you waiting to hear from the hospital?"

I nodded. I realized that under the woolen clothes, I still wore my wet bathing suit. I needed a shower. I didn't care. I tried to imagine my life without Ryan, to prepare for it. I would still go for jogs with Ice. I would go to work at the Pacifica Lab and continue the work we had begun on this expedition....what about Champ? My stomach felt worse. My throat ached from tightness. I tried to wipe my mind clean.

Brad came to the door. "Throttle down, George. The giants are falling behind."

"Where are we going?" I asked Brad.

"The west side of Guam. Remember when the giants headed for Uruno Beach, after the encounter at the base?"

I nodded.

"That's where their artificial-den community is located, about a hundred feet down. It's where these bitches belong, too."

The day dragged on. It was late afternoon. I sat in the bridge, too numb to hold a conversation. I was surrounded by my friends, but within me, I was alone.

Finally, the radio came on. I jumped. George unhooked the mic.

"Hello?" someone said. "Is this the *Cousteau?* The ship with the scientists?"

"Give it to me, George." Brad took the mic. "This is Captain Bradford Bellows of R/V *Cousteau.* Over."

"Oh," the caller said. "This is Doctor Sam Kramer of the Pearl Harbor Naval Base Medical Center."

I stiffened and held my breath.

Brad glanced at me. "Is this about Ryan Culley of *Cousteau*? Over."

"Yes, it is."

I stood up, my hands pressed to my chest.

"How -- how is he?" Brad asked. "Over."

I squeezed my eyes shut as I listened.

"He came through the surgery. He's now in ICU."

I flopped back into the chair.

"Well," Brad said, "well, what's the prognosis, Doctor? Over."

Mini came quietly through the door holding a sandwich.

"His condition is critical," the doctor said. "He has two punctured lungs, but fortunately, his heart wasn't punctured. There are other complications, though. We'll know more in twenty-four hours. If he makes it through the first twenty-four, he'll stand a better chance."

"Thank you, Doctor," Brad said. "Please have someone keep us posted. His fiancée is on board. Over."

"Oh, I didn't know," Doctor Kramer said. "Is she *there*?"

"Affirmative," Brad said. "Over."

"Well, tell her there's hope. There's always hope, and we're doing our very best for him.... Oh, over."

"Thank you, Doctor," Brad said. "R/V *Cousteau,* out."

"Yes," Doctor Kramer replied. "The medical center here. Over and out here too."

Brad hung the mic on its holder. "You heard what he said, Tess. There's hope."

I nodded.

"Tess?" Mini extended the sandwich to me. "You really should eat something."

Brad squatted beside me and took my hands. "Tessica, as your boss, I order you to take a shower, get into some nice clothes, and pack a bag."

I looked at him.

"While I call for a Coast Guard helicopter to pick you up and take you to the Pearl Harbor Medical Center."

"What about a diver?" I asked.

"I called the naval base. They have a SEAL team, if we need them. What say you?"

"I -- I say yay."

*****

I showered, put on my green dress, tied my hair back with the blue scarf, and hooked on the shell necklace and earrings. I wore sandals instead of the white heels. I tried to put on makeup but my hand shook too much. I packed a small bag and went on deck to wait for the helicopter.

Mini smiled when she saw me. "He'll love the way you look."

"I hope."

Later that afternoon, the helicopter approached. The basket was lowered to the stern.

Brad hugged me. "Take care of yourself, too," he said. "And tell Ryan he'd better get his ass back here if he wants to get paid." He took my arms and held me away to look me up and down. "I'm jealous."

George hugged me. "Bring me back some candy bars?"

I nodded.

Mini helped me into the basket and handed me my bag. "Remember what I said, Tess. *Talk* to him. Tell him how much you love him. Tell him about your future together. And have a doctor look at the burns on your legs."

I nodded and she squeezed my hand.

As the basket lifted, I watched *Cousteau* shrink to a white dot in a sea of blue that seemed endless

CHAPTER TWENTY SIX

I left the taxi and hurried into the medical center.

I told the receptionist who I was there to see, and she called for a nurse. A heavyset staff nurse with a mop of red hair twisted into a bun, and turned-down lips, came to the desk and escorted me to ICU.

The room smelled of medicine. An unnatural hush hung like a silent eulogy. Pale sunlight filtered in but couldn't warm the white walls.

"How is he?" I asked as the nurse led me to a bed, shrouded by a white curtain.

"You'll have to ask Doctor that."

My mouth felt dry as she quietly pulled the curtain aside.

"Ryan?" I whispered and sat on the chair beside his bed. "Ryan?" He was so pale and still. His eyes were closed.

"You can stay for a half hour," the nurse told me, checked her watch, and closed the curtain around us.

Culley was surrounded by a maze of humming machines, tubes, IV bags.

"Ryan, I'm right here with you." I kissed his limp hand. "It's Tessie, hon."

There was no response.

I put my head in my hand. I had no tears left.

A doctor threw open the curtain. I jumped. He was short and muscular, with quick motions. The staff nurse was behind him.

""How is he?" I asked and stood up.

"It's too soon to tell." He scratched his beard.

"Are you Doctor Kramer?"

"Yes."

"I'm Tessica Hoffman, Ryan's fiancee."

"Oh." He shook my hand. "Nice to meet you. Will you wait in the hall, please. It'll be awhile."

I nodded. "Can I stay with him overnight, Doctor? I won't bother anybody."

He turned to the nurse. "Let her stay. It might do him some good."

The nurse's lips turned down even more.

I took my small bag and walked down the hall, looking for a bench. I passed rooms with old people who lay under white blankets. Some glanced at me as I walked by, without smiling. A man held the hand of a pale woman who lay in a bed with her eyes closed, her mouth slack.

I found a bench and sat down heavily. There was no joy here. Not even the usual amenities of a smile in passing.

I unzipped my bag with trembling hands and took out my Q-Tree. I started to cry and waited until I got a grip on myself. A nurse passed and I put my head down. Then I pushed the button for my parents' code.

"Hello, Tessie?" my mother said.

"Oh, Mom, hi. It's so good to hear your voice."

"What's wrong, Tess? You don't sound good. Are you *all right*?"

"I'm fine, mom. It's not me. I'm OK."

"What is it, Rachel?" I heard my father's voice call from the background.

"It's Tess," my mother told him. "Something's wrong...no, she's all right, David. Tessie, what's wrong then?"

"It's Ryan, Mom." I started to cry again.

"What happened?" my father asked. Then his voice grew clearer as he turned on his own Q-Tree. "Tessica, what's wrong, baby?"

"Oh, Dad, it's Ryan. He got hurt. He's in the hospital. I'm here with him now."

"How bad is it?" my father asked.

"It's bad, Dad. He has two punctured lungs."

"Two.... What *happened* to him?" he asked.

"He got hit by a giant octopus," I said.

There was a pause.

"Dad?"

"I'm here. Where were *you* when this happened?"

"I was in the boat," I lied.

"What does the doctor say?" Mom asked me.

"He -- " I tried to answer, but my throat choked up.

"Tessie?" Mom said. "Are you there? Turn on your camera. You're scaring us."

"OK." I turned on the camera and I saw their worried faces as they studied me. "The doctor says they'll know better after twenty-four hours. I'm so scared, Dad!"

"When did it happen, baby?" Dad asked.

"I don't know. Maybe...maybe, I guess early afternoon."

"David," Mom said to Dad, "I think we should fly out there and be with Tessica."

"No, Mom," I said. "I have to go back to the boat...either way. Mini and George, and Brad, they're all very supportive. H-How's Chris?"

"Chris is fine," Mom said.

"His hockey team took first place in the state tournament," Dad told me.

"We're very proud of him," Mom added.

"Give him my love," I said. "Tell him that I'm very proud of him, too. I wish I were home with you guys." I put a hand against my clenched stomach.

Doctor Kramer came into the hall and motioned for me to come back to ICU.

"I've got to go, Mom. Dad. The doctor's calling me."

"Take care of yourself," Mom said.

"And stay in touch, baby," Dad added.

"I will," I told them. "I love you. I love you all."

"We love you, too, baby," Dad said. I heard the catch in his voice.

"OK." I broke the contact as the staff nurse strode past me, staring straight ahead. I felt like putting out a foot and tripping her, but I didn't.

I looked at Doctor Kramer questioningly as I returned to Culley's bed.

"He's holding his own. For now. What hit him, anyway, a Mann truck?"

I shook my head. "A giant octopus."

"Well," he said, "that's got to be a first."

*****

I stayed the night with Culley, holding his hand, talking to him. I told him about our future together and all the good years we would have.

Once, his eyes flickered.

"Ryan!' I said. "Hon? It's me. It's Tess!"

But he was still.

A young Asian nurse brought me a tray of food. I thanked her and found that I was hungry, after all.

"I'll get you some salve for those burns on your legs," she told me.

"Thank you."

She returned with a tube of over-the-counter salve and applied it for me. "You have to take care of yourself, too," she said. "For his sake. "

I nodded. "I will."

I talked to Culley all that night, as though my energy would sustain his life. But the next morning, there was still no response from him.

A different doctor came by and examined Culley.

"What do you think, Doctor?" I asked.

"Well, he's making it through the first twenty-four. So far. I don't want to get your hopes up, but he's young and strong, and I think he's a fighter."

"Oh, he is!"

The doctor smiled. "Keep talking to him." He pulled the curtain around us and left.

Nurses came by throughout the day, taking his blood pressure and oxygen level, changing empty IV bags and giving him medication through the bags.

I fell asleep and was awakened by some kind of alarm. I heard running feet.

"Ryan?" I jumped up. "Ryan!"

The nurses ran to another bed. I heard a curtain being flung aside. Voices whispered urgently. The bed was rolled out. Someone said "surgical suite!"

I fell back into the chair. My heart pounded as I stared at Culley.

By late afternoon, I estimated that it had been more than twenty-four hours since the octopus hit him. I tried not to get my hopes up, but the mind takes its own paths and I thought about what I'd say to him when he woke up. I went through various scenarios to keep my mind busy.

That night I held his hand and slept on an extended recliner two nurses brought in for me. They gave me a thin white blanket.

I awoke when early light probed the curtain. I had dropped Culley's hand onto the bed. I held it now and looked at him.

His eyes were open and staring. "Ryan." Fear struck me like a blow. I jumped up. "Ryan!"

He blinked and looked at me.

"Oh, God. Oh my God. You're awake!" I forgot all my scenarios.

Two nurses ran to the bed and threw aside the curtain.

"He's awake," I told them. "He's awake!"

Culley smiled wanly and said something.

"I leaned close to him. What, hon? What did you say?"

"Your green dress."

"Yes, baby. I wore it for you." Tears slipped down my cheeks.

He lifted a hand weakly to my face. I leaned closer and he brushed the tears with a thumb. "You look great," he whispered hoarsely.

One of the machines began to beep.

"Is it the nightingale?" he said.

I laughed through tears. "No, baby, it's the rooster. It's morning, no matter what the clock says."

I called my parents with the good news and told them they'd get to meet Ryan when we came back to California.

Dad turned on his camera. "You see these white hairs?" He lifted a strand.

I laughed. "Which ones am I responsible for?"

"All of them!"

*****

In the days that followed, Ryan was able to sit up. The doctor wanted him in a wheelchair as soon as possible. They worried about pneumonia if he remained lying down. Each day he went for physical therapy, and each day I saw him gain strength. His color was better, too.

"You know," he said while we ate lunch one afternoon. "I was in a valley, Tess. A beautiful valley."

I stopped eating. "You mean while you were in a coma?"

He nodded. "There were thousands of us, all going in the same direction."

"Where to?"

"I don't know, but I wanted to go there. We all did."

"Was it a dream?"

"It was as real as the two of us sitting here."

"You're scaring me, Ryan. I'm glad you didn't go."

He scratched his cheek. He needed a shave. "You brought me back."

I drew in a breath. "I did? By talking to you?"

"Yeah. I didn't want to go back, but you called me."

"I...I kept talking to you. You *heard* me?"

He nodded. "A few of us turned back. Most went on. You know, I'm not afraid of dying anymore."

"Oh, that's just great! What about me?"

He smiled. "Maybe when we're ninety or so."

"OK. Remember that next time you decide to save mankind's collective ass instead of your own!"

*****

I strolled beside Culley in his wheelchair through the hospital grounds. The path was lined with tropical plants. The days were tropical warm.

We spent hours talking, and planning our lives together. We grew closer during that time than we'd ever been.

When Culley was able to stand and walk, he was discharged from the hospital, with specific orders not to even think about diving. The water pressure on his chest could open up the surgical incision and the inner stitches. They wanted him back for checkups.

I had washed my dress and now I wore it for our home-coming. I bought ten candy bars at the hospital gift shop before we left.

"For George?" Culley asked.

I nodded. "But don't tell Mini."

*****

We were air-lifted to *Cousteau* at the government's request, because of the importance of our work.

Culley was lowered first in the basket. I followed.

By the time I reached the deck, Mini, Brad, and George were gathered around Culley, who sat on a beach chair in the stern.

"Damn," Brad said with a broad smile, "now I have to pay you."

"Don't make me laugh," Culley said. "It only hurts when I laugh."

I dropped off my bag in the cabin and put the candy bars under George's pillow.

Brad was telling Culley what had happened since he'd been attacked. It wasn't much, really. *Cousteau* had led the juveniles, with the ring leader still in the cage, back to the community dens, at a hundred feet offshore on the west side of Guam.

"Hey," I said as I listened from behind them, "what am I, chopped liver?"

Brad turned. "Now that's a yummy dish," he told Culley.

"She's taken," Culley said, "dress and all."

Mini stood up and we hugged.

"I've been so damned worried about *both* of you," she whispered. "Welcome home." She kissed me on the cheek.

"Oh, Mini. It's so good to be home," I said.

George smiled at me. "Welcome home, Tessie."

"That goes for me, too," Brad said and reached out a hand. I took it and he squeezed.

"George, come here." I motioned him away from the group. "The Tooth Fairy left you a present under your pillow," I whispered as we walked toward the cabin. "But don't eat them all at once or you'll *need* the Tooth Fairy."

"Oh," he whispered back. "Oh, thank the Tooth Fairy for me!" He giggled as he went into the cabin.

I took George's chair and sat next to Culley. "Brad, he has strict orders from his physician not to dive."

"And not to laugh," Culley added.

Brad lifted his hands in a defensive gesture. "Far be it for me...."

George came out of the cabin chewing a candy bar.

"Where did you get *that*?" Mini asked and slid me a look.

"Oh." George hurried back into the cabin.

"Did the juveniles stay at the dens?" Culley asked.

"They're back with their moms," Mini said. "It looks like they're there to stay. I think the adults are teaching them some manners, and, you'll be glad to know, Tess, very possibly their language."

"That's incredible," I said. "How do you know it's language?"

"Government linguists are already working on deciphering the giants' patterns of flashes," Mini said.

"Syntax?" I asked.

"Well," Mini continued with a smile, "there's a German linguist, Conrad Hass. He's studying copies of the ROV tapes that George sends him. Hass believes he's detected the forty-five degree angle that indicates patterns of speech."

"It's Greek to me," Brad said.

"Then our work here is done?" Culley asked. He looked tired.

"Not exactly," Brad replied. "The government's asked us to continue studying the giants. They want to know if the juveniles remain in the den area, and how they interact with the adults. They've asked for as many tapes of the giants as George can provide with the ROV." He absently fingered his necklace. "The Navy is scouring the Pacific for other gangs of rogue juveniles."

"To bring them home?" I asked.

Mini nodded. "Finally, Tess, it's hands off the giants, unless they attack. There's a program being hatched to plant den communities on the east side of the Mariana Islands."

"To monitor for earthquakes?" I asked,

Mini nodded. "Like the Stromboli octopuses. It seems that the giants are faster at detecting undersea earthquakes than the ocean sensors. If it works, the government will plant dens all along the west coast of the U.S. too."

"That's great," I said. "That's a real accomplishment for all the work we've done."

Mini patted Culley's shoulder. "There's nothing more for you to do, Ryan. Just get your strength back. We'll do the rest." She leaned down. "Is there anything you desire, sire?"

Culley looked at me and grinned evilly. "Yeah, but the doctor said I can't have it just yet."

"How about a beer instead?" Brad asked.

"Beer sounds like a good second-best," Culley told him.

"Your wish is my command." Mini went into the cabin.

"I'm right up there," I told Brad. "One step above a cold beer."

"George!" I heard Mini call, "what the hell are you eating? What are all these candy wrappers on the floor?"

"Uh, oh," I said and moved my beach chair closer to Culley for protection. I realized, from all the aches I felt, just how exhausting these last few weeks had really been, both physically and emotionally.

Brad stood up. "Minerva's on the war path. Think I'll retreat to the helm. Take care of your guy, Tess."

"What do you *think* I've been doing?"

Mini passed Brad with Culley's beer and a handful of candy wrappers. She strode to the stern. "Tessica!"

"I know. I know," I said.

She stuffed the wrappers into her pocket and opened the beer for Culley. "George is going to end up with diabetes."

"Not with you watching over him," Culley said and sipped the beer. "Man, that's good. Glad you've got nothing against beer."

"Would *you* be in trouble." Mini stared out to sea. "There's a ship approaching."

I scanned the water. "You mean that bump on the horizon?"

"It's been growing," Mini said.

Culley lifted himself to see it. "Mini, would you ask Brad if she's contacted us."

"You don't think they're pirates?" I said.

"Not this close to shore," Culley answered. "But they're headed our way."

Mini went to the bridge. I heard her talk to Brad. She called back. "No. No radio contact."

143

Culley got up and walked gingerly to the bridge. I walked beside him, ready to grab his arm if he stumbled. He studied the distant ship through binoculars. "She's flying the red, white, and blue ensign from her flagstaff," he informed us. "She's flying a private signal from the bow staff. I can't make it out yet." He sat down and continued to study the boat. "There's six boats. "Oh, shit," he finally said.

"What? Pirates?" I asked.

"Worse." He lowered the binoculars. "Their private signal is two hands. The name of the flagship is *Hands of God's Vengeance*.

"You mean the looney tunes from the televangelist show?" Brad asked.

"The same." Culley put down the binoculars. "The flagship's a yacht, about forty feet. There's five boats with her.

As the flagship came closer, I saw the hands from Michelangelo's *Creation of Adam* painted in broad strokes on her gunnel.

"These guys are worse than pirates," George said from the bridge door. "They don't want your money." He made his way to a chair and plopped down. "They want your souls." He put a hand to his stomach. "I don't feel so good."

"Why don't you have another candy bar, George?" Mini said.

"There aren't anymore."

"Jesus Christ!" Mini threw me a look.

I shrugged innocently.

Minerva," Brad said, "suppose you bring our weapons on deck."

"It can't hurt." Mini got up and went out on deck.

"It's just a precaution, Tess," Culley told me. "There's no law out here."

"OK," I said. "Just remember to stay out of that valley."

"What valley?" Brad said.

"I'll tell you about it sometime," Culley said.

Brad took over the helm and unhooked the radio mic. "*Hands of God's Vengeance*, this is R/V *Cousteau*. Over." There was no response. Brad repeated the message. There was still no response. "I'm going on deck." He put on his captain's hat. "George." He gestured toward the wheel as he left the bridge.

"Oh, creepers." George got up and held his stomach as he went to the helm.

"I'd ask Tessica," Brad told George, "but she looks worn out. You, on the other hand, are sick through your own gluttony. Be ready," Brad called back to George, "With an order from me for full speed."

George nodded and belched.

Culley and I got up and followed Brad.

"OK," Brad said with a sigh, "let's see what these looney mothers want from us."

Mini came back with the weapons and laid them on the deck near Brad.

"Oh, no," I said when I saw two men on *Vengeance* standing in the bow. The other five boats were strung out behind her.

One man was dressed in a suit and tie. His wavy hair was pure white, as though dyed. His features seemed to be sculpted out of rock, with a broad slit for a mouth. He was tall and arrow straight. The other man was the televangelist from the TV show who preached death to scientists, and the end of the world. He wore his crimson robe and his fiery expression. His hair and beard were long and jet black.

"This is the captain of R/V *Cousteau*," Brad called from the gunnel. "State your business with us, *Vengeance*."

The man in the suit saluted our flag, the national ensign, then saluted Brad. "I request permission to come aboard, Captain," he called, "to visit a fellow seafarer."

"Well at least he knows protocol," Brad said.

A young woman carried a boy, perhaps two years old, dressed in a tie and a suit over his diapers, onto the deck. The five other yachts stayed behind their flagship.

"What do you guys think?" Brad said.

Culley studied the other boats. "I don't think we have a choice."

"Do you intend to bring the boy?" Brad called.

"Affirmative," the man answered.

"What the fuck, let's go for it," Brad said. "As Culley says, 'we don't really have any choice in the matter, now do we?' Permission granted," he called.

Two crewmen, dressed as choir boys, lowered a small dinghy with the white-haired man, the boy, and the televangelist on board. The televangelist guided the small craft to *Cousteau's* side.

We lowered the ladder and gathered around it, except for Culley, who hung back, the rocket launcher and rifles at his feet. The launcher was loaded again with a rocket.

The televangelist tied the dinghy to the ladder while the suited man was careful to climb up with the child in his arms. Brad reached down and lifted the boy onto the deck. The two men came aboard.

The suited man carried an attaché case. I saw him flick a glance at Culley, who watched them with a stony look.

The boy was a cute little guy with dark hair and eyes, and round cheeks. I thought of Champ.

"Minister Jonas Gantry," the suited man said, and shook hands with Brad. Jonas' deep voice held an air of dignity. "This is my brother, Elmer, and my son, Elmo."

Mini had been right, I realized. Elmer *did* wear eye liner.

"Captain Bradford Bellows." Brad introduced Mini and me and gestured toward Culley. "Ryan Culley, my first mate."

Jonas nodded at him. Culley didn't return the gesture. He was playing the hardass. I lowered my head and smiled. *Good cop, bad cop,* I thought, with Brad as good cop. I think Elmo was intimidated by Culley. He pressed against Jonas and Jonas put a protective arm across the boy's chest.

"Why didn't you answer my radio message?" Brad asked Jonas.

Jonas spread his hands. "Unfortunately, our radio no longer works."

Brad glanced down at Elmo. "Do you have any idea how important a radio is out here?"

"We know. God knows we know. With a little help from the Lord." He crossed himself. "And a little good business, He will provide a radio."

"So to what do we owe this honor?" Brad asked.

"Well, you see, Captain Bellows, we're a sea-going ministry." Jonas gestured toward the stern, with its beach chairs and a small table. "May we?"

Brad nodded. We all went there and sat down, except for Culley. Jonas lifted Elmo onto his lap, unzipped his attaché case on the table and opened it up. There were samples of wedding invitations, marriage certificates, photos of bridal bouquets and veils, gold wedding bands, and sketches of garlands of flowers, some for weddings, others for funerals.

"I am certified to give Sunday mass," Jonas explained, "and hear confessions and give absolution. I'm authorized by the entire state of California to officiate over weddings, civil and religious denominations, including gay and lesbian same-sex marriages." He flicked a glance at Mini. "And interracial marriages." He turned toward Culley, who remained standing over the weapons. "And to hear the sins and give absolution to Wicca and pagan churches."

"But are you an *ordained* minister," Mini asked.

"Oh, most certainly, madam. I received my ordination credential package on line from the Church of Happily Ever After. I carry my ordination certificate, which I can print out for a nominal fee. Elmo here speaks in tongues. Elmo? Speak."

"The child began to babble."

I didn't understand any of his tongues.

"That's enough, Elmo." Jonas smiled and patted Elmo's shoulder.

Elmo looked up. "Pop?"

Oh, how cute, I thought. *He calls his father pop.*

Jonas reached into an inner pocket, took out a lollipop, unwrapped it, and handed it to Elmo. "Just lick it. Don't chew it."

Elmo nodded and licked.

Jonas cleared his throat. "If it's a fire and brimstone sermon you desire, Elmer here can provide that. Elmer?"

Elmer stood up. "Prepare for eternity!" his deep voice boomed. I jumped. "For it is at hand, my brethren, and be you not ready, you will spend eternity in the fires of hell! And those most evil of all men, the scientists who interfere with God's vengeful minions, the Krakens, will burn in -- "

"That's enough, Elmer!" Jonas quickly put a hand on Elmer's arm. "Sit." Elmer sat down.

"Jonas," I said, "isn't your Vengeance of God's Hands Church implicated in the death of two geneticists at an Arkansas university?"

"Madam." Jonas stiffened. "We were wrongly accused, and exonerated of all guilt in the matter. The murderer was a Russian hit man, a lost soul who was paid to kill the two scientists. He escaped by taking a plane back to Russia."

"Who paid him?" Mini asked.

"The wives of the murdered men, as it turns out. They discovered that their husbands were...excuse me, ladies," he lowered his voice, "were visiting prostitutes, and the two women conspired to have their husbands killed for their life insurance policies."

"What are all those other boats doing with you?" Brad asked.

"Oh. Those are our apostles and part of our sea-going ministry," Jonas said smugly. "That one there," he pointed to a boat, "is *Sister Crown of Thorns*. Sister carries a nice selection of wooden crowns, complete with real thorns." He looked at us expectantly.

We remained silent.

"Well, the boat to her port side is *Brother Sandals and Robes*. His sandals come in all sizes, for men and women, and including children." He lifted Elmo's leg. The boy wore tan sandals with colorful golden crosses.

A breeze came up and swept my hair in front of my face. I brushed it back and realized that Jonas' thick white hair remained in place.

"Beside him is *Father Crucifixes for Christians,*" Jonas continued. "Father carries a very nice line of inexpensive life-size crucifixes, and deluxe real-wooden crosses. His life-size Jesuses fit perfectly on the crosses, and are made from plaster of Paris. They're a bit pricey." He smiled and ran a hand through his stiff hair. "The largest boat, there in the back, is *Mother's freight and Faith.* She carries most of our inventory.

"And that last boat?" Mini asked.

"Ah, *The Sons of Water Into Wine.* Yes. They stock a very nice selection of red wine, and award-winning zinfandels and champagne from California, and an excellent variety from French vineyards."

Brad fingered his necklace. "What say you," he asked Mini and me, "to a case of assorted zinfandel, some full-bodied red wine, and award-winning champagnes? On the Pacifica Lab's tab."

Mini shrugged. "Well, then, why not?"

"Do you do assorted?" Brad asked Jonas.

"Oh, most certainly. We do custom orders at no extra cost."

"Do you carry beer?" I asked.

"Yes, Madam. And assorted candies."

"No!" Mini said, and glanced toward the bridge. "No candies!"

Jonas sat back. "As you *wish,* madam."

Brad gave Jonas his Pacifica card. Jonas flashed it with a device he took from his inner pocket, and handed the card back to Brad. He pulled out a Q-Tree and contacted *Water to Wine.*

"You do a good business?" Brad asked while *Water to Wine* launched a dinghy and headed for *Cousteau.*

"We manage to make ends meet." Jonas said. "Of course Sunday mass is a big-money day, but weddings are what keeps the ministry afloat. Wedding guests are always in a giving mood." He crossed himself. "Lord be praised."

Elmer and Elmo also crossed themselves.

The dingy arrived. The young boy aboard struggled to hand up a closed case. Brad and Jonas leaned over the ladder and hefted it on board. The boy thanked Brad and left.

Jonas extended his hand to Brad. "Thank you for doing business with us, Captain. Enjoy your wines." He grinned broadly and shook Mini's hand, then mine. "If you ever need our services again, contact us on your Q-Tree instead of the radio." He glanced at Culley and cleared his throat.

The three boarded their dinghy and headed back to the flagship.

People waved from the other boats as they passed and we waved back.

A juvenile female giant, with a male on her head, followed the last boat.

"Mini!" I shouted and grabbed her arm.

"I see her!"

"Hey!" I waved my arms at the boat. "*Hey,* there's a giant following you! Brad," I called. He was on the bridge. "Tell them there's a giant on their tail."

Brad came on deck. "I already *did.* They said it's a pet! They feed her, and the male on her head, and the two juveniles play with them in the water and the female protects them from predators." Brad shrugged broadly.

I looked at Mini, who was staring after the boats. "Go figure," she said.

CHAPTER TWENTY SEVEN

We set a course for Northern California. Mini, George, and I spent a lot of time in the small lab, studying our samples and communicating with scientists all over the world.

Mini was in contact with the sea-going Hands of God's Vengeance revival show to get details on their two juvenile pets. It seemed that the giant, accompanied by her tiny dark male, had been swept out to sea by the tsunami. She was cut and battered from scraping against coral, and was probably starving. The revival people fished for her and fed her. A paramedical on board one of the boats even treated her wounds. They had lowered a portable dive platform underwater where she could rest while the boats were underway.

"She's intelligent enough," Mini said, "to know they were helping her." She twisted a lock of hair. "Of course there have been many reports of a rapport between dolphins and humans, and even in rare cases, killer whales and humans."

"You know, I've heard old whaling-boat stories of orcas," George said. "They used to lead the boats to whales, and then the whalers rewarded them with the whales' tongues."

"Nice!" I said.

"It was a long time ago," Culley said.

"I heard a story," I told them, "where a husband and wife scientific team swam with the same pod of orcas every day in a harbor. One day, the husband, diving alone, died tragically. The wife knew it because the killer whales were very upset."

"I've met them on dives," Culley said. "They were curious about me. On one dive, a young male circled me, and then he swam away. He came back with the matriarch."

"What did she do?" I asked.

"She looked me over, probably told the kid it was just another scrawny human, and they both swam away." He chuckled. "I guess I wasn't worth their time."

"That's OK, hon," I said. "You're worth my time."

*****

One evening, as we approached Pearl Harbor to refuel, take on provisions, and have Culley go the medical center for his post-operative checkup, Mini got a call from Airman Elijah Jones. He was due for shore leave the next day and he was wondering if Mini might join him for a week.

"What say you, Captain?" Mini asked Brad with a broad smile.

"I say that if I say nay, my life will be pure hell."

I was glad for Mini, and the rest of us. It was a much-needed vacation for the whole crew.

Culley and I decided to take a plane back to the Anderson Air Force Base

148

on Guam and visit Champ. George and Brad wanted to take in the sights and check out the restaurants.

Culley and I stopped to buy Champ a toy model of a white giant with a charcoal male glued to her head.

"Aren't you the two divers who discovered the Krakens?" the salesman said."

"Well, we helped," I told him.

"We're the two divers," Culley said. "Don't be so modest, Tess."

The salesman grinned broadly. He put the toy giant in a bag, and extended it to me. "I want you to have it, Miss Hoffman, free of charge. Wait till I tell my girlfriend I met you two!"

"Thanks," I said.

"Maybe we'll get the same results in a restaurant," Culley said as we left the store.

"Sure, hon," I said sarcastically, "and maybe free dentistry, too."

Gloria was on duty at daycare on the base. "He'll be happy to see you," she said, and led us to Champ's crib. He was asleep.

"How's he doing?" Culley whispered.

"Better than we expected," Gloria told him. "It's pretty amazing how resilient these kids are."

"It comes with being a dominant species," I told her.

Gloria looked at me blankly and Culley chuckled. I realized I wasn't talking to a scientist.

"Just kidding," I said. "I'm really glad he's doing so well." I glanced at Culley. "When do you think," I asked Gloria, "he'll be ready to be adopted?"

"A month, maybe two at the most. We like to get them into secure, loving homes as soon as possible."

Culley slid me a look. "A boy for me?"

Gloria glanced from me to Culley. "Well, she said briskly, "I've got some paperwork to do." She went to her desk.

I stared at Champ and held the rim of the crib. "What say you?" I whispered to Culley.

"I say with your work and mine, we'd be raising him on a boat."

I nodded. "I could home-school him."

"Tess, are you *sure* this is what you want? You understand that your life's changed forever when you have a kid?"

"Well, I helped raise my brother Chris. That's my only credential."

Culley smiled. "He is a cute little rug rat, but you know he might have problems."

"Hon, don't say yes unless you're very certain that this is what you want too. If you don't feel right about adopting him, I'll understand."

Champ woke up and rolled onto his back. He smiled when he saw me and reached out his little arms.

"Champie." I picked him up and showed him the toy octopus. "Look what we brought you."

He took the toy and turned it around. Then he tried to chew off the male glued on the female's head. Champ's bottom was wet. "Uh, oh." I grinned at Culley.

"This time you change him, Mom. You better get used to it."

"Oh, Ryan! Is that a yay?"

He smirked.

I felt a welling of love for Culley. I hugged him with one arm. "Did I ever tell you how much I love you? You're my world."

Gloria came back with a big smile on her pretty, young face. "I did the paperwork." She laughed. "It's the adoption application. You two will have to be married, though, before we can let you adopt him."

Culley looked from me to Gloria. "Did you two broads cook this up before we came here?"

"*Culley,*" I said, embarrassed for him.

Gloria laughed. "I live on a mostly male base. I've been called worse."

We were allowed to take Champ with us for the afternoon, to a carnival. His round, little eyes grew wide at the colorful rides, the raucous music, the ice cream cone Culley bought for him, He dropped it and cried as he tried to reach down and pick it up.

"OK, Dad," I said, "dig into those deep pockets and buy your son another cone."

He did.

The tantalizing aromas of sweet candies and hot popcorn emanated from booths. The ground beneath our shoes was sticky with smears of food.

Culley had to sit down. The next day he was due for his checkup. He couldn't hold Champ against his chest. The incision was still too sensitive. But he had his backpack with the holes in it and I wore it.

I looked at families strolling with their children and I felt a sense of peace. Perhaps this was what our lives would be like from now on. A family, and relatives, and friends.

It wasn't to be.

That afternoon we returned a very tired Champ to daycare and Gloria's kind hands. We had signed the application forms and Gloria assured us that if we married, he would be ours. She promised to stay in touch about his condition and let us know when we could pick him up for good, as our son.

They had to do a background check on both me and Culley. I felt a bit apprehensive on what would find out about Culley's checkered past. Stealing a car at sixteen couldn't be all that bad. That was the same year he'd found his mother dead in her car.

We flew back to Pearl Harbor.

Mini and Jones met us at the airport and invited us for dinner at the rented cottage they shared for the week. Mini didn't look too happy.

That afternoon, the six of us gathered in the small, neat cottage. Mini was unusually quiet. Jones was his usual ebullient self.

Brad and George told us about their adventures in sight-seeing and eating at various ethnic restaurants.

"Did you find a French restaurant?" I asked Brad.

"We did," he said, "but it was no Armand's, I can tell you."

"It was good," George said.

Brad looked up at the ceiling. "And that, ladies and gentlemen, is coming from a chocolate gourmet."

I waited until after we had eaten the chicken dinner Mini and Jones had prepared for us. I smiled secretly at Culley.

He nodded.

"Well, guys," I started, and let out a breath, "I've got some good news to tell you."

They all grew silent. "Firstly," I said, and took Culley's hand, "Ryan and I have decided to tie the knot." I kissed his hand.

Mini put her fingers to her lips. I saw tears start in her slanted, black eyes. "Oh, Tess." She got up and hugged me. "Congratulations! Do I get to hug Culley too?"

"Very gently, Mini," I said seriously.

She hugged him and planted a kiss on his cheek.

"Hey, that's extra," I said.

"Halleluiah!" Jones clapped his hands. He stood up and danced around the room. "Halleluiah. Praise God! There's going be a wedding."

Mini lowered her head.

"Congratulations," Brad said. "Though I'm not surprised." He shook Culley's hand delicately. "You're getting a handful, my man. You'd better keep a whip handy for when she growls."

"Thanks, a lot Brad," I said. "Always good to get a recommendation from my boss. I hope I never need another job!"

"Congrats, Tess, Ryan," George looked subdued.

"Thanks, George," I said. "Well, that's just *half* the good news."

"You won the lottery," Brad said.

"Better," I told him. "We're going to adopt Champ."

Brad got up. "That *does* call for a celebration." He opened the bottle of champagne that he had brought with him and poured it into water glasses.

"Ryan," Mini said, "would you prefer a beer? I have beer in the refrig."

"When I turn down a cold beer," Culley said, "you'll know I'm dead."

"Don't even kid about that, hon," I said.

Mini got the beer and opened it for Culley.

"A toast," Brad said and raised his glass. We all raised our glasses, except for Culley, who raised his beer can.

"To a long and productive life," Brad said. "Live long and prosper." He drank.

Where had I heard that before? I couldn't remember.

The champagne wasn't all that good. I think Brad overpaid for it.

Later that evening, while Culley, Brad, Jones, and George watched a football game, Mini and I went for a stroll in the cool evening air.

"So, how goes it with Jones?" I asked.

She sat down on a carved, stone bench. We were surrounded with bushes and trees. "He's, well, not exactly what I expected."

"Oh?" I sat next to her. "In what way?"

"He's really into the God thing, you know?"

"The God thing? Like how?"

"Like he's a creationist."

"Oh. Does that stand between you two?"

She shrugged. "The only time it doesn't is when we're in bed."

I waited.

"There's more to a relationship than good sex, isn't there?' Mini asked.

"Absolutely, if it's going to be long-lasting."

"I don't think it will be."

"I'm sorry, Mini."

"You know, I told him that we have nothing in common to talk about."

"What did he say?"

"He said so what?" She spread a hand. "He said God loves us both. What is there to talk about?"

"Uh, oh."

She snapped a leaf off a bush and studied it. "He has no curiosity about the world, Tess, or the whole universe! He knows *nothing* about science."

"Mini, did you expect him to? He's an airman. He has different skills."

"I know. Like Culley. But Culley's smart, and curious about the world. He doesn't walk around with blinders over his eyes, like a horse!" She crumbled the leaf, "You know, George is so much more intelligent and interesting than Jones."

I felt shocked. "George? Well, I can understand that. George is a brilliant, intuitive scientist."

"Yes!" She flipped the leaf away and stood up. "I've never told him that."

I was at a loss. "You...you two have always been very good friends."

"I realize *now* it's been more than that."

I stood up slowly. "You and George?"

"Why not?"

I stared at her. "Oh. No reason. No reason. What are you going to do?"

"I intend to pack my bag and catch a ride with you guys back to the boat. We can leave tomorrow for the mainland and home, if you like."

"With George?" I said dumbly.

"Of course, Tess. With George."

"Oh, sure. When are you going to tell Jones?"

"Half time! He won't even talk before half time." She strode back to the cottage, slammed open the white picket fence with the flowered arbor, went up the pink rock path, and threw open the blue door with the painted clouds and cherubs."

I sat down again. I yanked a leaf off a bush, crushed it and breathed in its bitter aroma.

I heard yelling from the cottage's open window. George came flying out, followed by Brad.

"Dammit, Culley!" I whispered. "Where the hell are you?"

He walked nonchalantly through the doorway, still holding a beer. Mini came out last, her bag in hand, and strode down the path.

"Fallen woman!" Jones yelled from the open door.

"Screw you!" Mini answered.

"Whore!" Jones slammed the door.

As Culley approached, I smiled brightly. "Must be half-time," I said.

"How'd you know?"

"Just intuition."

Culley looked back at the cottage. "I wanted to see the rest of that game."

*****

Culley's post-surgery checkup went well. The doctor told him he had the constitution of a bull elephant.

"A bull elephant in must," I told the doctor

The doctor blushed. I was sorry I said it.
Culley winked at me.
*****

We were on board *Cousteau*, having breakfast together. Brad was sautéing a shrimp in white-wine dish, with home-made biscuits. George was close to drooling as he waited.

Mini came into the cabin tying a green scarf in her hair. She sat next to George. "Good morning," she said and smiled at him.

George took his gaze off the frying pan and slid her a look. "Good morning. Did I do something right?"

She nodded. "You usually do, Georgie."

"Georgie?" he asked.

Culley lowered his head. I saw him smile. I had told him what Mini said the evening before.

Mini put her arm around George's shoulders.

He stiffened. "To what do I owe this pleasure?"

"Call it an epiphany," Mini said. "A realization of the brilliance of your mind and the sparkling quality of your conversation." She gestured toward the wine in Brad's hand. "More sparkling than champagne."

"Champagne?" Brad turned the bottle, read the label and shook his head. "White wine."

George sat with Mini's arm still draped around his narrow shoulders. "Now I *know* I did something wrong. He straightened. "Oh, you! You discovered my cache of candy bars, *didn't you?* Oh! Don't tell me you threw them overboard." He took her arm from off his shoulders. "You *did,* didn't you?"

"Georgie, what say we go to the lab for some privacy. There's things I want to talk to you about."

George breathed in the aroma of the frying shrimps and wine and closed his eyes as Brad added more wine. "Right now?" he asked Mini in a squeaky voice.

"OK, sweetie." Mini tickled him under his chin, "it can wait until after breakfast."

George looked around suspiciously.

"Go with the flow," I told him. "She *means it*. Georgie." I nodded for emphasis.
*****

Brad set a course for Northern California and home. Mini, George and I had enough data to keep us busy for a long time. Culley and I planned our wedding, with our friends and families. The future looked bright. Until I got the call from Gloria.

"Hello, Tess?" she said.

"Yes, this is Tess."

"It's Gloria."

"Oh, hi, Gloria. How are you?"

"I'm OK," she said. "Just a bit overworked."

Her voice sounded strained.

"I'm sorry. How's Champ?"

"Oh, he's fine."

"Is something wrong? You sound worried."

"I don't know how to tell you this."

"Tell me *what?*" I felt a sudden premonition that scared me.

"Well, it seems that Champ has an aunt, his mother's sister."

"Oh?"

"She was in the hospital after the tsunami hit and she had no idea that Champ had survived."

"Gloria, you said that we could adopt him. It was just a matter of *time*."

"I know. Maybe I shouldn't have spoken so soon. We had no idea that his aunt survived. Her house was in ruins and Champ's grandmother died there. They took away the bodies so fast, and we didn't know Champ's last name. I'm so sorry, Tess, but for Champ's sake, and by law, he has to go to his aunt. His real name is John. They call him Johnny."

"John," I said numbly. I think it was hearing his real name that made me realize the bond was broken.

"OK. Well, thanks for calling."

"His aunt really wants him, Tess. We think she'll give him a good home, with his own people."

"OK." I broke the connection and went to Culley, who was resting in his bunk.

When he saw my expression, he sat up. "What's wrong, Tess?"

I told him about the conversation. "We can't *have* him," I said.

"Oh, baby." He embraced me. "I'm sorry. I'm really sorry."

"They said it was best for him. His real name is John. Our little Champie."

"That's not his name, kid. And we're not his people. He's already used to living on Guam. It's best for him." Culley hugged me.

"OK," was all I could manage.

*****

In the days that followed, as we headed home, I felt bereaved.

"Do you still want to marry me?" I asked Culley while we were alone in the cabin.

Culley was lying down in his bunk again. He looked stronger these days, but he still got tired fast. "Cut it out, Tess."

"Well, I don't feel like a complete woman anymore."

"Come here." He sat up.

I walked over and sat beside him.

"Would I marry a woman who wasn't complete? Let's see. You've got a head, ears, shoulders, arms."

I laughed and gently pushed him away.

"Ah, I was just getting to the good parts." He took my head in both his hands. "You're my lady, and if you ever forget that, it's the whip...the whip."

We kissed.

"We'll have children," he said. "Remember? Designer kids? A boy for me and a girl for you."

"OK, hon. It's probably better for Champ...Johnny, to be with his own relatives."

"It's really where the kid belongs."

George came into the cabin. "Did you hear?"

"No, what?" I said.

We were still sitting on Culley's bunk.

"Am I, uh, interrupting anything?"

"For God's sake, George, what *happened?*" I asked.

"There's illegal fishermen catching giants."

Culley and I looked at each other.

"Where?" Culley asked.

"Over the dens. There's an Asian market. They've even got a brand name: Steak of the Sea. They say it tastes better than lobster and you can order it in any Asian restaurant. They slice the meat into steaks. And not only that...."

"What?" Culley said.

"There's a black market in the traditional Asian medicine shops for the suckers, the siphons, and even the eggs. The buyers think they hold curative powers."

"How long has *this* been going on?" I asked and stood up.

"And where the hell is the Coast Guard?" Culley said.

"Well, the trawlers keep track of the Coast Guard," George told us, "and they go in to fish when the Coast Guard's not around. Mostly at night. With no lights, you know?"

Brad came into the cabin, followed by Mini.

"Did you hear?" Mini said.

I nodded. "George just told us."

Brad sat at the table. "The government's decided to lay down dens around uncharted atolls. They're hoping it will at least slow down the traffickers."

"What if the government used public service announcements," I said, "and explained to the people that there *are* no curative powers in any part of a giant's body. No more than in any other octopus species. It's just not true!"

"Tell that to the nut cases who pay thousands of dollars for bear bile and rhino horns," Culley said.

"I've visited an Asian country," Brad told us, "where you can buy a snake to boil down and drink like tea. If you have a stroke, don't drink the liquefied powder they give you. It could be dried cockroaches." He looked up. "So why not giants? I'm wiped out. Could somebody get me a cup of coffee?"

"Sure, boss." I poured it and set it in front of him.

Culley came to the table. "The question is, what can we do about it?"

Mini sat next to George and he smiled and leaned against her. "These giants are incredibly smart as animals go," she said. "If only we could communicate the danger of bait and hooks to them. The ones that get hooked are brought up and don't get a chance to communicate to their buddies."

"But how could we do it?" I asked.

"You know," George said, "there was a case of an African elephant whose baby was killed by a tribesman. The elephant mom went into the village, took a human baby right out of his mother's arms with her trunk and laid him on the ground."

"And?" Culley said.

George sighed. "Then she killed the baby's mother."

"The giants," Mini said, "have proven to be more tolerant than that. They're more like dolphins. Those guys have saved drowning people by getting underneath the person, lifting him, and giving him a ride to shore."

"And look at how we repay them," I said, thinking of the slaughtering of dolphins that still went on."

"Well," George said, "well, the dolphin and human genome are basically the same. But mollusks?"

"The camera eye of humans and octopuses are similar," Mini said, "but it's just a case of convergent evolution. The thing is, octopuses have complex, 'clever' brains. We really don't know what these giants are capable of learning, or feeling, or *doing*, for that matter." She twisted a lock of hair. "If we could somehow show them the danger of a fishing line, and bait, and the hook, they might be able to communicate it to their fellow giants."

"I hope they don't go extinct," I said, "before we manage to communicate that bit of info."

"I'm afraid the work will be for others to take up." Brad sipped his coffee. "We've been called back to Pacifica Lab. Sea Worthy needs *Cousteau* for other scientific expeditions. Our work here is finished, boys and girls." He looked around. "I, for one, am glad it's over. The director couldn't ask for more than we've given her, and I'm anxious to get back." He closed his eyes.

"Is everything OK, boss?" I asked.

"Oh, I got a call from Harley this morning." He blinked back tears.

"Do you want to talk about it?" I said.

"There's nothing to talk about. He wants to break up."

We were silent.

"Did he say why?" Mini finally asked.

"He said I'm gone too much of the time. He's tired of being alone, and anyway...." He wiped his eyes on his shirt. "He met someone."

"Do you think," I said, "there's a chance for the two of you if we get back soon?"

Brad fluttered a hand. "Maybe. I don't know. We had planned to have a celebration dinner at Armand's when I got back. George, do you have a candy bar you can spare?"

"I'll see what I've got left." George opened his drawer and rummaged through it. He pulled out a candy bar and came back to the table. "You like Three Musketeers?"

"I'm sure I would," Brad said. "and I'll probably like the candy bar too." He took it from George's hand and unwrapped it. "Thanks, Georgie." He studied the bar, sighed, then took a bite. "Ah," he said as he chewed, "not as black and sweet as Harley."

"Is Harley black?" Mini asked.

"Black and sweet as a Hershey bar," Brad told her.

She patted Brad's arm. "We'll all keep our fingers crossed for you, boss."

"Thank you, Minerva. You four have found each other, while I...I spend *my* nights alone."

It was hard to hear Brad talk that way, instead of his usual, bantering style. I felt tears in my own eyes. I got up, went to him, and kissed him on his cheek. "We all love you, boss."

"I appreciate that, Tessica. But I need a *real* lover."

"Brad," I said, "you once told me there are more fish in the ocean."

"But who likes fish?" he said.

"We're on our way home," Culley told him. "Maybe things will work out."

Mini sat down and smiled at George. "What did Georgie say, 'Home is where, when you have to go there, they *have* to take you in'."

"Well." Brad sighed. "Maybe not. it's more like you can't go home again."

CHAPTER TWENTY EIGHT

The day dawned clear, the sea was calm. Waves slapped the boat's sides as we headed north by northeast, toward Northern California. I sat in the bow and thought about Ice. I realized just how much I missed him, and how much I wanted to see his fuzzy, adorable face. "I'm coming, Ice," I whispered. There was an ache in my heart for champ, but, as Culley had said, time would heal it. Well, I had no choice in the matter.

"You're looking good," I said to George as he walked to the bow. He had lost some weight. "Are you off the candy kick?"

"You know, I am. I didn't realize it, but I am! I don't crave chocolate anymore."

"Compliments of Mini?"

"Yes, I guess so." He sat down with a dreamy look and brushed his hair back over his head. "She's wonderful, Tess." He chuckled evilly. "Jones doesn't know what he lost."

"She sure is wonderful." I smiled. "His loss is your gain. You look happy, George."

"I don't believe I've ever been happier in my life. I walk around in a daze."

"I know the feeling," I said, but I wanted to laugh. George *always* walked around in a daze.

We were passing two uncharted atolls in the distance, northeast of the Hawaiian Islands, about halfway home to California. The atoll to the west was larger, and looked green. The one east of it appeared to be almost flat.

I squinted, my hands over my eyes, at a bump in the narrow passage between the atolls. "Is that a ship?"

"Where?"

"Between the atolls. Culley!" I looked up at the bridge windows. He was at the wheel. "Is that a ship?" I pointed to the atolls.

He lifted the binoculars to his eyes. "Sure is," he said. "A trawler."

"What's a trawler doing on a coral reef?" I asked.

"Good question," he said. "Hey, boss."

Brad was also on the bridge. He stood up and studied the ship through binoculars. "It's a fishing trawler."

"I'm going to get Mini." George went to the lab.

"Mini," I said as she walked to the bow, "do you think the Coast Guard might have planted dens there?"

She grasped the rail and studied the atolls. "It's a prime area for them. There are plenty of fish on coral reefs for the giants, and sharks come in to feed. You wouldn't think humans would bother them in the middle of nowhere. You see that narrow passage between the atolls, where the trawler seems to be cruising?"

"Yes," I said.

"Great place to lay eggs and have them aerated by the rip tides between the atolls." She looked up at the bridge. "Boss, don't you think we should check this out?"

"I'd rather just call it in to the Coast Guard," Brad said. "We don't know what we're up against with the trawler. Suppose it's an illegal boat with some heavy artillery? We've been there before, you know, with the pirates."

Mini, George, and I went to the bridge.

"The Coast Guard's too far away to get here in time," I told Brad, "if they're harvesting giants,"

"It's our duty to get their ID and call it in to the Coast Guard," Mini added, "in case the trawler decides to leave."

"What do you think, Ryan," Brad asked.

"It couldn't hurt to have a look. We can always outrun a damn fishing boat."

"All right," Brad said, "but just a look. We're not equipped to deal with illegal fishing boats, if that's what she is."

Culley turned *Cousteau* toward the atolls.

Brad put on his captain's hat.

"Should I get the weapons?" I asked.

"Why not?" Brad said. "Let's all get paranoid together."

Mini threw an arm around George and he leaned against her. His eyes came up to her breasts. I had to smile.

I went for our weapons and came back to the bridge with our rocket launcher, the rifles, my gun, and the Mark 3.

Brad studied the trawler through binoculars. "Dammit. I hope I'm not seeing what I think I'm seeing."

"What do you think you're seeing?" Culley asked.

"Have a look." Brad handed him the binoculars.

Culley studied the boat. "Those mother fuckers," he said too softly.

"What is it?" I asked.

"You might not want to see this, Tess," he said.

"I can take it if you can, big guy."

"OK." He handed me the binoculars.

I focused on the trawler. "Oh, no!"

A juvenile female giant was being dragged over the side of the boat, thrashing as she fought the hook which must have been imbedded in her beak. She was flung into the boat and two men lifted clubs and beat down on her. Her tentacles flailed. The men paused and looked toward our boat, then continued to beat her.

"Oh, God," I whispered and lowered the binoculars. "We've got to *do* something!"

Culley looked at Brad.

What's going on?" Mini said.

"They're killing a juvenile," I told her.

"Let me see."

I handed Mini the binoculars.

She raised them to her eyes. "Those bastards! Oh." She lowered the binoculars. "I think she's dead. They're dragging her to the stern."

Brad," I said, "come on, we have to do something about this."

"We are, Tessica!" Brad replied. "We'll get the boat's ID and report them."

"There must be dens down there." George squinted through a window. "If only the other giants could be warned."

"How?" I asked.

George shrugged.

"What if we rammed them?" I said.

Culley shook his head. "They're bigger than us, Tess. It would sink *Cousteau*."

As we approached the trawler, she turned on her engines and plowed through the inlet, away from us. I watched her disappear behind the larger atoll, to our portside.

"She's running from us," Culley said.

Brad unhooked the radio mic. "This is Captain Brad Bellows of R/V *Cousteau* to the fishing trawler. Over."

No response.

Brad tried again, with the same results.

We hit the crashing waves in the inlet. They rebounded off the shallows and came back at us from all directions, seething up our hull. Brad was steering us through, when the trawler reappeared and turned her bow toward us.

"She's preparing to fire on us!" Brad shouted from the helm.

"Uh, Oh." George backed into a wall.

I heard a boom. An exploding missile tore the surface off our starboard bow. Water rained down onto the deck.

"Jesus," Culley exclaimed. "Brad! Turn her around."

"She'll hit us amidships," Brad said.

"She'll hit us anyway," Culley told him. "They're firing missiles. Turn her around!" He ran on deck. "C'mon." He waved to Mini, George, and me. "Launch *Nomad* and grab some stuff."

Another boom split the water off our port bow.

"We've got a rocket launcher," I said.

"Their missile launcher is a hell of a lot more powerful," Culley told me.

Brad came flying onto the deck. "That's enough for me!" He ran to help us with *Nomad*.

"Did you get off a mayday?" Culley asked.

"I did," Brad said, "but I didn't hang around to wait for an answer. These mother fuckers are out to kill us!"

Mini and George helped me load our dive gear into *Nomad*. Culley came onto the deck with the weapons and threw them into the craft.

I grabbed two tanks from the wet room and dragged them to the deck. George lowered them into the craft. "Let's go. Let's go!" he cried.

"I'll get the other two tanks," Mini said. She blocked Culley, who was headed to the wet room for the tanks. "Let me get them," she told him.

I was glad when he nodded and went into the cabin for more stuff. Not only shouldn't he be diving, he shouldn't be lifting heavy tanks.

We jumped into *Nomad* and lowered her as another missile exploded near her bow.

Culley turned on the motor as soon as we hit the water. We unhooked the small craft and plowed toward the stern of *Cousteau*, where the trawler couldn't get a clear shot at us.

We were closer to the big atoll. Culley turned *Nomad* behind it, out of sight of the trawler.

"They'll expect us to land on this atoll," Culley shouted. "Let's fool the son o' bitches and go around behind them and head for the small atoll."

Another boom lifted a wave, but *Cousteau* was intact. Then she was out of sight as we skirted the big island.

"You know what?" George said.

"What?" we all said in unison.

"I don't think they're out to sink *Cousteau*. I think they wanted to scare us off the boat."

"Shit!" Brad said. "I think he's right. Now they can take over *Cousteau* and kill us in this inner tube."

"Out of the frying pan," I said as we swung behind the big atoll. If I wasn't holding on so tight, I would've chewed a nail.

Culley slowed the craft to a crawl as we approached the inlet from the back of the big atoll. *Nomad* was lost between crashing waves. I watched the trawler swing past *Cousteau* and continue around the big atoll, searching for us. Culley cranked on the gas and we flew across the inlet, bouncing on top of waves, and to the back of the small atoll.

"Great plan, Ryan," Brad said. "Now what have you got in mind for us?"

"I don't know," Culley responded. "I'm making it up as I go."

"Keep making it up," George said.

We found a flat beach with scrub bushes and weeds, on the far side of the small atoll.

"This looks as good as any place on this sandbox," I said.

"Yeah." Culley agreed. "Get ready to lift the motor out of the water. He drove the craft onto the beach and Mini lifted the motor just before we scraped bottom.

We jumped out and dragged *Nomad* up the beach, all but Culley, who ripped off a dried bush and swept our tracks to the grass line. "We can't take any chances." He pushed sand up to the top of the pontoons to camouflage the craft. The rest of us joined in. Brad disconnected the motor from the wooden stern and he and George hefted it inside *Nomad*. I took my dive knife from my bag and used the serrated edge to saw off trunks of small bushes. Mini spread them around the boat.

It wasn't the trawler, but a skiff that slowly cruised, close to shore, around the small atoll. They were leaving nothing to chance.

My heart was thumping We flattened ourselves in the sand behind *Nomad* and Culley took my hand.

"It's all right, Tessie," he said. "We still have the rocket launcher."

"OK."

Someone in the skiff stood up and trained his binoculars on the beach.

"Hey," he called, "if you're out there, come on out. We won't harm you guys. We just wanted your boat."

"Screw you," Mini whispered.

"Mother fucker!" Brad said as a seagull landed on his back and pecked at him.

Don't chase him," George said. "We don't want to give away our location."

"I'll have the bastard for supper! Owww!" Brad exclaimed as the gull pecked again.

"We'll be back for you," the guy in the skiff called. "At first light. You had your chance to surrender, assholes. Now you're dead!"

The skiff continued on and I think we let out a collective sigh of relief.

Brad made a grab for the seagull but missed. The bird squawked and flew away. "What the hell do we do now," Brad said. "If we call for help on a Q-Tree, the trawler will hear our broadcast."

There was nothing more to do in daylight. We stayed low until darkness closed in from the east.

With night as our cloak, lit only by a sliver of moon, we hiked across the atoll to see what was happening in the inlet. *Cousteau* was anchored beyond the inlet, her dark shape outlined by stars.

The trawler was also anchored, with lights on inside her cabin. Sound carries across water and we heard talking and laughing. If the Coast Guard had been on its way, the criminals would've intercepted broadcasts and they'd be gone by now.

"Suppose we head for Hawaii in *Nomad?*" I suggested. "When we get far enough from here, we can call for help."

"Tessie," Culley said, "it sounds like a good plan, but we've got maybe a hundred miles on *Nomad's* fuel. If we call for help when we run out, it'll be a race between the trawler and a helicopter from Hawaii. These guys don't want witnesses to their illegal fishing, and we're about a thousand miles northeast of Hawaii." He rubbed his forehead. "And about a thousand miles from home."

"Oh," I said. My confidence had stemmed from Culley's strength and courage, his ability to choose the right plan in an emergency. I think we all felt that way. Now, with Culley worn out and still in pain from the surgery, we were like a pack that had lost its alpha male.

"We could climb aboard *Cousteau* at night," Brad suggested.

Culley shook his head. "They might have guards posted on *Cousteau,* just waiting for us to show up."

"You know," George said, "with the price of giant octopus on the black market, and the medicine shops... If you weigh that against our lives -- "

"We come out second best," Mini said.

"We'll have to take turns on guard duty until morning," Culley told us.

Culley and I held hands as we walked through soft sand. So did Mini and George.

"George," I said, "do you think there's crawly things?"

"I'm sorry, Tess, but yes, all sorts of crawly things."

"I'm going to sleep inside the inflatable!" I said.

"But what are we going to do in the morning?" Mini asked, "when they send their skiff to check out *this* atoll?"

"You know," George started.

"Tell us, George," Brad said.

"Well, suppose we sink the trawler?"

"You know," Brad said, imitating George, "well, suppose we chew the hull with our teeth?"

"Sea cocks," George said.

"Who's going to open them?" Culley asked.

"Uh, I was thinking Tess," George said, "with her dive gear."

"Think again," Culley told him.

"We could row there in the dark in *Nomad*," I said, "with the motor shut off. All I'd have to do is go over the side, open the underwater sea cocks, and the ocean would do the rest."

Culley sat down on a blanket, his back against *Nomad*, and ran a hand over his chest. "You'd have to shine a light. And what tool are you going to use to open the sea cocks?"

"You guys could keep *Nomad* between me and *Cousteau*," I said. "If there are guards on board *Cousteau*, they wouldn't see the light."

"There's a toolkit in *Nomad's* stern," Brad told Culley.

"It's only for the inflatable's small motor," Culley said. "Tess, there's too many *ifs*. Let's have something to eat and get some sleep."

I sat down beside him and he took my hand. "I guess...." he started.

We all listened.

"We send Tess and Mini to hide out in the trees and we face the fuckers from behind *Nomad* tomorrow, with the rocket launcher and our rifles. With sand piled inside, *Nomad* is as good as any fortification, except for a rocket or a missile."

"That's your plan?" Brad said.

"I'm out of ideas!" Culley admitted and closed his eyes. He rested spread fingers across his chest.

I stared at a sky full of stars and wondered if Rámon was right about his compassionate god.

Because I had a plan.

George is a night owl, so he was glad to take the first watch, toward the inlet side of the atoll. He brought a couple of sandwiches and a thermos of coffee with him. Culley, Mini, and Brad ate at *Nomad*.

"Aren't you hungry?" Culley asked me.

"No," I lied. "My stomach's upset. Too much excitement for one day." I smiled. "We need to spread it out more."

It's not good to eat just before a dive.

It wasn't easy to stay awake while the three of them fell into an exhausted sleep, wrapped in blankets in the soft sand. Our gear from *Nomad* was spread out on another blanket to keep the sand off it.

Maybe something of Culley's courage had rubbed off on me, because I felt confident and determined as I got quietly into my wet suit, mask, both mine and Culley's weight belts, as part of my plan, my buoyancy compensator, gloves, a compass, my knife, a torch, a light that dangled from my belt, and Culley's mark 3. I was loaded for bear. Or illegal fishermen.

This would be a free dive, with no tank. The sound of the bubbles could give me away.

I carried my fins to the water's edge by the light of a sliver of moon with a star hung beneath it. Their positions gave them the look of a question mark.

"Are you asking me why, God," I whispered. "And is this part of your plan, too?" I looked at the indifferent stars. "Or am I just talking to myself?"

At the water's edge, I put on my fins and manually blew air into my buoyancy compensator to make up for the weight belts. I slipped into black water and snorkeled out and around the back of the small atoll, as quiet as a fish with my fins slightly under the surface. The Milky Way was a curved sweep of stars. Billions and billions of stars, so thick here in the blackness of the sea, they looked like a belt encompassing our planet. How much could we possibly matter? The only thing between us and the forever stars was an image of God that we projected out there.

If you're up there, God, I thought, *please let me succeed. Not only for my sake, but for four good people.* I suddenly realized how Culley must have felt when he laid his life on the line to save others.

There was *Cousteau* and the trawler, both anchored away from the inlet's inexorable current. Disturbed seagulls cawed and lifted off the water as I passed them. *Shut up!* I thought.

I struck out toward the trawler, wondering what predators might be on the prowl beneath me. Sharks often look for wounded fish that flap on the surface. They're easy prey. So was I.

The trawler's cabin was lit. A square of light hanging between the blackness of sea and space. I saw movement within, and voices that carried across the water.

Cousteau was dark and silent. I doubted there were guards on board. These smug bastards thought we were a helpless bunch. In their devious minds, tomorrow we'd be dead meat.

Night was my camouflage as I swam to the trawler's stern. Something bumped me and I gasped, but I dared not turn on my light. I kicked out with my fins, but only hit water. *A passing fish,* I thought, *that was curious about this strange creature in his world.* It's happened to me before on night dives.

I heard a thumping on the side of the boat. I stayed close to the hull to hide as lights came on. My heart thumped too as I heard running feet on the deck.

The thumping continued and I moved quietly past the stern to have a look on the port side. Stirred phosphorescence lit my path. I swam slowly to keep it down to a minimum.

Damn!

Lights showed a struggling juvenile giant hooked by her beak, and being hauled up the side of the boat. The large hook kept her beak open. It's a wonder she hadn't drowned on the way up.

No, you don't, you bastards! I thought and swam to the line that held her. I reached up, grabbed the line, in the darkness just past the beam of light, and slashed it with my knife. The giant splashed back into the water and disappeared beneath the surface. She still had the hook in her beak, but at least she was free.

"What the hell?" someone on board exclaimed. "The line just went slack. Where the hell did she *go?*"

"She bit through the fucking line," another man said. "I'll be damned. I didn't think they could do that."

"They *can't* do that!" the first man said. "What the hell's going on? Hey, captain!"

More footsteps on deck.

I moved quietly back to the stern and unclamped a weight belt. While the slime balls argued over whether or not a giant could snap the line with her beak, I quietly wrapped the weight belt around the propeller and the shaft, pulled it tight, and snapped the buckle shut.

"Did you hear something?" someone on board said.

"Ah, for Christ's sake, you're always hearing something! It's your fear talkin', man!"

Keep thinking that, you miserable excuses for human beings! I wrapped the second weight belt quietly around the other propeller and shaft and pulled it taut.

I realized that anger kept down fear. *Stay angry, Tess.*

I let the air out of my buoyancy compensator underwater so it wouldn't make a hissing sound. Then I made my way along the starboard side of the hull to the anchor line at the trawler's bow. I swam out, my fins underwater, to where the anchor line met the water, drew out my knife and used the serrated edge to cut the line underwater, where there'd be no sound.

The trawler's bow began to drift toward the inlet in the light breeze of a current.

I swam back to the stern and cut their second anchor. *Eat that, you pieces of slime!*

"The anchor!" someone shouted from the trawler.

Yeah, both anchors! I thought. After what they'd done to the juveniles, I had no pity for these greedy bastards.

"What the fuck is going on?" someone called from the deck. "We're adrift."

I reached the dinghy, which was tied by a tow line to the trawler's stern. I was about to cut the line, but lights swung across the surface. I took cover behind the dinghy and pulled my snorkel from under my mask strap. It might be seen above my head.

After a few quiet breaths, I filled my lungs and slipped underwater. With a hand on the dinghy to guide me to its bow, I rose to the surface, reached up and sawed through the tow line.

"There he is!" someone shouted.

Oh, shit! I dived and swam back to the dinghy's stern for cover.

"The bastard's behind the dinghy. Kill him! We need that dinghy to get to *Cousteau!*

You can try, I thought. I checked my compass, took a few deep breaths to build up oxygen in my lungs, dived, and kicked hard as I headed for the middle of the inlet by the glowing light of the compass. Here, the running current would carry me away from the trawler.

It's hard to dive with a wet suit and no weights, but as I went deeper, the air in the suit compressed and it was easier to stay down.

To get to Cousteau, one of them had said. So there weren't any guards on *Cousteau.*

When I finally had to surface, the trawler and the dinghy were adrift in the current. I sleeved my snorkel back under the mask strap.

I heard a sound like some supernatural cat screaming as the trawler's engines came to life and the propellers were sheared by the lead weights.

By now Culley and my friends would be worried about me. I couldn't help that.

I smiled, there alone in the sea, and angled out of the current toward the small atoll. *Thank you, God,* I thought.

Quite a night's work, Tessie, I told myself. *Ryan's gonna be pissed, but he'll love you for what you've done.*

I angled toward the small atoll as the running water carried me past it.

When the current dissipated beyond the inlet, I turned on my light and started the long swim back to the atoll, moving between coral mounts. Small fish were attracted to my light, but it was good to see that there were no large predators. We humans are creatures of light. Our primitive ancestors retreated to caves when the sun went down.

Suddenly, out there, alone in the blackness of sky and sea, I realized what I had accomplished and the chances I'd taken. I started to shake. *I hope Ryan isn't too pissed.*

I remembered a story I'd read about a helicopter pilot in a war during the last century. He said he was calm while missiles were fired at him from the ground. He almost felt disconnected from the battle. But afterwards, sitting in the officer's club, he would begin to shake, and couldn't stop.

Culley and the others were waiting for me on the inlet side of the atoll. I turned on my light and came up on the ocean side. The trawler and the dinghy were floating out to sea. *Bon voyage,* I thought. "Hey, guys!" I called, "are you looking for me?"

My knees went weak as I came ashore and had to carry my weight again. I slid down to the wet sand. My right leg wouldn't stop shaking. I held it in both hands, but it continued to shake. *Here we go,* I thought. *The aftershock.* I gripped my knee harder. My throat felt tight, too.

"Tess!" I heard Culley call. "Tess! Is that *you?*"

I felt dizzy.

"It's me," I said shakily. "Ryan. It's *me.*" I tried to get up and fell back again. Culley ran up to me. "Tess! Are you all right?"

"I don't feel so good." I tried to stand again, but I couldn't.

"Are you hurt?" Culley said.

"No."

He sat beside me and held me. "Jesus Christ, Tess. What did you do?"

"Don't be mad at me. Please." I laid my head against his arm. "Don't be mad." My energy drained like bubbles in an opened bottle of champagne. I looked up at the Milky Way. It blurred into a smear of running milk. Then the milk ran out and I felt Ryan brace me as I fell backwards.

CHAPTER TWENTY NINE

Somebody had dressed me in my woolen shirt and pants. I had a good night's sleep, wrapped in a blanket, but morning dawned drizzly and miserable. I sat up. Sky and sea competed for the color of lead. There was no place to get out of the rain, except *Cousteau*, still anchored where the crew of the trawler had left her.

Nomad was gone. The trawler and her dinghy were also gone, with the tide. I looked around. "Ryan?"

I was alone. Just me, the seagulls, and the damn red crabs. "Mini?" They couldn't have been *that* mad at me. "George? Boss?"

I heard the sound of a small motor. *Nomad* swung around the north side of the atoll and Culley, at the wheel, steered her up the beach. Mini, Brad, and George were with him, laughing and talking.

"Oh," I said. "There you are."

Culley got out and approached me, grinning.

"You're not mad?" I asked him.

"Me mad? I'm mad as hell." He sat next to me and put an arm around my shoulders. "I'm supposed to be the hero. You're stealing my thunder." He kissed my cheek. "And I don't faint when it's over."

Once on board *Cousteau*, I took a shower while Culley made a breakfast of scrambled eggs and toast. When I came into the cabin, Mini, Brad, and George gathered around me.

"Can I touch you, oh, brave Valkyrie?" Mini said. "What the hell did you do to their propellers?" She sat next to me and laughed.

"Well, I told her, "We don't have any more weight belts."

"I noticed that," Culley said from the stove. "We've got a couple of spares, unless there's another boat you want to destroy?"

"Maybe some other night," I answered.

"To the victor go the spoils." Culley put a dish of bacon and eggs in front of me. The smell made me realize how hungry I was. There's nothing like a long dive to make a person famished. I chewed a mouthful of eggs.

"You'll make her a good wife," Brad told Culley and chuckled.

"How do you like your eggs, boss?" Culley responded. "Once over your head, lightly?"

"That's egg on your face," George said and grinned. He tilted his head toward Mini and she kissed his cheek.

Over breakfast, I told them the details of what I'd done. Brad had called in the trawler's ID number to the Coast Guard after I set her adrift.

"You know what?" Brad said, imitating George.

"What?" George leaned forward. He didn't get it.

"Be nice, boss," Mini said, "or I'll sic Tess on you."

Brad went to the refrig and took out a bottle of champagne. "I think Tessica's night's work calls for a celebration."

"This early?" I asked.

"Early, late," Brad responded. "What's the difference?" He uncorked the bottle and poured champagne into plastic cups. "Minister Gantry's finest!" He lifted his glass. "A toast! To the Noblest Valkyrie of them all."

We solemnly touched glasses and drank.

"And to going home," Brad added.

"Uh, maybe we'd better not drink to going home just yet," I said.

"No, no, no!" Brad hit his forehead with his knuckles. "I want to drink to going home!"

"Home is the hunter," George recited sadly, "home from the hill, and the sailor home from the sea."

"Nevermore!" Brad added. "Lay it on me, Tess. Did California sink into the sea?"

"The dens," I said. "I cut a juvenile off the fishing line while they were reeling her in."

"Another toast!" Brad said.

"We didn't finish the first one," Mini reminded him.

"You cut her off the line, and?" Culley asked me.

"Well -- " I started.

"Oh, God!" Brad sat down. "Now you want to go down to the dens and get the hook out of her large, solid-as-a-brick-shit -house beak!" He leaned close to me. "You don't need your right arm anymore, lefty?"

Culley put his elbow on the table and his head in his hand.

"I guess," George said, "what you want to do, Tess, is teach the giants how to avoid hooks? Then they can communicate it to each other?"

I nodded and bit a nail.

Culley took my hand and held it.

"Suppose," Culley said, "you wait for the doctor to give me permission to dive. Then we'll go down together."

"How are we going to get back here, Ryan?" I asked. "We have to turn over *Cousteau* to Sea Worthy. The Lab's research vessel *Reverence* is lying broken on a reef, and we can't come out this far in your sixteen-foot Boston Whaler. I'd bring the torch with me on the dive, and the Mark 3."

"Culley," Mini said, "give me some dive lessons. I'll go down with Tess."

"This is no dive for a novice," Culley explained. "You could get yourself and Tess both killed if you panicked."

"I've never panicked in my life," Mini said, a bit offended, by the tone of her voice. "Well, maybe when I was trapped in that air bubble inside *Reverence*."

"You've never been down a hundred feet in a swift current in a community of giants," Culley told her.

Brad had been quiet. He poked at the scrambled eggs in his dish with a fork. "Suppose I contact your physician, Ryan, and see what he advises?"

Culley nodded.

Brad got up and went to the bridge. Mini and George followed, to give me and Culley some time to talk.

I looked at my hand and smiled. "My nails are growing."

He nodded.

"Would it help," I said, "if I tell you that I'll be very careful?"

"It should," he said. "But it doesn't." He pushed away his plate and let go of my hand. "I'm sorry I came on this expedition."

I swallowed to hold back tears that burned without falling. "Are you sorry you met me?"

"I'm sorry I could lose you. I'm sorry I could finish this trip without you. I'm sorry I could go back to living alone!"

"I could not love thee dear, so much," I said, "loved I not honor more?"

"Fuck honor! I prefer a long life with you." He touched his chest. "I'm going to lay down for a while." He went to his bunk.

A few minutes later, Mini, Brad, and George came into the cabin.

"Did you get in touch with Ryan's physician?" I asked.

Culley sat up.

"We did." Brad nodded. "Doctor Kramer. I'm sorry, Ryan, but he said no way. He said the pressure on your punctured lungs would open the stitches and you'd bleed to death."

Culley laid back down and stared at the ceiling. "Do what you have to, Tess. I wash my hands of it."

My friends looked from Culley to me. I let the tears slide down my cheeks without wiping them.

Into the lion's den, I thought. *But that's where you have to go if you want to study lions,*

*****

"Hello, Mom?" I said into my Q-Tree.

"Tess, how are you?'

"Fine, and you and Dad and Chris?"

"We're all...OK here. How's Ryan?"

"Much better, Mom. He's recuperating."

"That's wonderful news, Tessie. Are you on your way home now?"

"That's what I'm calling about. No, not yet, Mom. It turns out there's some more work to do."

"With the giants?"

"Well, yes."

"Tessie, what's going on? You don't sound right."

"Nothing, Mom. I just wanted to hear your voice. Is Dad home?"

"He's...no, he's not home right now."

"What is it, Mom?"

"Well, Tessie, I didn't want to worry you, with your work and all, but two days ago your dad was mowing the lawn, and -- "

"And *what?*"

"He got a pain in his chest."

"Oh, no."

"It was a mild heart attack. You know how I always tell him to cut down on meat and ice cream?"

"Yes. How is he?"

"He's in good spirits. The doctor wants to keep him in the hospital for observation. Just for a few more days. Then he can come home."

"Oh, thank God for that. Can I call him?"

"No, not today, Tessie. He's still in ICU. Just as a precaution, but no calls and no excitement. The doctor wants your father to stay on a strict diet and get more exercise when this is over."

No excitement, I thought. "How's Chris taking it?"

"He's scared, but he won't admit it. You know, he's like his father."

"Mom, do you think Dad will change his diet and get the exercise he needs?"

"He will, or he'll answer to me!"

"Good for you, Mom. I always said that Dad isn't afraid of anything in this world except you."

"He'd better believe that. I want him with me for a long time."

"Mom, when you go to see Dad, tell him I love him. And tell Chris, too."

"I will, Tessie. I was just leaving for the hospital when you called."

"Oh, OK. You go ahead. I love you, Mom."

"I love you too, baby. Take care of yourself."

"I will, Mom. Goodbye."

"Goodbye, Tessie."

I broke the connection and went to the lab to talk to Mini.

She looked up from the microscope. "What wrong, Tess? You look worried."

We sat down and I told her about my dad's heart attack. "He's not supposed to have any excitement. If something goes wrong on this dive.... Mini, what would you do in my place?"

"That's a tough one. Suppose you leave it to other divers to go down there and try to get the hook out of her mouth?"

"Who else would do it? She could starve to death by then, and the other giants *still* wouldn't get the idea of what a baited hook looks like. They *have* to see that the hook is hidden inside the bait. With all the illegal fishing for giants, it's imperative that they learn about hooks and bait."

"You're making a good case for doing this dive. I've been thinking about it. We could lower the shark cage, tie you to a tether line in case the current takes you, and Georgie would track you with the ROV."

"But Ryan's really mad at me."

"Well, look at the dive *he* made to get a giant into the shark cage." She put her thumb and forefinger close to each other "He came *this close* to losing his life. If you hadn't been there, he wouldn't have made it back."

"What about my father if something happens to me?"

She put her long arm around my shoulders. "Tess, the dive is your call. But you can't live your life for other people, no matter how much you love them."

I patted Mini's knee. "As usual, you're very wise, and very right. Mini?"

"Yes?"

"If anything happens to me -- "

"Tess, *don't.*"

"No, listen. Will you promise you'll find Ice a good home? My parents are not dog lovers."

"I promise."

"Thanks." I stood up and checked my dive watch. "Slack tide's in an hour or so. I'd like to go down in about a half hour from now."

Mini stood up. "Are you going to say something to Ryan before the dive?"

I sighed. "I don't think he wants to talk to me."

*****

As I suited up, I tried to regain the air of confidence and self-assurance that had seen me through the trawler dive. But my mind strayed to images of the people involved in my life. We were like a web. Break one strand, and the entire web suffers. And God, who sits on the sideline like a spider, if He exists at all, monitors His web with an invisible touch. To what extent does He control the living strands? I put on a neoprene glove and looked at my hand. *Who moves my hand?* I thought. Is it my own will that drives me to make this dangerous dive, or am I a pawn in God's web? I *think* I have free will. But is this dive into the den of giants really my idea, or part of a higher plan? And how much does my life matter in that higher plan?

"What are you thinking, Tess?" Mini asked as she picked up my fins and mask.

"Oh...nothing."

We went on deck. The sky was clear, a great blue cushion that protects us from the silent, black infinity of space. The sea, that servant of wind and moon, reflected the blue of the sky, and the white of clouds in its frothing waves.

Whoever planned this dive, me, God, or some entity who sits and chuckles in the wings of the human drama, the die was cast.

George and Brad came out from the bridge. "Tess," George said, "I'll be following you with the ROV." He put a hand on my shoulder. "Best luck."

"Thanks, George." Culley was in the cabin. I glanced at the closed door.

"Remember, Tessica," Brad said, "if things go badly, get into the shark cage and let us know where we need to stop the cage for you to decompress. There's an extra tank in there and some cut up fish so you can bait the hook and show the giants what bait is all about, if mollusks are capable of understanding the concept of a baited hook."

"OK, Boss," I said.

"Don't shortchange them, Brad," Mini said. "The giants are proving to be the smartest of the very clever cephalopod species."

I put on my weight belt. Brad lifted the tank and helped me into my buoyancy compensator, which was attached to the tank. Mini stuffed the torch and the Mark 3 inside the compensator. I strapped on my knife, purged the regulator with a blast of air, rubbed defogger into my full-face mask, and glanced back as I heard the cabin door open. Mini handed me my fins and helped Brad swing the shark cage over the side.

"Oh, hi, Culley," George said as he passed the open cabin door on his way to the bridge and the ROV controls.

Culley came on deck and stared at me, unsmiling.

I lifted a hand and waved slightly.

He walked toward me. "I want to check your gear." He checked the gauges on my dive computer. Then he checked the straps on my fins to make certain the rubber wasn't dried and cracked. He checked the connection between the tank and the regulator.

"Do I pass inspection?" I asked.

"As your dive master, or as the man who loves you?"

I smiled. "How about the latter?'

He tucked a loose strand of my hair under my hood. "Don't stray too far from the shark cage. We won't let it touch bottom, so it won't raise sand. It's going to drift near you, in case you need it."

I nodded.

He fitted the full face mask over my head and checked the communication system. "Don't hesitate to abort the dive and get into the shark cage if things go bad."

"OK."

If they squirt acid, and you're in the cage, stay there! We'll pull you away from it."

"Sounds good."

"But most of all," he said.

"What?"

His tone softened. "Remember that I love you."

"That's what I needed to hear, hon."

Tears glazed his eyes. "When this is over -- "

"You'll buy me lunch at that Jewish deli you found?"

He smiled. "I'll even try a knish." He checked his watch. "It's coming on slack tide. If you're going to make this dive, you'd better do it now."

I took his hand. "I love you, tough guy."

"I love you back."

Culley watched as I went over the side and into the big blue.

With the shark cage following me down to my left, and the ROV tracking me on my right, and a tether line attached like a harness, I wondered if we hadn't made too much of the danger of this dive.

I held onto the cage and let it bring me down, to conserve air and my energy.

Below, a city made of violet domes materialized on the sandy bottom like a fantasy viewed through clouds. As far as I could see in either direction, domes painted to look like bright rocks swayed from their anchors. Fish had already taken up residence in the domes' crevices, unaware that they were sushi for the giant inhabitants of the dens.

As I sank lower, the blurry white blobs on the sand materialized into white giants, adults and juveniles.

The cage stopped while the ROV went ahead to inspect the city closer. Some giants slithered across the bottom. Others stayed in dens, with their tentacles dangling outside.

They probably have eggs, I thought.

Juveniles played like young dolphins, jetting and chasing each other. One held a dead crab, while others tried to snatch it away from her. I thought of young, predatory mammals who often engage in this game of tag with a bone or a piece of meat. A few adults kept an eye on the kids while they played.

Babysitters, I thought. This, too, was not unheard of among wolves, and other mammals and primates.

It seemed that when the octopuses went communal, instead of living as loners, the social aspects of their "clever" brains kicked in and changed their behavior to suit an environment of close, cooperative living.

"Lower the cage," I said into the mic of my mask. "This is pretty incredible, guys. It's like a chimpanzee family. Mini?"

"Yes, Tess. I'm here."

"Not only am I seeing cooperation among the giants, but babysitters. And youngsters are interacting and playing games."

"George is getting it all on the ROV camera. We're up here with our mouths hanging open."

As I swam down, I saw strands of eggs that swayed with the light current, in the interior of dens.

"We see it on the ROV screen," Mini said. "This is fucking incredible."

"Tess," Culley said, "have the giants made any aggressive moves toward you?"

"No, but I intend to get closer and hopefully find the juvenile with the hook. Oh, wait a minute. Crawling and pulsing around one den were the juvenile, charcoal males, playing among themselves. An adult female stayed close to them and watched their antics. A beautiful angelfish swooped down and zeroed in on a male.

Unimpressed by the fish's good looks, the babysitter lashed out with a tentacle. The angelfish escaped, but didn't hang around.

The hatchlings, still brown with acid mucus, stayed close to the giant females. Skeleton heads and remains of fish and shellfish were strewn behind the dens, much as neat apartment dwellers might leave their garbage in one pile.

"There's the males!" I said.

As I swam above the dens, watched by the giants, trailed by the cage and the ROV, I came upon the dens of the adult males. Two to three feet long, the charcoal adults lived apart from the females and the kids, as male elephants do, and even some tribal humans. When the juvenile males saw me, they retreated to their dens.

By all appearances, this was a thriving, well-organized community.

"I wonder if it's matriarchal?" I said.

"This just keeps getting more and more spectacular," Mini said. "It seems that the giants' apocalyptic encounters with humans have pushed them to take a giant, evolutionary leap, if you'll excuse the pun, or go extinct."

"They made the right choice," I said.

"This behavior is unprecedented with marine life," George added. "Maybe because they have arms."

"Be careful, Tess." It was Culley's voice. "They could still see you as the enemy."

"I will, hon."

"Let me get my two rubles in, Tessica," Brad said. "Get what info you can gather without losing your right arm, OK?"

"OK, boss."

I swam down slowly, my arms tucked across my chest, instead of dangling, to show that I came in peace.

I had an idea!

I opened the shark cage, took out a chunk of fish, and extended it to an adult who was close by.

We stared at each other. while she slowly flashed in neon waves across her body.

Some of the adults and kids came closer and watched. Curious hatchlings swam around me. I hoped they wouldn't brush against me with their acid mucus. A juvenile female squirted acid, then jetted away to hide inside a den.

I backed away from the dark smear of acid in the water. My friends were watching, I knew, but they stayed silent to allow me to concentrate.

Maybe I should have brought a crab as an offering? I thought. It's one of their favorite foods.

The gathering of white giants parted and a huge female approached.

The matriarch?

My friends moved the shark cage closer to me. The ROV maneuvered between me and the female.

"Lower it, George," I said. "You're blocking the view."

He did.

I extended the fish to the matriarch and quietly waited. For some reason, I wasn't afraid. I sensed intelligence here, and culture, and a thought process.

I ventured a little closer. There was still no response from the matriarch. I swam to the bottom, about fifteen feet further down, laid the fish on the sand, and backed away. The outgoing tide was beginning its slow tug.

The matriarch flashed to a large, adult female close to her. The female flashed back. Then the matriarch moved toward the fish.

Relax! I told myself as the excitement of the moment made me breathe faster. *Relax.*

She brushed a tentacle lightly across the fish, then folded it in the tentacle. I could almost hear the Triumphal March from Aida, complete with dancers and horses, as she accepted my offering and brought it back to the community. She ripped it into pieces with her beak and others snatched the drifting pieces.

"Yay," I said softly into the mic.

"Yay," my friends took turns answering.

"Don't let your guard down," Culley said. "They might know you're carrying weapons and just want to lure you in."

"OK, hon. But if you could feel the sense of community here."

"Listen to what I'm saying, Tess!" Culley said.

And then they brought her out.

The juvenile with the hook still embedded in her open beak. The attached fishing line floated around her. She leaned against the adult who carried her to me.

"Do you *see* this?" I said quietly into the mic. "Do you *see* it?"

"We're watching closely," Culley told me.

"This is incredible!" George said.

The adult laid the wounded juvenile near me and backed away.

I approached her quietly, with no extra motions, the way Culley dives. She jetted backwards when she saw me and drifted to the bottom.

I followed her slowly, barely kicking, exhaling, which helped me lower myself to the sand. Anything I could think of to allay her fear of me.

How ironic, I thought. We had all been so worried that they would attack me, and here I was, trying to gain their trust.

The hatchlings swirled around me but kept their distance.

I looked at the matriarch, who watched, with the rest of the community, and thought of first meetings between Western man and the Chamorro people. While there was no comparison here to humans, the sense of first contact was evident.

I reached the wounded juvenile. She began to slither backward. The matriarch flashed and she stopped. I reached out and gently stroked the juvenile's tentacle. She jerked but didn't jet away.

"Tess," Mini said, "your boyfriend looks like he's going to faint. Be careful, OK?"

"Promise," I whispered.

I gently lifted her tentacle. She flashed, perhaps like a kid begging the dentist not to hurt her. The hook was embedded in her mouth, behind her open beak. If she was thinking *please don't hurt me!* I was thinking *please don't squirt me!* I grasped the hook and gently moved it back and forth.

She jumped.

This is going to hurt, I thought. *But it's for your own good.*

I held her open beak with one hand and pulled on the hook.

Nothing.

I looked at the matriarch.

She slithered forward and embraced the juvenile. The juvenile wrapped her tentacles tightly around the matriarch like a kid clinging to her mother for comfort. The juvenile flashed quick patterns that ran across her mantle.

Fear, I thought.

The matriarch flashed back, but in long, slow lines that spiraled her mantle and might be comforting to the youngster.

Now or never, I thought. *Hang on, kid.*

I twisted the hook to free the barb and yanked. The juvenile jerked and the matriarch gripped her tighter.

"Damn it!" I said into the mic, "it's really in there." I took a breath, twisted the hook again and yanked hard. The hook, surrounded by blood, ripped free. The juvenile jerked back again, and fought to jet away, but the matriarch clasped her tightly.

I held up the hook for all to see and strung out the line in my hand to show that it was attached.

The matriarch gathered the juvenile in her tentacles and took her to an unoccupied den.

I went into the shark cage, got the other chunk of fish and came out. While the giants gathered around me, like a fantasy forest of great white trees with dangling roots, and the juveniles peeked out from behind the adults, I baited the hook and made certain it was hidden inside the meat.

One adult caught it in a tentacle and studied it. Others reached for it and it was passed around.

I checked my pressure gauge. I was low on air. I went into the cage and switched to the fresh tank.

"Culley?" I called.

"Yes, my Valkyrie?"

I laughed. "Send down another tank at my decompression stop, will you?"

"I already did. You coming up now, or did they invite you to stay for supper?"

"Probably better than cold sandwiches," I told him.

I went back to the community, to say a "goodbye" of sorts, when the matriarch came close with a tentacle wrapped around something. She extended a live lobster to me.

Payment! I almost laughed.

I took it and held it by its spiny carapace in my gloved hand.

"This is fucking surreal," Mini said.

I stroked the matriarch's extended tentacle, and then I began to swim up.

The community accompanied me to my decompression stop, then they jetted back down. I waved my arm in an imitation of a tentacle.

The water around me was empty again. The city below was blurred in the poor visibility as the current's surge strengthened and stirred up sand that closed the scene beneath me like a curtain that dropped at the end of a play.

"Did this really happen?" I said into the mic. "Or did I dream it?"

"If you dreamed it," Brad said, "Ryan wouldn't be laid out in a beach chair with Mini fanning him."

"C'mon, Brad," I said, ""you're scaring me." I put the lobster in the cage.

"Just kidding," he responded, "but I'm not scaring you half as much as you scared the tough guy."

CHAPTER THIRTY

This time we did celebrate our homecoming, with a bottle of Gantry's champagne. This bottle was nothing to write home about either. If it were award-winning, I'd like to know in which country it had gained that distinction.

Brad was about to throw the live lobster into boiling water.

"No, wait a minute, Brad," I said. "You can't do that to a living creature."

"What do you propose?" he asked, "that we dunk it in Gantry's champagne and get it get drunk first?"

"Well," George offered, "lobsters are cold-blooded. If you put him in the freezer for fifteen minutes, he should go into a state of hibernation."

"So," Brad said, "then we kill a hibernating living creature?"

"Well, you see," George told him, "he'll be dead in the boiling water before he wakes up."

The hibernating lobster was tasty. I shared it and we all got a piece. I thought of how the matriarch had shared the chunk of fish I gave her. I'd seen nature films where male chimps shared the meat of their hunts with females, who were then more willing to mate with them. We humans are just a little more subtle about it, like candy on Valentine's Day.

We were all glad that the cruise home was uneventful. We'd had enough events to last us for a long time.

Mini and I stood on the portside rail as we passed the atoll where *Reverence* lay broken on a coral mount. We were silent as memories flooded back.

Mini rubbed her arms as though she were cold and nodded toward *Reverence*. "That's one boat I don't ever want to see again."

I knew she meant her terrifying experience when she was trapped in *Reverence's* cabin, inside the air bubble. I put an arm around her.

"And if it hadn't been for Brad," I said, remembering when he stopped me from going over the side of the boat after the giant had tilted it, "I wouldn't be here."

"And if it hadn't been for you," Mini said, "Culley wouldn't be here."

We chuckled.

"I guess," I said, "Brad and George live charmed lives."

"They're both dyed-in-the-wool survivors," Mini said.

"If it's OK to ask," I said, "how are you and Georgie getting along?"

"He's great, Tess. "You know, I didn't realize that I loved him until I spent that time with Elijah. I was bored stiff! I found myself yearning for George's company and a stimulating conversation on some moot point in science."

I nodded. "You two have always had a love of brilliant debates."

She giggled. "The only time we're not debating is when we're in bed."

"Well." I laughed. "The word *intercourse* has two meanings."

"And we've been exploring them both!"

"Mini," I said seriously, "will you do me the honor of being my maid of honor?"

"I can't!" She laughed.

"Oh?"

"I figure on a double wedding when we get back."

"Congratulations." I put an arm around her waist. "My dear friend."

I thought of Brad. Who was this Harley Davidson that he couldn't see what a catch Brad really was?

*****

As we approached the San Francisco harbor, news helicopters swooped low to film us. Private and Coast Guard boats came out to accompany us home. A San Francisco fire boat put on a display of sprayed water that shot upwards around the boat and left a mist behind it.

Culley volunteered to steer *Cousteau* to the berth. I don't think he's comfortable in large crowds. He prefers a few good friends. The rest of us lined the bow and waved.

"So this is what it's like to be a celebrity," Mini commented.

"I guess," I said. "My arm's getting tired from waving."

"Wave with the other arm," Brad suggested. "If all these people could come out here just to greet us, we owe them a wave."

I waved with the other arm.

We disembarked and were inundated with questions from the media and spectators alike. George was in his element with all the fanfare and admiration. Mom and Chris couldn't make it. She spent her days in the hospital with Dad.

my Q-Tree rang. I opened the connection and saw Mom's face.

"Mom," I shouted above the din."

"Tessie, you're home!"

"Yes, Mom. I'm on the wharf."

"What's all that shouting. Is something wrong?"

"No, Mom. I pointed the Q-Tree at the crowd. "It's our welcoming committee. How's Dad?" I put a finger in my other ear to drown out the noise.

"He's fine. He's coming home tomorrow. I wanted to tell you, baby, you can go ahead with your plans for the wedding now."

"That's great, Mom! I'll tell Ryan. I can't wait to see all of you."

"Me, too, baby."

"I've got to go, Mom. It's pure insanity here."

"I love you, Tessie."

"I love you, too, Mom."

I broke the connection and the journalists descended like predatory birds.

Brad handed out public service announcements he had written about our experiences with the giants and the preliminary conclusions we'd drawn, but the journalists wanted direct quotes on camera.

Finally, squad cars pulled up, lights flashing. The officers got out.

"Time to leave, folks," one of them called and waved his arms as he walked toward the crowd. "There's too many people on the wharf. Let's go."

"Time to go home now," another officer called. "Getting close to supper time."

"Aw," a teenaged boy said. "I was just gonna buy a Dungeness crab!"

"All right," the officer said, "buy your crab and eat it off the wharf."

"Now let's go, people!" another officer said.

The crowd quietly disbursed.

The police left when only a few people remained on the wharf.

Mini and I were relieved. We sat on a bench and waited for Culley and George to tie *Cousteau* to the dock. Pacifica Lab was sending out a van to pick us up.

"Who's *that*?" Mini pointed to a black man who stood on the wharf like a model posing for a shoot in Gay Today Magazine. He held his head high. His eyes were shielded by dark sunglasses. His feet were braced apart. A black leather vest covered his bare, hairless chest. His pants, too, were black leather. He wore a leather strip necklace with a silver clasp. A striking man. People who strolled on the wharf noticed him as they passed by.

Mini lowered her head. "Give me a fucking break!"

"Tell me about it," I said. "We're both taken, Mini. Remember?"
"I'm trying to."
"Try harder!"
We laughed.
Brad strolled up to the man with his personal bag from the boat slung over his shoulder. "Why did you come to meet me, Harley?" he asked. "Is your new paramour too busy to keep you interested?"
"Oh my God," I whispered. "That's Harley!"
"Don't be cruel to me, Brad," Harley responded in a voice that seemed too high for his strikingly masculine appearance. "It didn't work out between us." He took off his sunglasses.
"So now you've come crawling back to me?" Brad said.
"I thought we might try again." Harley pursed his lips and furrowed his brows to accent his hurt feelings. "I guess it took me a while to realize that I love you."
"Until someone else comes along? I was always faithful to you, Harley."
"Well, I suppose that's easy when you're on board a boat with four straight people. I had to deal with loneliness and opportunities."
"I had opportunities when we went ashore."
Harley sighed heavily. "What do you want me to say, Brad? I'm sorry. OK? I was wrong. OK?" He drew his lips down and sniffed. "I've really missed you and all the good times we had together."
"How long will *that* last?" Brad asked, "until the next guy comes along?"
Harley fluttered a hand.
"Oh, look," I whispered.
"Yeah," Mini said. "He must have taken lessons on hand fluttering from Brad."
Harley reached out and fingered Brad's necklace. "I was thinking...." He shrugged.
"That's good to hear!" Brad said sarcastically.
"You're so cruel to me, Brad. I was *lost* without you."
"I was lost, too, you know," Brad admitted.
"Well, then, what do you say we go for it, you and me?" He smiled and unbuttoned one of Brad's shirt buttons.
"Go for what?" Brad asked. "Dinner at Armand's? I guess we could do that without you making a commitment."
Harley sighed. "I was thinking, Brad, more like dinners for the rest of our lives together." He blew Brad a kiss.
"Oh, my God!" I whispered. "Mini, I think -- "
"He's about to *propose*," Mini whispered.
"Are you saying what I *think* you're saying?" Brad asked Harley.
"Well, same-sex marriages are legal in California."
"Mini!" I said.
"Quiet, Tess," Mini warned. "They'll *hear* you."
"Oh!" Brad covered his mouth with a hand. "Are you proposing to me?"
An older couple walked by. The man took the woman's arm and hurried on.
Harley embraced Brad. "Well, what do you *say*? Can you stand me for the rest of your life?"
"I...I say yay!" Brad exclaimed and wrapped his arms around Harley's back.
"Oh, Mini!" I grabbed her hand.
Harley picked up Brad in an embrace that lifted him off the ground.
"I think," Mini said and grinned, "he just swept Brad off his feet."
"Halleluiah," I whispered, imitating Elijah Jones, "there's going to be a wedding."
"And Brad and Harley make three weddings," Mini said.
Brad and Harley noticed us.
Mini watched them approach. "Who's going to marry this group?" she whispered

to me.

We looked at each other and said together "Minister Gantry!"

"What?" Culley said as he walked up to us with his dive bag slung over his shoulder, on his way to *Shearwater*, his Boston Whaler, further down the dock.

"There's going to be a wedding, Ryan," I told him, "and it's going to be one for the books!"

"Uh-oh," Culley said.

"What?" I asked. "Are you having second thoughts?"

"The barbarians are at the gate," he said.

I turned.

The police had just let in the media people who had been eagerly awaiting their turn. They were charging across the dock, cameras and mics held aloft.

George came out of *Cousteau's* cabin with his bag. His eyes widened when he saw the journalists. I thought he'd retreat back into the cabin, but he hurried to join us, with a bounce to his step and a big grin on his pudgy face.

But Brad and Harley looked uncomfortable as we were swamped again. They let go of each other's hands and moved apart. I felt bad for them. How must it feel, I wondered, to have accomplished all that Brad had done, and still feel like an outsider?

We fielded questions from the new wave of journalists, then excused ourselves as the Pacifica Lab van drove onto the wharf to pick us up.

I realized, with a sense of loss, that for the first time in two months, my friends and I would not be together.

*****

Culley came with me to pick up Ice. He was curled up, asleep on a blanket on my neighbor's porch.

"Ice!" I called as I opened the creaky gate.

He raised his head and looked around.

"Hey, Ice!" Culley called, "your girlfriend's here."

"Culley!" There was a man mowing a lawn next door.

Ice howled like a wolf when he saw me walk up the path. Huskies don't bark much, but they're great at howling.

I squatted. "Icey!"

It was a mistake. He charged down the steps, knocked me over, and jumped on me. I tried to get up but he licked my cheeks so hard I rolled to my stomach to hide my face from him. "OK, Ice. OK!" I said. He jumped on my back and licked my neck.

Culley laughed so hard he fell to his knees.

"How about you get him off me?" I muttered through my fingers as Ice nibbled on my ear.

"Not while I'm learning his moves."

"You bastard," I said.

My neighbor, a retired English teacher with thin, white hair that lifted in the breeze, and a cane, came out of the house. "He's been crying for you for two months, Miss Hoffman." He pointed at Ice with his cane. "The next time you go chasing after giant octopuses, you'd better take him with you because he loves with a love that is greater than love."

*****

My apartment smelled musty after two months of closed windows. Culley and I opened them.

I called my mother. Dad was home, she told me, and feeling tired but crotchety, like his old self.

"Mom," I said, "we're planning the wedding. There are three couples now and it's going to take place on the wharf."

"Three couples...on the wharf? I-I'm not going to give Dad the details just yet. I'll wait until the doctor says he can take some excitement."

"Sure, Mom. Culley and I figured on that. Give Dad and Chris a kiss for me."

"Me, too," Culley said.

"Is that my new son in law?" Mom asked.

"That's him in all his glory," I told her.

"Good!" she said. "I hope he's a pisser, like your father and Chris."

I glanced at Culley. "You won't be disappointed, Mom."

Culley came up and hugged me from behind as I broke the connection. "Who's getting married?" he asked.

I turned in his arms. "Losing your courage, tough guy?"

He hugged me tighter. "Who, me? Mr. Commitment?"

I put my arms around his back and stroked his hard muscles. "Have you been taking steroids just for me?" I kissed him.

"Don't do that unless you mean it."

"I never do anything I don't mean," I said.

Ice trotted in from the backyard.

"Oh, no," Culley said. "Guess I'll have to fight him to see which one of us wins out to mate with the female."

"You really are a pervert." I kissed him again. The fire was rising in me. "But then, I always had a thing for perverts."

Culley carried me to my bed. "Don't expect this carrying service for the rest of your life." He plunked me down on my bed.

I got up and lowered the shades.

Culley tried to grab Ice but Ice was wise to him now. He jumped on my bed and whined.

Culley picked him up and carried him out the door.

I laughed as Ice tried to squeeze back in. I got undressed as Culley nudged Ice out and closed the door.

"Ah," I said. "Poor Ice."

"What about 'poor me'?"

He turned around and saw me naked. "I'm afraid I'm going to be attacked by a wild woman."

"C'mere, Mr. Tough Guy," I said, "I want your body, for what it's worth."

"Whatever meager attachments I have, they're all yours."

I helped him out of his clothes and looked down. "Oh, I wouldn't call it meager. Not great. But not meager."

"I've been told by women that I'm well endowed." He put his arms around me and kissed me.

"Those days are over, stud muffin."

Ice heard us talking and whined.

Our lovemaking was passionate. My climax was like nothing I'd ever felt before. It was as though we were one entity, meant to be joined forever.

When it was over, I didn't want to part from him. I suddenly realized that Ice was still whining and scratching at the door.

"Should I let the poor bastard back in?" Culley said.

"No. Not yet. Not yet, hon."

I realized there was another orgasm building inside me. I arched against him and pressed him against me. "Oh, Ryan!"

He began to move inside me again and I clung to him as I climaxed."

We were both breathing hard.

"Was it good for you?" he asked. "Because you wore me out, woman."

I laughed.

"You want to order that pizza now?" I said.

"Can do. But I got to tell you, the sausage isn't so hot anymore."
"I'll take what I can get."
"I'm not so sure I want to marry you anymore," he said.
"Oh?"
"I'll probably die young of a heart attack in the middle of sex."
"But think of the interesting corpse you'd leave."

We parted and Culley sat up. "I'm going to let Ice in before you kill me while I'm still young."

"Ryan," I said as he reached the door.

He turned. "What now? You want my body again?"

I smiled. "I love thee to the depth and breadth and height my soul can reach," I recited and smiled.

"Did you just make that up?"

I laughed. "I forgot to tell you I'm also a great poet."

"Right." He opened the door, then covered his crotch as Ice came flying in and knocked over a chair.

CHAPTER THIRTY ONE

I'll never forget the wedding. Neither will Minister Gantry, or Mom and Dad, or the guests, I'm certain.

It was held on the San Francisco wharf. Minister Jonas Gantry's team from the boats set up an arbor, adorned with artificial flowers, as the altar. A faded red carpet was rolled out as an aisle for us to walk down. Chairs with drooping white bows on the backs were lined up in rows. A flimsy table held treats and kool-aid, and a large wedding cake as the centerpiece. Above our heads, a flowered blue canopy enclosed the wedding party in case of rain. A ripped edge flapped in the breeze.

Mom, Dad, Chris, and Ice attended, and relatives and friends of all three of us marriage couples.

It was so good to see my family again.

"Dad," I said, " how are you feeling now?"

"So your mother went and told you and scared you!" He slid a glance at Mom.

She grinned and patted dad's paunch. She wore a lovely pink satin dress for the wedding. "I need all the help I can get, David, to keep your hands out of the refrigerator."

Mom is tall, stately, and dark-haired. I look a lot like her. Dad is a bit shorter, with lighter coloring and rounded features. Chris is out of Dad's gene pool.

I watched my young brother saunter up to Culley, who looked so handsome and so uncomfortable in his rented tuxedo from Gantry. It was a size too small.

"So," Chris said, "you're the great, commercial diver, huh?'

"That's me," Culley told him.

"Well, what makes you so great?"

"I was born great." Culley smirked. "What makes you such a hardass?"

Chris laughed sharply. "I was *born* a hardass."

"C'mere, wise guy." Culley put an arm around Chris' shoulders and squeezed. Chris sleeved an arm around Culley's waist. "You're lucky you're my wife's kid brother, you know?"

"So, do me something," Chris said brashly.

"I never pick on brats."

"So," Chris said, "you gonna teach me to dive?"

"Why should I do that?"

"Because you're gonna be my brother in law! And I'm gonna be a great diver."

"Like me?"

"Better."

183

Culley looked at me and chuckled. "Tell you what, brat." He sat down. "I'll teach you to dive if you teach me how to be a hardass."

"You got a deal!" Chris said.

"I think," I told Mom and Dad, "that I see a budding relationship. Birds of a feather."

Dad shook his head. "If Ryan can stand Chris."

"It might be a close race, Dad, as to which of them can stand the other longest."

"I hear you hate school," I heard Culley tell Chris, "and you're going to run away and join a circus. What's your problem with school?"

"It sucks!"

"Yeah, I hated it, too."

"Did you quit?" Chris sat on the ground, cross-legged, next to Culley.

"At sixteen."

"Did you run away from home?"

"No. I stole a car."

I saw Chris' eyes widen.

"They didn't catch you."

"Yeah, they did. I went to jail."

"You were in jail? What's it like."

"Sucks worse than school."

"Well, I'm not going to steal a car."

"You might end up stealing food." Culley leaned forward. "Tell you what, brat. You stick it out in school, and I'll teach you to dive. Deal?"

"Will you teach me to be a commercial diver like you?"

"I hate to burst your bubble, but you've got to go to school for that. Dive school."

"Does it suck?"

Culley smiled. "Not if you love to dive. But first you've got to graduate from high school."

"I knew there was a catch!'

"There usually is, in life." Culley brushed a hand through Chris' sandy hair. "But you'll have a head start."

"How?"

"Well, that bargain we just made."

"Oh, I'll teach you to be a hardass."

"And I'll teach you to dive. You know what it's like to dive for lobsters at night with a light?"

Chris shook his head.

"You'll find out." Culley got up. "C'mon, brat. We gotta go make you my brother in law." Culley winked at me as they walked over.

I smiled back. He was already a part of my family.

The wedding cake, a gift from Harley's parents, the Davidsons, who attended the wedding, was adorned with the conventional tiny statues of a couple. The real three couples were anything but conventional.

I wore my green dress. My veil and artificial bouquet were all Hands-of-God's-Vengeance rentals.

It was time for the marriage vows. I felt a little scared as Gantry played The "Wedding March" on his Q-tree while we six walked down the red-carpet aisle, in three pairs, to the altar. Chris stood on the side. He was my best man.

"Dearly beloved, Minister Gantry began in his deep, rich voice, "we are gathered here in the sight of God to marry -- "

I heard screams.

Gantry's pet juvenile giant, with the charcoal male plastered to her head, had surfaced and crawled partway out of the water between *Vengeance's* docked boats.

Ice went berserk. He ran to the dock's edge, leaped into the water, and attacked the juvenile.

"Ice. No!" I shouted.

People near the water overturned their chairs in their rush to get away from the giant.

I kicked off my shoes, threw down my bouquet and ran to the water's edge, with Culley and Brad right behind me.

One of the teenage boys aboard *Mother's Freight and Faith* jumped into the water and tried to separate Ice and the giant.

Someone screamed. "The Kraken is eating a child!"

"Ryan!" I shouted. "She'll kill Ice."

Ryan squeezed out of the jacket of his tuxedo as he ran to the dock and dived in.

I heard my mother shout "No, Tess. Don't!" as I dived into the water.

Brad followed.

"Oh, Brad," Harley shouted, "she'll kill you." He ran back and forth on the dock. "Brad, don't leave me now!"

Mini stood at the edge of the dock. "I can't swim!" she yelled. to Harley.

"Me either," Harley yelled back.

Ice bit the juvenile's tentacle.

"Oh, no!" I swam toward him with Culley and Brad beside me.

The juvenile wrapped a tentacle around Ice and lifted him out of the water, then slammed him down and held him underwater.

"Ice!" I screamed.

Culley dived and emerged with Ice. The tentacle was still around Ice's body. Brad and I helped Culley pull Ice to the dock while the teenaged boy shouted "No, Whitie!" to the giant. "No. Go back, girl." he smacked her tentacle. "Back!"

Culley bit the tentacle and Whitie let go of Ice. The boy guided Whitie back to her underwater dive platform. She flashed red while the tiny male ran around her mantle in circles.

With his ears flattened back on his wet head, Ice wrapped his front legs around my neck. Huskies are not water-loving dogs, especially underwater-loving dogs.

Culley hefted Ice, who was shaking, onto the dock. Then Culley lifted himself to the low platform and helped me and Brad out of the water.

"Ice," I called, but he was panicked. He ran to the wedding party with his dripping tail between his legs, to seek the protection of humans, and shook himself off next to Elmer Gantry, who sat in the front row, dressed in his crimson robe. Elmer got hit with most of the spray. He threw Ice a fierce, eye-liner look. Ice retreated to my mother, who had sat back down after we emerged from the water, looking pale. Ice jumped on her lap.

"Oh, shit!" my mother exclaimed and got up, brushing off her pink, satin dress with the handkerchief she had used to wipe tears over the coming marriage of her daughter.

Still frightened and shivering, Ice trotted to the table with the wedding cake and crawled under it.

"Ice!" I called as I reached the table.

At the sound of my voice, he lumbered back out and hit a table leg with his wagging tail. The table went down. The cake slid off.

Culley and I stood there, staring, dripping, as Ice licked cream off the cake.

"I'm so glad you brought Ice along," Culley said. "Now we've got something to tell the grandkids about our wedding that won't bore them to death."

A police car, sirens wailing, lights flashing, pulled up. Two officers jumped out of the vehicle, their hands on the butts of their guns.

"What's going on here?" one shouted.

"A wedding," George squeaked.

"We got a call that a Kraken was attacking a kid," one officer said and looked around. "Where is it?"

"There is a Kraken," Brad told him as he and Harley, who was still dressed in his leathers, sauntered over. "But it's OK, officer." Brad brushed back his wet hair, "the Kraken's a pet."

The two officers stared suspiciously at Harley.

"Is he a Hell's Angel?" one asked.

"Oh, no," Brad exclaimed. "No." He took Harley's hand and patted it. "He's just gay."

I knew Brad was enjoying this carnival scene and playing it to the hilt.

"We're about to get married." Brad smiled broadly.

"Congratulations," the officer said without returning the smile. He looked at me with my wet, clinging dress and dripping hair under a lopsided veil. He frowned at Ice, who still licked the wedding cake. He glanced at the artificial bouquet on the ground, that had cracked in half when I dropped it, and threw his partner a look. His partner motioned to the police car with his head. They got in and drove away.

"Enjoy the doughnuts, boys," Brad called and waved.

Culley took my hand. "We came here to get married," he said and led me to the altar, "and goddammit, "we're going to get married!"

Culley and Brad and I left a puddle on Gantry's red carpet as we stood before the minister under the arbor. Mini and George held hands next to us. So did Brad and Harley.

The wedding guests grew silent as Minister Gantry began, in his deep, rich tone: "Dearly beloved, we are gathered here in the presence of God to witness and bless the exchanging of vows between...uh." He unfolded a piece of paper and read from it. "Between Harley... Harley Davidson?" He glanced at Harley and cleared his throat. "And Bradford Bellows, and between Minerva Johnson and George Backer, and between Tessica Hoffman and Ryan Culley, in the covenant relationship of holy matri-money, I mean matrimony!" Gantry's cheeks flushed.

The words he said afterward faded into the background as I gazed out over the water. We had opened the sea like a ripe fruit and discovered just a very few of her sublime wonders. What other revelations awaited those who dared to plumb her depths?

"Tessica?" Minister Gantry said, " I asked you if you take Ryan Culley to be your lawful wedded husband?"

I took Culley's hand. He stared into my eyes with such love that I felt my lips quiver.

"I will," I said.

"Please say 'I do'." Minister Gantry sighed.

"Oh, I do," I said.

He asked Culley the same question. Culley's throat must have been choked, because he cleared it. "I do," he said.

Chris came up, winked at me, and handed Culley the ring.

"Thanks, brat," Culley whispered.

I put out my left hand and Culley slipped the ring on my finger. "With this ring," he said, "I thee wed. And with all that I am, I honor you."

"Oh, Ryan," I said. "I take thee to be my constant friend, my faithful partner, and to honor you with all that I am too."

I heard my mother sob. I glanced back and caught Dad wiping a tear.

Ice was chained to Dad's chair.

"You may kiss the bride," Minister Gantry said to Culley.

Culley took me in his arms. "I will," he said, "and I will always love you, my Tessica."

We kissed to the cheers and claps of the wedding guests.

I heard a deep-throated sob. I turned and saw Elmer Gantry wipe a tear on his robe. The eye liner smeared under his eyes.

"Amen!" Minister Gantry said and snapped closed his good book.

Brad turned to the congregation and gestured at the fallen cake. "Now," he said, "who wants a piece of wedding cake?"

George stepped forward and was about to say something but Mini yanked him back.

"How about a nice, award-winning glass of champagne for all?" Minister Gantry said and rubbed his hands together.

I looked at Ryan. "Home is the hunter, home from the hill." A westerly breeze wafted in and brought the smell of the open sea.

Ryan smiled. "And the sailor home from the sea."

END

Adult Science Fiction:
Sojourner to the Stars: Book One - The Loranth
(The Jules Rammis series)
Sojourner to the Stars: Book Two - Halcyon Nights
(The Jules Rammis series)
The Empty Hands

Children's Books:
Snowflake's World: Book One - The Deadly Sulphur Mine
Snowflake's World: Book Two - The Enchanted Portal
at Haunted Lake
Snowflake's World: Book Three - The Quest for New Eden

jeankilczer@centurylink.net

CPSIA information can be obtained
at www.ICGtesting.com
Printed in the USA
BVHW042319010520
579061BV00012B/1884